BETWEEN

❧ FRACTURE ❧

LINES

JULIEN BRADLEY

WISE
CREATIVE · PUBLISHING
Ink

ISBN 13: 978-1-63489-225-4

Library of Congress Catalog Number: 2019937276
Printed in the United States of America
First Printing: 2019

23 22 21 20 19   1 2 3 4 5
Cover and interior design by Steven Meyer-Rassow

Wise Ink Creative Publishing
807 Broadway St NE #46
Minneapolis, MN
www.WiseInk.com

*To my wonderful family—your love and support
never cease to astound me.*

Dedicated to our heavenly angel Jordan Michelle

CHAPTER 1

JASON

Jason Monroe sat in a booth near the back of the hotel lounge, nursing a glass of twelve-year-old scotch and a grudge. He read the final investigation report, basically accusing him of threatening a potential business partner and carrying a concealed and unregistered handgun in the state of North Dakota. He had no problem owning up to the gun charges—after all, carrying a gun was a constitutional right. The company ethics committee disagreed and had assessed him a hefty fine, all because he'd said a few curse words toward an antagonistic woman. His old man pulled him off the Altman mineral rights and land acquisition as a result. It was ridiculous.

Altman's former business partner Senator Kip Ferguson and that bitch heiress Ramona Strong had filed a restraining order against him, prohibiting him from going anywhere near the negotiating table. *Must be nice to have the local law enforcement in your back pocket*, Jason mused. It was a sweet setup; too bad it wasn't his. Located in the Bakken basin of North Dakota, the Altman estate and business holdings included two operating oil wells plus thousands of acres of land, with mineral rights intact. Landing the deal would have secured Jason's legacy among the international oil conglomerates. Now . . .

Then, there was his presumed friend and legal counsel for Monroe Oil Company to contend with. John Finch had threatened to pull out of the project if Jason stayed on, as if he had that kind of advantage. The old man, however, had sided with the lawyer over his own son. *The ungrateful backstabber.* It would have been a sweet ride to the top for his former friend had he stuck with Jason; now he would be destroyed, along with his career. The bitter thought brought bile to his throat. "By the time I'm through with you and that bitch," Jason muttered, "she won't be able to give away the property." The thought brought a sadistic smile to his face, and he took another drink.

Plotting his revenge, Jason failed to notice the brutally handsome man stealthily making his way toward the booth until the contract for hire sat down in the seat across from him. A waitress materialized to take the man's order. "I'll have a club soda," the gun for hire said in a smooth baritone voice.

As the waitress left, the hire removed a manila folder from a leather satchel and slid the surveillance pictures across the table. Jason returned from his reverie and mindlessly thumbed through the photos. They were aerial views of the Ferguson farmstead framed by a stark winter landscape, along with curbside shots of Senator Ferguson's home in Williston. A few shots of the attorney showed Matthew Ferguson leaving his home in Bismarck.

"See the swelling in his face and the darkened eyes?" the private investigator said, pointing to the attorney. "He'd been in one hell of a fight. Rumor has it, his own brother did it."

Jason gave a disinterested grunt.

The gun for hire lifted a brow. "Of course, it's just a rumor."

The waitress returned with the club soda, smiling at the handsome man and offering a menu. Feeling slighted, Jason said, "Bring me another scotch, and not this watered-down shit." He held up his tumbler of melted ice without looking up at her. The waitress snatched the tumbler and left without remark.

"You get more bees with honey," the hire said, amused.

"I don't want bees, I want a goddamn decent scotch."

The gun for hire tapped the photo in Jason's hand. "That one is of Ms. Strong in front of her farmhouse in southeastern Minnesota. See the bluff in the background? It's rural, but not as remote as it may appear at first glance. Her neighbor's driveway is off to the right side of her property, separated by a small dry run set back further from the road up in the hillside. See?"

Jason examined the picture.

"Her house is set closer to the road with the barn and other outbuildings set further back near a holding pond below the bluff. Not easy to get in and out of without being detected. The property is on a main county road, and for her being the only one in the house right now, there is quite a bit of foot traffic. It seems along with her veterinary clinic, she also boards some of her client's animals. She just had a couple of Weimaraners and an American foxhound she's been rehabilitating—good security alarm."

Unimpressed, Jason asked, "Have you been inside?"

"Of course. Nothing of extreme value. Petty thievery—flat-screen, laptop, some electronics, a small safe in the office sitting in plain sight. You'd never know she was a multimillionaire. She's got her father's war memorabilia from Vietnam and Medals of Honor he earned in the Air—"

"Yeah, yeah, blah, blah." Jason shoved the photos away. "What else you got?"

The hired man's jaw twitched. "This is Altman's farm in North Dakota—much more remote, easier to access, but a top-notch security system, military grade. I would suggest leaving the hangar alone and going for this cluster of outbuildings here and this little shed here. Leave the cabin by the lake."

"Why?"

The hire shook his head. "The hangar siding and doors are made of steel. The cabin's too much of an outlier. It's not worth it."

Jason crumpled the aerial photo in his fist, remembering the humiliation at the cabin. He'd been on that frozen swamp with the makeshift ice rink a few months ago. Someone had taken a shot at him. He felt the fear prick at his neck, the phantom warmth of urine trickling down his cold leg. He wanted it to burn, all of it. "Do you have anyone in mind for the job?"

"A few. I strongly discourage using anyone local. There are several guys out there working the oil rigs desperate enough for the money who have the criminal records to do it, but everyone knows the Fergusons, Altman too—and I mean everyone. I haven't found a single hater among the community, except that property management and real estate owner you told me about. Besides, if any of the locals got wind about the plot, they'd probably dole out their own justice and lynch the bastard responsible."

"Saves me the trouble and expense," Jason mumbled.

The gun for hire leaned forward. "Expense, perhaps, but the incident would eventually ricochet back to Monroe Oil. You don't need that kind of blowback."

Jason felt the weight of a mercenary's gaze judging him. *Who does this asshole think he is?* He'd used him on past projects. The thug was reliable, proficient in his work, and well compensated. He had an underlying tone of arrogance that Jason found annoying but had let slide in the past. The thug had always known his place—until now.

"Afraid your hands will get dirty?" Jason challenged.

"The dirt won't be on my hands," the thug said coolly.

Was this guy trying to piss him off? Maybe he had the wrong man for the job. Their previous business dealings had been petty intimidation, illegal setups, and bribes, nothing with a potential body count (unless one counted that middle management paperweight who'd committed suicide after his extramarital affair with an underage male went public). This time was different. Everything was on the line.

The fate of Monroe Oil and his reputation were both at stake. Challenging Altman in probate was Jason's idea, and he'd invested considerable time and resources toward the project. Finch had been right about one thing: the woman wasn't going to sell, not to him. Not until he forced her. In a hostile takeover, fatalities were an inevitability, especially when engaging an enemy as entrenched as the Fergusons and Altman. Jason conceded the obvious power F&A Oil held locally, and they had allies in high places, but so did he. He wasn't about to let a couple of Midwest, Podunk farmers with a little military background humiliate him or scare him off. He would have Ferguson and Altman's mineral rights, no matter what or who required elimination. Then, he'd decimate their company, along with the land, beyond salvage.

The gun for hire's voice took on a menacing tone. "You don't fuck around with this one. Spend the money on a professional and do it right."

Jason looked his employee in his cold, dark eyes. "That's why I hired you."

The hire gathered up the photos and finished his soda. "Are there any other services you'd like to negotiate?"

The waitress returned with Jason's scotch, no ice, and set it on the table. "Last call, gentlemen. Can I bring you anything more this evening?"

The gun for hire pulled a fifty out of his wallet and handed it to the young woman. She couldn't have been more than a sophomore in college, with average looks, medium height, and box-blonde hair. Her steel-blue eyes, her only remarkable feature, widened at the sight of the fifty. A dimple popped out on one cheek when she smiled and said, "Is this for both tabs?"

Jason snatched the money and threw it at his employee. "Hell no, I'm paying for the drinks," he snarled, reaching for the wallet.

Cool, and confident, the hire picked up the bill and handed it back to the waitress.

Flabbergasted, she said, "Sir, the designated driver drinks are always free."

He gave a silky laugh. "I wouldn't work for this man if he were the last soul on the planet. It's my tip to you. He can pay his own tab."

Blushing, the young woman kept the bill, then turned to Jason expectantly. Going one better, he pressed a hundred-dollar bill into her hand, winked, and said, "Bring me another scotch, and charge my tab to my room. You can keep the tip, sweetheart."

Confused by the sudden change in behavior, the waitress grabbed the empty glasses and walked back to the bar. When she was out of earshot, Jason leaned an elbow on the table. "Won't work for me, my ass."

The gun for hire waved his hand. "Semantics. Any other request?"

"Yeah, I want you to add Finch to your watch list. He's been avoiding me lately. I need to know what he's been up to. Plus, find out what happened to kid brother Ferguson. He's low-hanging fruit."

The hire stood as a young man in jeans and a tight-fitting T-shirt approached the booth. "You know my fee schedule," he said. "I'll expect it in my account by noon tomorrow. The standard finance fee applies for every fifteen minutes it's late." He tipped his head to the young man. "Good evening."

Jason's eyes followed the mercenary. "Asshole," he muttered. When the thug was out of sight, he slid to the end of the booth. He was tired, needed a shower, and wanted his goddamn nightcap.

A tall young man with a bodybuilder's physique and shaved head blocked his way. "I'm sorry, Mr. Monroe, but your credit card has been declined. How would you like to close out your tab?"

Jason looked up at the imposing figure. "What do you mean? There's plenty of money. That's my business card." He scanned the room. "Where's my waitress? I want my scotch." The hulking youth towered over his seated position like a bully on a playground. It was embarrassing. Stirring up a commotion, Jason snapped, "I shouldn't even be paying for drinks. My company owns this pathetic dump. Now run it again, you incompetent prick, and don't come back with your lame-ass excuses."

A security guard walked up to the table and joined the scene. They argued back and forth like that for a while, until the hotel manager finally arrived. He was a middle-aged man, overweight, and wore a wrinkled tie. He said, "My sincere apologies, Mr. Monroe, but there seems to be a mistake."

Jason was seething. "You bet your ass there's been a mistake. I promise you, you're all going to be out of a job when I'm through with you."

"There seems to be plenty of money on the account," the manager persisted. "It's—"

Jason went into hysterics. "I told you. Now run the goddamn card."

"The credit line is not the problem, I—"

"Why are you still standing here and not running my card?"

"The problem, sir," the hotel manager said with excruciating patience, "is that you are not an authorized user."

"What?" It had to be the most humiliating moment of his life.

After several phone calls that got several more people involved than Jason would have wanted, he learned the cold, hard truth. His old man had cut him off. Mortified, Jason threw his Amex card at the manager. "Take off the gratuity charge. I've paid enough for your cheap liquor."

Security escorted him from the lounge. Exhausted by the ordeal, Jason crossed the lobby floor, ready to crash for the night. The desk manager said something to the guard, who then snatched him by the elbow and steered him toward the desk.

"What the—"

The night manager addressed him pleasantly. "Good evening Mr. Monroe. I'd like to talk to you a moment about the credit card you are using for your stay with us."

CHAPTER 2

MASSEY

Senator Kip Ferguson lumbered through his son's office door. Massey stood from his desk, where he'd been studying the application map for the proposed Dakota Access Pipeline route, and said, "Hey, Dad, done with your appointment already?" He looked past Kip. "Where's Poppy? Didn't she go with you? What did your cardiologist have to say?"

Kip ignored the questions and walked straight to the mini-fridge, grabbing a Pepsi. Cracking it open with a flourish, he took a noisy swallow. "Damn doctors. Whatever happened to the tried-and-true Western medicine approach of *Name it, drug it?*" It was a rhetorical question. Ever since Kip's angioplasty and stent placement three months back, he'd been unbearable to be around, mostly due to his restrictive diet. Massey felt sorry for his stepmom, who bore the brunt of his father's frustration. A twinge of guilt niggled him for not chiding the old man for drinking the pop. Then he figured, *Why waste words on deaf ears?*

"First they starve you to death, then they take away what little pleasures you have left in this miserable life."

Massey refrained from responding. His father had a good life—he was bitching about the booze. A PTSD casualty from his tour in Vietnam, Kip had been self-medicating with alcohol for years and was a high-functioning alcoholic. Still, the years of abuse and excess were catching up. Massey hoped his dad had enough sense to know his cardiologist wasn't bullshitting when he told him the next step was open-heart surgery—if he didn't have a stroke or heart attack first.

Kip changed topics. "Has Mony had any luck finding the missing deed?"

Another sore subject—the threat of mortality only heightened Kip's determination to start a drilling project right away. The problem was, the probate hearing and the missing title and deed to the twenty-acre parcel of land were far from resolved.

"No," Massey said, "but I'm thinking we should go over to Buddy's place again and check things out."

As if the thought had just occurred to him, Kip said, "You don't think Mony accidentally tossed it out when she cleaned the house?"

"I spoke with her over the weekend," Massey told him, "and she assured me that everything sent to Goodwill was clothing, household knickknacks, and small appliance stuff, not paperwork." It was a partial truth. He had talked with Mony, but they hadn't discussed the deed. It would be better if his dad didn't know she would be attending a veterinary conference this week in Chicago,

John Finch's territory. Not that he would disagree with his dad's concern regarding Mony's too-close proximity to the enemy—they just didn't need to be micromanaging her life.

"What about the boxes Nathan supposedly stored in Buddy's room?" Kip asked. "Has she gone through any of those things yet?"

Another sensitive topic.

"She promised to call me when or if she came across something that looked important. Besides, she hasn't found the combination to the padlock on the safe."

"All she needs is a good bolt cutter for that. I think she's stalling. You need to stress to her how important this is. I've got that jackass Monroe breathing down my neck and—"

"Dad," Massey said, tempering his tone. "Monroe's an idiot, and his half-assed team couldn't find their way out of an open paper bag. The court will rule in our favor. Besides, Mony won't let you down. If it's there, she'll tell us. In the meantime, I think we should go through the house again, maybe the hangar too. Buddy's filing system for the crop-dusting business was marginal at best, but it's worth a look." Massey had another motive for going to the Altman farm that had nothing to do with titles and deeds, but he kept that to himself.

Kip's voice brightened a little. "Yes, good thinking. I hadn't thought about looking through any of the archived records. Plus, I need to take inventory. When's the soonest you can come to Williston?"

They settled on a date and his father left. Massey sat

down and leaned back in his chair, staring out at the bluff overlooking the Missouri River. A May 2014 edition of the *Bismarck Tribune* lay open on his desk, next to the oil pipeline map. The proposed DAPL route would stretch from Watford City, located in the heart of the Bakken oil fields, and run all the way south to Patoka, Illinois, some 1,100 miles away. The pipeline was slated to cross the Missouri River some ten miles upstream. The announcement wouldn't go public until June, but as a legal advisor for the city of Bismarck, Massey couldn't support it as a viable option. For one, its proximity to wellhead source and protected water areas presented a significant risk to municipal water supply wells. Two, it would be difficult for the pipeline to stay five hundred feet away from homes, as required by the North Dakota Public Service Commission. Three, Federal pipeline regulators would likely classify the proposed route as a "high-consequence area," which meant in the event of a pipeline spill or breach, it would have the most significant adverse consequences. Still, the pipeline had to cross the Missouri River somewhere, and no matter where it crossed, the surrounding wetlands and the river itself would always be at risk for possible contamination. Even small spills of petroleum products, like the one near Lake Sakakawea, had a damaging effect. These sorts of projects never had good safety track records, no matter how much propaganda DAPL organizers fed to the public. Massey wondered what Mony, being something of an environmentalist, might think of the issue.

The daughter of his father's former business partner,

Mony Altman Strong, and her late husband had been outspoken opponents to frac sand mining, a key component to drilling. It was crazy to think of her owning an oil business. Her dad had not only willed the oil business and his wealth to his only child, but he'd included Massey's brother, Nate, as well. Neither were much interested in drilling, a position which infuriated Massey's old man to no end.

"Excuse me, Mr. Ferguson," his administrative assistant's voice came over the interoffice comm. "You have a call from Norman Stapleton on line one."

Massey felt his jaw clench at the mention of Mony's former custodian; he'd been waiting for the call. He picked up the handset. "Put it through, Jesse, and buzz me when I've reached fifteen minutes. It's my turn to pick up the boys from school and get them to hockey practice. I don't want to be late." Maybe he was a so-called big shot in town, but he took his turn carpooling during a busy workday. Even the governor couldn't bump his commitment, and the governor knew it.

There was a smile in his admin's voice. "Yes, Mr. Ferguson."

Massey answered with his best perfunctory greeting. The last thing he wanted to do was agitate a man who'd seemed morally justified in tormenting an innocent child just because she'd been an inconvenience so many years ago. Plus, Norman Stapleton seemed to be slipping cognitively since his hip surgery. Trying to hold a conversation with the man was like beating your head with a baseball bat. Stapleton had once made a career as a banker and investment advisor, and he'd been proficient at his job during the pinnacle of his career. That was no longer the case. Massey was surprised it took this long for the vultures to begin circling at the fresh scent of easy money.

"Mr. Ferguson," Norman said, "there is a matter of grave importance I wish to discuss with you."

Massey waited silently during the spiel, but he already knew the issue. Norman had been hounding Mony since the beginning of the year with a claim that her mother, Stapleton's wife Charlene, had a letter written in Buddy's handwriting claiming entitlement to his military pension. Massey had never seen the letter, which Charlene had allegedly received shortly after Buddy's plane went missing for several months in the mountains of Vietnam. Massey didn't necessarily doubt the letter's existence, but Stapleton's claim that Charlene had entitlement to the military pension was preposterous. After a reasonable amount of time, he said, "Of course, Mr. Stapleton. I will put you in touch with my admin and arrange a mutually acceptable time to talk. Good da—"

"What's wrong with the present?" Norman retorted. "Is my time less valuable than yours?"

Massey felt the knock of the bat against his brain. "I'm off to a scheduled meeting," he said flatly. "I'm transferring your call to—"

"Charlene has a letter in Altman's handwriting that proves she's entitled to his military pension," Norman said in a persistent, almost desperate tone. "You can either talk to me now, or we can settle this in court."

Massey had heard the threat before, several times—nothing had come of it. "Contact your lawyer, Mr. Stapleton," Massey said with advisory purpose. There was no way he was going to get into a debate with an early-dementia senior with an overinflated sense of entitlement. "Good day." He would have added, *Sir,* but the title Stapleton forced Mony to use when she was his ward felt undeserved.

The workday ended; eager to get home for supper, Massey retrieved his briefcase and headed toward the door. He should have kept going, but as he passed his admin's desk, Jesse said "I know you're on your way out, but I think you're going to want to take this call. It's counsel for Monroe Oil."

And the hits just keep on coming. Massey breathed a deep sigh before he picked up the phone. "Massey Ferguson."

There was a pause—then, "You know, I finally made the connection now that I heard you say it out loud. It's a tractor, right?"

Massey recognized the voice and said, "Yes, it is. Being a city man, I'm surprised you would even know that."

"I thought I'd get your answering service," the attorney continued. "I didn't think you'd be working this late."

"It's late for you as well, Mr. Finch, and you're an hour later than me," Massey countered, trying to hold back a smile. He liked the notion of Monroe Oil's legal team leader burning the midnight oil. It smelt of desperation.

"Oh, I'm just killing time," Finch said nonchalantly. "I have a dinner date with opposing counsel's client. She should be landing shortly."

Massey doubted it, but he played along. "You called to tell me about your dinner plans?"

"I think it's time you and I have another face-to-face, without our clients this time," Finch said more seriously.

"Why, is Mony's presence too much for you to handle unless she's in the missionary position?"

"Found your brother yet?"

"Why? Are you looking for a rematch?"

"I just spoke with a Norman Stapleton. Is he going to be a problem?"

Massey's fists clenched involuntarily.

"I'm not sparring for a verbal altercation, I—"

"Like hell."

"Look." Finch's voice sobered. "I can see the writing on the wall. Ramona Altman's inheritance will happen without so much as a blink, but you'll still have to deal with what to do if you don't have that title or deed. I thought you and I could have a civil discussion free from client drama or emotion, and maybe to come to some mutually acceptable agreement."

Massey smiled but kept it from his voice. "You thought wrong, Mr. Finch. There is no drama or emotion, and there is no discussion without all F&A Oil owners present."

"Including your AWOL brother?"

"Especially my brother."

Finch let out a deflated breath "Very well, Mr. Ferguson. I'll see you in a couple of weeks." With that, he hung up.

Half past seven in the evening, Massey pulled into his

driveway. He was tired, irritated, and hungry and still had a mountain of work ahead of him. His boys clambered out of the SUV, unloading their gear with the finesse of two bulls in a china shop. He laughed.

Derrick and Devon chattered about their day to their mom as Massey walked through the kitchen. He was half listening. Mulling over the events of the day, he wondered if staying in the oil business was worth the effort, especially when two of the owners didn't want it and the third was getting too old to continue an active role.

His wife, Michelle, came up behind him and slipped her arms around his waist. It felt good.

"I know that look," she said, leaning her cheek against his back. "Someone has been pulling your chain."

Massey pivoted in her arms to face her. "I'm going up to Williston tomorrow with Dad to look for that damn missing title. He's making himself sick over it."

"So, not a good report from his cardiologist?" Michelle asked.

"Nope. I don't think it matters one way or another having the deed—the property belongs to Mony and Nate based on adverse possession—but it will give Dad something to do until the probate hearing in a couple of weeks. Then, I'm going to put him to work finding out what merit a *Dear Loved One* letter holds when it comes to claiming military death benefits."

"Stapleton call again?"

"Yup. The man is aggravating. Dad still has connections in the Air Force, and his investigating might take his mind off drilling."

"But isn't it a bad time to drill with oil prices dropping?"

Massey nodded. "We'll likely be in a bust by the end of the year."

"Then why is your dad so fixated on drilling, and why is Monroe still after F&A Oil?"

"I think Dad's been carrying the sword in this fight so long, he doesn't know how to put it down. For Monroe, or any conglomerate, getting their hands on prime real estate like Mony and Nate's land—with established wells and mineral rights intact on the North American continent—would be the find of the century. Even with the drop in oil prices, F&A Oil has market sustainability for decades to come. This is our children's legacy as well as a burden."

Michelle kissed his cheek. "Sounds like a rock-and-a-hard-place scenario. What are you going to do, hon?"

"Proceed judiciously," he said, kissing her lips. "I've contracted a private investigator to follow Nate's former band members. He has to be with one of them. It's time to flush him out of hiding. He's had a long enough cooling-off period to get his head out of his ass. Next, I need to light a fire under Mony to look through Buddy's memorabilia. If she doesn't have time to do it, I'll do it myself. There must be something in that safe about the deed. Things like that just don't disappear. As soon as we clear probate, we need to be ready to drill, dropping oil prices or not. As long as this country relies on fossil fuel, we have a product to sell."

His wife cupped the cheekbone Nate had cracked during their brawl. "Are you sure you want Nate and Mony back mucking things up?"

Michelle hadn't forgiven Massey's brother for putting him in the hospital. He was, however, willing to put it aside for now in order to keep the oil business running. "I have no other choice," he said softly. "Buddy made his decision. My job is to honor it."

"Buddy should have left the business to you," she said sullenly.

He didn't entirely disagree.

CHAPTER 3

MONY

The two women left the theater with arms linked, laughing like a couple of schoolgirls. Mony was glad she'd arranged an early flight into Midway to spend time with Juanita. Massey tried to talk her out of it, of course, citing the many dangerous aspects of a possible run-in with opposing counsel. It was overkill. To conciliate his objection, she'd told him she needed the CEs for her practice and the conference in Chicago worked into her schedule, as well as instructing him to mind his own business. It was more explanation than she'd ever allowed her deceased husband. Bob knew better than to interfere. Besides, she was desperate for girl talk, and she'd be goddamned if she was going to stop living her life just because John Finch resided in the city.

"Let's cross here," Juanita suggested. "I know a great little restaurant nearby I think you might like."

Mony did the touristy thing, gawking up at the surrounding buildings. She looked like an out-of-towner, but she didn't care. Half-jogging to keep up with her friend, she tried to comprehend the appeal of the big city. To her, it felt like she was just another cog in a massive wheel, grinding for some corporate purpose. Juanita however, thrived in it.

Despite being opposites, the two women had struck up a friendship on a train ride to Minneapolis and had kept in touch ever since. In a recent conversation, Mony could tell something weighed heavily on her friend's mind. She hoped a day of entertainment, libations, and gourmet food would loosen both their tongues.

Seated at a table in a cozy nook, Juanita grabbed the wine menu, picking out just the right bottle to pair with their meal. As they wined and dined, she filled Mony in on the latest.

It seemed Juanita's husband, a veteran police officer for the city of Chicago, had recently lost his K-9 partner of eight years to gunfire during a narcotics raid. "He's in a terrible funk," Juanita said, refilling both wine glasses. "In his twenty-seven years on the force, I can't recall anything shaking him as bad as the loss of Karl." Karl was the name of the Belgian Malinois her husband had trained as a pup. Mony noted a hint of disdain at the mention of the dog's name. "You'd think the damn dog was a person or something."

Being a veterinarian, Mony had witnessed firsthand the grief associated with the loss of a beloved animal. It was a mutual emotion; her late husband's dog Shep had nearly succumbed to grief after he'd died. To help the dog heal, Mony hauled the German shepherd out to the cemetery every day for over a month so that he could mourn his master's passing. There was a powerful bond between two-legged and four-legged.

The waitress bought tea and dessert, signifying Mony's turn to talk. There wasn't much to tell. She didn't want to bore Juanita with the oil business, the probate hearing, or the day-to-day of a veterinary clinic. And her business partner, Nate Ferguson, had fallen off the radar for nearly five months now, with no hint of resurfacing anytime soon.

"No one can stay gone forever," Juanita said, scooping into her decadent dessert. "Besides, why do you keep pining for this guy? Seems to me, he's brought you nothing but heartache."

That wasn't quite true. Mony had been equally culpable for the pain in Nate's life, especially when she'd married Bob. "I wanted to tell him that he was Dane's biological father. He left town before I had the chance. Maybe he'd have left anyway, but at least he'd have known the truth."

"Why tell him at all? Your husband raised him well, and your son's a grown man."

"Bob was a wonderful dad," Mony said wistfully. "I don't know that I would have ever told Nate, if it hadn't been for Bob's untimely death."

"Then why tell him now?"

How could she explain the deep and powerful connectedness she had with Nate, when sometimes even she didn't understand it? Theirs was a bond forged in the foxhole of childhood abandonment, sealed in a naïve promise to always look out for the other without conditions. Forsaken by their mothers, on a stormy night in July they'd each found sanctuary in one another's arms and had been holding onto each other ever since.

"I hoped the transparency would help us reclaim our relationship."

"Maybe your time has passed," Juanita said thoughtfully. Difficult as that thought might be, it was one Mony shared as well. "You always give me an honest perceptive. Thank you, my friend."

Juanita reached over and patted Mony's hand. "It's always easy finding solutions to someone else's problems."

As they prepared to leave, a small group of businessmen entered the restaurant. Mony looked in their direction and paled.

Noting the reaction, Juanita asked, "What's wrong?"

Mony whispered, "Don't look."

Juanita averted her eyes, but not before cataloging the details of the four men who were being seated on the other side of the dining room. Mony recognized one immediately, a tall man with shoulder-length raven-black hair and a killer smile. Massey's warning echoed in her head as the self-possessed man took his seat.

Juanita leaned into her and asked, "What do you want to do, Ramona?"

"Let's head over to Macy's like we planned."

Her friend nodded and took the lead, whispering, "You're explaining this as soon as we're out of the restaurant."

Mony thought they'd made a clean escape when, less than a hundred feet from the restaurant, she heard her name like the crack of a whip.

"Ramona!"

John Finch walked briskly toward her, weaving in and out among the pedestrian traffic in his two-tone oxford shoes, completely in his element. The man exuded urbanity in such an Old Hollywood sort of way that she had to steel her breath. It wasn't difficult to see why she had fallen for him on the train. It didn't hurt that he was equally good in bed. That all happened before she'd discovered what, and whom, he represented.

"I thought that was you," John said by way of greeting. He extended his hand to Juanita. "Sorry to intrude— I'm John Finch. I wasn't expecting to see Ramona in town until early tomorrow. I'd like to speak to her for a moment, if you don't mind."

Juanita shook his extended hand. "Please to meet you, John Finch. I'm Juanita. We took in a show, but you probably already knew that." She looked to Mony. "I think you might want to ask Ramona whether she wants to talk before you go schmoozing the friend."

Mony kept her arm linked with Juanita's, trying to remain calm, and reached for John's hand. The anticipated tingle of awareness surged between them. "That's okay, Juanita," she said, resisting the urge to retract her hand. "You'll find Mr. Finch can be very persistent." To John, she said, "I'm sure whatever you have to say can be said right here, Mr. Finch. It isn't classified or anything. Is it?"

The foot traffic on the sidewalk flowed around the three-person island, a minor inconvenience. John steered both women out of the mainstream toward a bay of windows at the front. "No, it's not classified," he said with a charismatic smile, "and call me John. I just wanted to ask how long you planned to be in Chicago, and if there was any chance you had time to meet with me, say, this evening?"

Juanita laughed. "You get straight to the point, don't you, Mr. Casanova?"

John's smile didn't falter. "I've learned if I don't pin Ms. Strong down to a commitment, she's liable to flitter off to something else."

Mony's offended protest, "I don't flitter," was essentially ignored. John and Juanita continued their banter back and forth while she analyzed her situation. She'd anticipated a run-in, just not quite so soon, and she wondered if he were having her followed. The thought both annoyed and exhilarated her. Despite her precautions, if John could trace her to the restaurant—*Crap.* She wasn't ready to deal with him yet. Juanita and John looked at her expectantly.

"It's a brief stay, Mr. Finch. I—"

"Please, call me John."

Mony stammered as her equanimity began to unravel. "I'm in town for a conference—"

"The veterinary conference," he finished. "Yes, I know. You're presenting tomorrow. I believe the topic is, 'Shock collars: does the punishment fit the crime?'"

Of course, he had her itinerary. "Actually, I'm part of a panel, not a—"

"Oh? I thought you were a keynote speaker. Hmm, I must have read the conference schedule wrong."

Juanita interrupted. "Can you wrap up your closing argument, Mr. Finch? We have some shopping to do today."

"My apologies for detaining you," John said, smoothing his tie. "By the way, how is Officer Jordan? It's a shame what happened to the dog, but better an animal than a person, right? I hope your husband will be returning from administrative leave soon. This city sure could use more men with moxie like him."

Mony noticed Juanita's dark complexion turning stony gray. It was bad enough that John had followed her— now he was harassing her friend. Mony's fingers curled into her palm. She wanted to punch him in his pearly white teeth. "What do you want, John?"

He took a subtle step back, his tone more contrite. "Ramona, listen, I just want to talk, that's all. Say around seven tomorrow?"

"Seven thirty," Mony countered. "I have your business card. I'll call you with a location." Ending the conversation, she gave a sharp tug at Juanita's arm, walking at a brusque pace. When they were almost a city block away, Juanita halted.

"Slow down, girl. I'm getting a charley horse."

Mony stopped and looked behind her. John had disappeared into the crowd. When she turned to Juanita, her friend had tears in her eyes. Mortified, she said, "God, I am so sorry you've been dragged into this mess. He had no right asking about your husband."

Crying, Juanita threw her head back with a laugh. "Did you see the look on his face when you snapped at him? Girl, I thought you were going to kick him square in the testicles. That would have been something."

Mony felt the tension leave her jaw and her shoulders

relax. How had she gone from fight to flight mode so quickly? She'd posed as bait a thousand times and kept her composure. How was this different? Looking to her friend, she found inspiration. Juanita was taking John's not-so-subtle remark into stride like a cop's wife, a trait worth emulating.

Juanita patted Mony's arm. "I think Mr. Finch is wrong about more men on the force with moxie. What they need is you." They resumed walking at a more leisurely pace. Contrary to her friend's opinion, it wasn't moxie but fear that made her volatile when confronted, a residual effect from her rape. As she mentally kicked herself for letting John rattle her, her friend said, "That man sure has a thing for you."

Mony stopped and shook her head. "No, no, you have it all wrong. He's the lawyer who works for the oil company that's after my father's company. He's after—"

"Your company," Juanita corrected. "And he doesn't give a damn about oil. He's after you. I don't claim to know as much about animals as you do, but I know a predatory gaze when I see it."

Mony had seen it too, and it sent her running. She could live with a purely sexual interest, if she could be certain that's all it was. Posing as bait was nothing new for her; in fact, it was a role she was very proficient when the enemy was clear. John was an enigma. He'd disarmed her with a smile and the element of surprise, and she'd choked. There was a primeval lust palpable between them which made it too easy to become subject to his whim and lose control of the situation. That simply couldn't happen. The future of her family's business depended upon her ability to seduce him, not the other way around. She'd assured Massey as much. Determined to keep that promise, she would have to stow the emotional hang-ups.

"And you've clearly got a thing for him," Juanita said, resuming the walk. "I could feel the arc of heat between you. Ooh, I can't wait to hear how this story plays out."

Mony didn't respond. Her interest in John could be his greatest weapon. She would have to let him see it, in order to make it hers.

CHAPTER 4

NATE

A sharp slap across the face jolted Nate from his drunken stupor. As he sat up, the room went instantly into a tilt-a-whirl spin. He retched. Someone thrust an empty pail in front of him and ordered, "Go ahead." Nate snatched the pail and leaned over the side of the bed, the onlooker watching with contempt. "Still think you can party like a rock star?"

Another volley, and he emptied the remaining contents of his stomach. With a tremulous hand, he set the pail on the floor and reached for the liquor bottle on the nightstand. "Oh, hell no," the disembodied voice scolded. A cup filled with an opaque substance appeared in front of him. "Here." Nate reached feebly for the glass, almost dropping it. He brought the thick, syrupy substance to his lips. The sickly sweet smell made him gag.

"Don't think, drink," the voice commanded.

Nate shuddered as he slammed it down, then handed back the empty cup, "Thanks," he muttered, "I owe you."

His benevolent helper snatched the cup from his hand.

"You bet your ass you do. But I'll settle for the blonde using my shower right now. Go back to sleep. I'll see you in a couple of hours." He was unconscious before his head hit the pillow.

He awoke sometime later to the mouthwatering aroma of bacon and cautiously opened one eye. He remembered where he was and felt the mattress beside him. He breathed a sigh of relief. *Christ, I really screwed up big this time*, he thought, and slung his feet over the edge of the bed to prepare to face the consequences.

Revived by the shower, Nate wrapped a towel around his hips and ventured out into the kitchen. A woman in a short, silk kimono stood at the stove scrambling eggs. Naked under the towel, Nate debated whether he should go put some clothes on, then thought, *Screw it.* If he'd fucked the woman last night, what laid beneath his towel was of no great consequence.

Dressed in similar attire, Trevor St. James—his friend and the homeowner—sat at the table, reading the newspaper and drinking coffee. Nate glanced over at the open living room shades. Blinding sunlight poured through the window. He turned his attention back to the kitchen.

"Hey," he said warily.

"Hey," Trevor grunted without looking up from his paper. The woman cooking at the stove responded in kind.

Nate opened the fridge, pulled out a container of orange juice, and chugged out of the carton. Out of habit, he walked over toward the sink.

"Nope." Trevor pointed to a tall cupboard at the end of

the countertop.

Tossing the carton into the trash compactor, Nate sat at the table. After a beat, Trevor flipped the paper closed, folding it neatly. He took off his reading glasses and said, "Are you about done with your self-destructive behavior?"

It was a valid question. He had immersed himself in some pretty high-risk behavior since arriving in Vegas—gambling, drinking, whoring around, but mostly wallowing in self-pity. Still, he didn't owe Trevor an explanation; he went with, "Yeah, sure."

"Doesn't sound very committed," Trevor replied. "What do you think, Gem?"

"Admitting there's a problem is the first step," the woman at the stove responded. She turned to face them. "Wheat or rye?"

"Rye," Trevor answered.

She looked to Nate.

"Sounds good."

The toast popped, and Gem moved into action. Clearly, she knew the space. She assembled the plates, served the men, and then joined them at the table. She reminded Nate of his favorite bartender back in Williston; the thought made him smile, but it quickly faded. He and Shannon had not parted on good terms.

Gem slid a coffee mug over to him. He reached for it, and she grabbed his hand. "In case you were wondering, I brought you home last night, though I doubt you remember."

He didn't remember, and said awkwardly, "Ah, thanks."

Gem released his hand. "Can you hand me the salt?" Nate obliged. "I've been monitoring you," she said, seasoning with a heavy hand and passed the shaker to Trevor. "You're damn lucky it's been mostly professional women who were hanging all over you. Although," she added, waggling her finger at him, "if you had brought home that skank from a few nights ago, I would have intervened. They'll rob you blind, cut your throat, or give you a nasty case of the clap, usually all of the above."

Nate took a bite of his eggs. He had no idea what she was talking about. His whole stay in Vegas had been one big blur since he'd arrived. Trevor had generously loaned out his place as a gift for Nate's pending nuptials to Mony, an event which never came to fruition. Trevor had been in Europe on extended business and told Nate he could stay as long as he wished. That was months ago. Nate took advantage of the offer, like a narcissistic bastard, leeching off his friend and hiding from his problems ever since.

"You're welcome," Gem said, and took a vicious bite out of her bacon.

Trevor shifted in his chair. "Now that we have that out of the way, don't leave me hanging here, man. What's going on with you?"

Nate took a deep breath and decided to go with blunt. "I fucked up really bad back home, and I guess I need to straighten my head out."

Trevor pursed his lips. "Details."

"A woman is involved, that's for sure," Gem interjected, "and someone close to you died, I think."

Nate looked stunned.

"Not the woman," Gem amended, "at least I don't think. But someone died recently, or maybe in the past, and you were just thinking about that person."

Nate shook his head. "No, not the woman. It was her dad who died recently. How did you know?"

Gem gave him a sly wink. "You talk in your sleep, sweetie. Oh, and you really should see your dentist about that teeth grinding, it's really bad."

The color drained from his face. *Shit, had he slept with her?*

Gem read his thoughts, "No we didn't fuck, if that's what you're thinking. Although . . ." She gave Trevor a suggestive look. "There was plenty of that noise coming from your room this morning. It made me hot just listening to it."

Nate stood abruptly. "I think I'd better go."

Trevor let out a boisterous laugh. "Man, sit down. If you think that's the worst thing that's gone on in the guest bedroom, you should have been here when T-squared stayed with us last winter."

"Yeah, we had to throw out that mattress after his stay," Gem chuckled.

They were referring to Mile High City drummer Timothy Thompson. Tim's antics were insane. Nate sat back down and took a sip of his coffee. It was the first time since he'd left North Dakota that he'd felt a sense of ease. Maybe it was because he was among friends who'd done crazier shit than he that he decided to go for it.

"I beat the shit out of my brother when I thought he'd had sex with the woman I wanted to bring to Vegas and marry."

Gem spit her coffee back into her mug, "Wow, that is fucked up."

Trevor lifted his brows. "Wait, you said *thought*. Are you saying he didn't?"

Nate shook his head. "I don't really know anymore. I don't think so. But it took me twelve hundred miles and a half a year of self-abuse to figure it out." *It had to be a lie,* Nate thought. A lie conjured up by jilted ex-lovers, passed on by a so-called friend.

"And the woman?" Gem asked.

Nate pressed his shoulders back into the chair and arched his head toward the ceiling. He hated to think about it. How could he have been so cold as to leave her like that without an explanation? It was the same way she'd left him.

Trevor slapped Nate's bare shoulder. "You and your women troubles. It reminds me of when you hooked up with me and Rocky in Denver. That was over a woman too, wasn't it?"

Nate kept his eyes trained on the ceiling.

"Holy shit, is it the same person?"

Nate didn't answer.

"You wrote your best stuff over that breakup. What was her name? Mary, Margie—"

"Mony. Her name is Mony." Saying her name aloud made him realize what an ass he had been. All the while he'd blamed Shannon for feeding him the lie, when he'd been the gullible fool. He should have trusted that Mony and Massey would never have betrayed him. He should have known it was all a lie.

"If it's not true, why don't you just go back to her?" Gem asked.

Trevor said, "Before you do, write it down, man; write it down."

Gem shot Trevor a scowling look. "Is that what you did the first time, take advantage of your friend's misery?"

Trevor responded in shock. "Are you kidding? You should have seen how messed up he was before he started writing music. When Nate focused his torment on paper, he'd penned some of the greatest heartbreak lyrics the world of rock and roll has ever known." He placed his hands over his heart. "People could relate. It was beautiful and cathartic."

"Loosely translated, you made a shitload of money," Gem grumbled irritably.

"Psssh, think what you want," Trevor said, impervious to the barb. "Nate has a gift, and a gift should be shared, not hidden under a bushel basket or something like that." Trevor was also an internet-certified minister for the Lady Luck drive-through chapel.

Nate wasn't listening, his mind still stuck on whether Mony would take him back. It hadn't been the first time he'd misjudged her, and despite all his impudent, self-righteous bullshit, she'd always shown him love and friendship. But this time was different; this time he'd hurt her when she'd been broken. Nate gave Gem a despairing look. Part of him wanted to believe Mony would still forgive him, but the greater part knew he didn't deserve it.

Gem kicked him under the table. "You aren't going to

know unless you ask her."

She was right. Still, he said, "I can't go back, not yet. If there is one thing that I've learned through my life's stupidity, it's that time heals—eventually. Every time I rush it, I make things worse."

"Hm, sounds like a song lyric." Gem kicked Trevor in the shin. "Ouch." He slid his chair away from the table. "So, Nate, what are your plans?"

Nate considered. He knew Mony had a temper and that she probably needed a cooling-off period. He'd shattered her trust; forgiveness would take a while. She also had major decisions to make regarding the oil business, as did he. If Mony had already made that decision, she hadn't shared that with him.

"Things are really screwed up between me and Mony. I'm not even sure Massey's still on my side. I thought I'd head out to the coast for a while, get my head together before I go back with hat in hand and beg forgiveness."

"You've done enough recuperating. Do some yoga, tai chi, or something for self-reflection and have a priest exorcise your demons."

"Demons? I guess that's one way to describe it."

"Who was she?" Gem asked.

Nate looked puzzled.

"The woman you cry out for in your dreams. Is it this Mony? Because I feel it's someone else."

Nate sighed. Had he resurrected that ghost too? What else had he exposed on his drunken rampage? "My mom," he confessed, "and it's not a dream, just a bad memory. She left me and my brother when we were just kids."

Gem's tone softened. "Why?"

Another difficult question, because the truth of it was that he didn't know why. "I was pretty small at the time. My dad never talked about it, and she never contacted me. All I have are these awful images in my head and a bunch of unanswered questions."

"Have you considered hiring a private investigator to look for her?" Trevor asked. "People do it all the time, and you've got resources, right?"

Nate and Massey had never talked about or even considered looking for their mom. Both maintained the fundamental belief that if their mother wanted to see them, she would be the one to initiate. After all, they were still pretty much where she'd left them, back in North Dakota. *But what if she was unable to contact them? What if she'd already died?* The thought made his stomach knot.

"Well," Trevor said, placing a hand on Gem, "I'd say it's high time you put that police academy training I paid for to use and do some private investigating."

Gem pushed his hand away. "I've done plenty to earn that training back threefold, but I'll help you, Nate, if you want. We'll call it, Operation Search for Ma Ferguson."

Nate took a drink of his cold coffee. "I haven't a clue where to start looking and I doubt my dad or Massey would be of much help."

"You leave that to me. We can talk later this afternoon about what you remember and take it from there."

Feeling inspired, Nate said, "Sure, why not. There's nothing lost by looking. And when I find her, I can decide then if I want to make contact or not." Then a terrible thought occurred to him. "Maybe she doesn't want to be found?"

"Cross that bridge when you come to it, Nate," Gem said.

Right. He pushed the thought from his mind. Focusing on the positive, his shoulders felt lighter walking to the bedroom to dress for the day. Perhaps learning what happened to his mom was the best place to start on his journey to healing.

CHAPTER 5

JOHN

John stood in the corridor outside the auditorium where Ramona was speaking. He'd heard bits and pieces of her presentation; she must have said something funny, because several times the audience broke into bursts of laughter. He leaned against the wall and began nervously tapping his foot. It had been reckless calling the attorney, but he'd accomplished what he set out to do. He'd rattled Ferguson. It was there in his voice. Despite the easy money, John had no plans of taking on Stapleton's case, but it was satisfying letting the attorney think so. Ferguson would have also warned Ramona to tread lightly in enemy waters. Except Ramona splashed around as if she owned the damn pond. He was beginning to understand her. Even the attorney couldn't tell her what to do. He found that very attractive.

It didn't surprise him that she'd stood him up the night before. Having no intention of meeting him, she would go about her business and leave town without a backward glance. He didn't view it as playing hard to get; it was just her way, and he rather enjoyed her making him earn her time. She showed interest in him, or so he let himself believe. She was just . . . *conflicted.*

The physical attraction and mutual enjoyment in one another's company made him believe it wasn't impossible for them to be together. There would be a certain level of discomfort leaving the familiar behind—that was to be expected—but the pros far outweighed the cons. She was his way out of his law firm. The commission alone convincing her to sell to Monroe would ensure his financial independence, a complete win-win. He would never be as wealthy as she. It was a factor he could live with. The sale of the oil business offered Ramona unmitigated autonomy. He would offer unbiased counsel and set her free from the shackles of running an oil business, if she'd let him. What they needed now was to get back to where they were before they knew one another's identity. He had a plan for that.

As the auditorium emptied, John considered his obstacles. It was mostly the Fergusons, especially the rock star. He didn't believe for one minute the moronic rumor Monroe fed him regarding the Fergmeister beating up his brother, or that he'd *disappeared.* From his observation, the brothers seemed tight, at least outwardly. It was the friction between the rock star and his old man which had been apparent. Young Ferguson maintaining a low profile was simply a ruse to confuse Monroe Oil. He'd tested his theory, mentioning the altercation to the attorney. It hadn't provoked much of a response. Still, there was something about the whole thing that didn't quite add up. He'd witnessed firsthand the intimate connection between Ramona and Nathan—it was a significant complication to his plan. Ramona held a strange notion that pursuing her personal interests was a betrayal toward her family. He could respect loyalty, but her relationship to the Fergusons was nothing more than a business arrangement. Businesses were a commodity, meant for purchase and sold at a profit.

John moved to the back of the room and watched people continue to mill around Ramona, vying for her time. She was patient with each person, personable and friendly. She looked up and saw him. Her smile didn't waver. That may have been for the sake of her audience. When it became apparent she was stalling, he approached the group and said politely, "I hate to break up this lively conversation, but I need to get our guest speaker out for lunch."

Acknowledging their cue, each shook her hand and left. Ramona walked back to the podium, where she gathered her things. Without looking at him, she said, "What makes you think I'm going to lunch with you?"

Not a sharp response, a playful one. John let her finish her task, then gently took her arm and escorted her out of the room. She didn't resist. It gave him hope. It was when they'd reached the lobby that she dug in her heels.

"First, where are you taking me?" she said in that sweet venomous way, warning him to tread carefully.

"You said you wanted to have lunch somewhere public, so that's where I'm taking you."

"Details," she said, impatience slipping into her tone.

John weighed his words. "If you haven't been to Navy Pier, I thought we could go there, have a picnic lunch, and enjoy some of the bright sunshine on this warm spring day. Have you been to the Pier?"

"No. I wanted to, but my timeline is tight," Ramona said wryly.

He smiled. "Do you need a jacket or anything before we go?"

"I suppose I should. I hear the wind off the lake still has a bite this time of year." She started toward the bank of elevators.

That went too easy, John mused. He was tempted to follow her, make sure she didn't give him the slip, but he stayed in the lobby. Fifteen minutes passed. John was beginning to assume the worst when she stepped off the elevator with a jacket draped over her arm.

"Lead the way," she said.

He'd taken his Lamborghini Aventador out of winter storage the week before just to impress her. She liked the metallic blue color. He wished he could have shown off its speed and powerful engine. He needed the open road for that. Maybe next time.

They hit the food court and stopped at America's Dog, where he bought two Chicago-style hotdogs, then sat down on a bench that overlooked the lake. Ramona ate the dog like a pro, oozing little of the toppings onto the wax paper wrapping. He was impressed. Afterward, they walked the Pier. She enjoyed the Smith Museum of stained-glass windows, the atrium, and the ballroom. She loved the gardens and took a ride with him on the Ferris wheel. They strolled along the boardwalk arm in arm as he entertained her with the history of the Pier and stories of Chicago. She was beginning to relax, the previous caution abating. He tried to segue the conversation toward business. She asked questions about the marinas along Lake Shore Drive.

"The Chicago Yacht Club is a few miles from here. Would you like to take a tour?"

"I'm not sure," she said. "You put me on a tight leash with that stunt you pulled, calling Massey."

John reared his head back. "I'm surprised you let him boss you around like that."

She shrugged. "I don't. But there's nothing to stop him from flying to Chicago and trying to retrieve me. Massey is extremely protective."

"Don't you think that's a bit of an overreaction?"

"A bit. But you don't know our history. Besides, my brother is a man who likes to control the outcomes. I'm sure you can relate."

John could relate. That was a problem. As much as he wanted to dislike Ferguson, innately, he liked the guy. "He's not your brother," he said coolly. Ramona looked at him frustrated. He placated her by holding his hands up in surrender. "Let me rephrase that. You can tell legal counsel to give it a rest. I'll be sure to have you back before your plane turns into a pumpkin or something."

She laughed, a sweet sound to his ears. "I already did. Let's go check out your hoity-toity yacht club."

Ramona gazed out the side window as he drove along Lake Shore Drive. He could see her reflection, wide-eyed with fascination as they passed Grant Park, the Museum campus, and the stunning Chicago skyline. He told popular tales similar to the ramblings of a tourist guide, then used the opportunity to segue to business.

"Have you given further consideration to Monroe's offer? I see he's upped his offering price. Seems like a good time to sell with oil prices dropping."

Her facial expression hardened. "I'd rather not talk about that."

"Just making conversation," he said casually. "Monroe Oil is one thing we have in common."

She turned to face him. "Don't remind me. Do you really want to ruin this lovely day talking business?"

He didn't. "Point taken," he said contritely. "Here's our exit."

He parked in the underground garage near the Monroe Station and said, "Ready for your boat ride? We catch the water taxi over there." He pointed toward the dock. "Then we shuttle out to the harbor where the yachts are moored."

She looked at the dock and stiffened.

"Don't worry, the moorings are extremely safe and provide excellent privacy for a relaxing evening aboard the yacht."

"Who said anything about staying the evening? I thought we were just checking it out."

There was an undercurrent of tension, and he cursed inwardly for bringing up the topic of oil. "Well the place is out there on the water, Ramona," he said, lightening the conversation. "We can make it a quick ride and—"

"It's not about the ride."

She continued to stare at the dock; he followed her line of sight, the larger picture, which put him and Mony on opposite sides, coming into view. Senior partners Quincy Goldman and Randall Rice along with Randall's son Ethan, son-in-law to Thomas Monroe, stood waiting for the taxi. She must have recognized them from his business luncheon the day before. *Shit.*

"Look, it's all right," he said trying to reassure her. "I'll call Lyn and let her know we won't be coming. She's been—"

"She?"

He heard the tone of amusement. "Yeah, Lyn is a member of my racing team. She's one of the best sailors I know."

Ramona watched pensively as the three men boarded the taxi. "And there will be no one else with us on the boat, no middle-of-the-lake rendezvous?"

The wariness was back in her voice, as if she were being lured into an ambush. *Perceptive,* he thought, since that was in essence what he was doing. "No, just you, me, and Lyn."

She watched the taxi clear the dock and chug out into the bay. The few minutes that passed between them felt like an eternity. Finally, releasing the tension from her shoulders, she said curtly, "Well, all right, then. We'd better get going if we're going to catch the next taxi."

As the *Lynnie Q* came into view, John felt the skip in

his heartbeat. The Westerly Cirrus was a fantastic little vintage cruiser and came fully loaded. He'd purchased her as a starter boat but kept her long after he'd moved onto a newer, much faster racing boat. She was sturdy, seaworthy, and in top-notch condition. She had sleeping room for four, but he'd remodeled for two sleeping cabins. He'd rigged her for single handle from the cockpit with a rolling furler. John used to tell people he'd kept the *Lynnie Q* mostly for cruising, but who was he kidding? He loved that boat. It always gave him a surge of excitement whenever he prepared her for sailing. That excitement increased exponentially as Ramona boarded the vessel.

Lyn came up from below deck, her smile wide. "Well, I finally get to meet the famous oil woman from the Bakken my little brother's been talking so much about." She wiped her hands on her shirt, took Ramona's hand and gave it a hardy shake. "Hi, my name is Lyn Finch. Welcome aboard the *Lynnie Q*."

Ramona looked at John. "Little brother?"

Lyn laughed. "He didn't tell you?"

John could tell the two women were going to hit it off nicely.

When they hit the open water, he forgot about plotting mergers and acquisitions. Lyn began engaging Ramona in the fundamentals of sailing; the other woman caught on quickly, an innate response to those who took the helm of their vessels. They rode along the Chicago shoreline for several hours. The wind was out of the north at a cool fifteen miles per hour. It made for a tricky return to the harbor, but the captain and crew were up to the challenge.

It was a thrill watching Ramona. She'd give her face to the sprays of water and wind—an act of defiance against nature, or an expression of equanimity and surrender. John manned the helm as his sister entertained Ramona with stories at his expense. He didn't mind and laughed along with them. It was a side of his life few were privy to, a curse of working for the most powerful and prestigious law firm in the city. At work, he was constantly under a critical microscope. Out on the lake, he could be his true self.

They returned to the mooring early evening, and Ramona helped John dock the boat while Lyn went below deck. They didn't work as well together as Mony and Lyn had. John was a split second too late warning Mony to duck as the bow came around, catching her on the forehead. Lyn returned moments later, carrying a picnic basket packed full of goodies. She set it on the deck and looked up to see the minor laceration above Mony's eye.

"Christ, John, I leave you for a second and you're already beating up the woman."

Mony laughed it off. "It's just a scratch, and you read my mind," she said eyeing the basket. "This sailing business burned off that hotdog we ate at the Pier about an hour into our trip." Lyn got Mony a cold compress, then together they unpacked the basket while John cracked open a bottle of wine. He liked the way Ramona and his sister interacted. They sat out on the deck, enjoying their meal as the sun began to settle over the Chicago skyline.

John was pleased at least part of his mission had been a success. He wanted Ramona to experience what life could be like beyond the oil fields of North Dakota, and in the short term, at least, he'd accomplished that. Speaking his musings aloud, he said, "It doesn't get much better than this."

"I think you're wrong about that," his sister said with a twinkle in her eye.

Lyn was as close to a best friend as any male counterpart John had in his life. She knew his heart and his mind, and never failed to support him in any endeavor. She looked at Ramona, who had become engrossed in the view of the skyline. *"Talk to her"* she mouthed silently. John shook his head.

Lyn smiled, then kicked back as they all enjoyed the rest of the wine and watched the approaching twilight.

CHAPTER 6

MONY

John's sister left after sunset with the excuse that her
wife would become worried if she wasn't home by
nine. If Mony had wanted to leave at a time of her own
choosing, that would have been her opportunity. She
stayed.

Before Lyn boarded the ferry, she surprised Mony
with a hug. "It was a pleasure meeting you today, Mony
Strong. I have to say, I was very impressed with your skill,
for a newbie."

Mony touched her forehead. "I imagine I could have
done a whole lot worse."

They bantered in true Minnesota goodbye fashion. She
seemed hesitant to leave. Mony wouldn't mind if she
stayed. Lyn had been a lot of fun and very easy to talk
to. Her presence defused some of the tension created by
John's searching for an opportunity to talk business and
the ill-timed arrival of his partners. She was grateful for
that.

Lyn whispered in Mony's ear, "He's crazy about you,

you know. Let him down gently when the time comes. It's going to take him a while before getting over you."

The remark caught Mony off guard. *Crazy in what way?* She held no illusion that today was anything more than an elaborate strategy to talk her into selling to Monroe masquerading as a lovely day sailing on Lake Michigan. She hoped John would be as perceptive as his sister.

Lyn pulled away and gave her brother a kiss on the cheek, then winked at them both. "Don't do anything I wouldn't do."

She left, and John and Mony settled out on the stern deck, drinking wine. The boat rocked gently as a breeze blew in from the northwest, carrying cloud cover that reflected the lights from the city. It was a beautiful scene. The soft sound of jazz wafted from below deck. He was clearly a fan, she not as much, preferring R&B. Jazz deviated too much from the melody, taking the listener on a convoluted journey of countermelodies and trills before winding its way back, yet it seemed to fit her mood as well as the current situation.

John rested against the long bench with his legs stretched out in front of him, cradling Mony between his arms and legs. She sat back against his chest, reflecting on the high points of the day. He'd designed each moment with her seduction in mind. It wasn't entirely an unpleasant thought, excluding the ubiquity of his hidden agenda. Inviting Lyn had been a nice touch—her presence lent John the illusion of being more humanly attainable. There was an easy rhythm between brother and sister as they worked the sailboat, a familiarity Mony admired.

But admiration didn't substantiate compatibility or the possibility of an actual relationship working between them.

John combed his fingers through her pixie strands of wind-tossed hair, the tactile stimulation soothing; she breathed a contented sigh. When she didn't think about the scumbag whom John worked for, she considered how easy it would be to fall for the guy. He was handsome, smart, charming, and a skilled lover. She'd become aware of how depressed and cranky she'd been as of late. Work and her hobby farm provided limited distraction; a good romance novel and a dog at her feet didn't cut it. She missed male companionship, and she missed having sex. Her deceased husband had evolved into quite a passionate partner. It hadn't always been that way between them. In the beginning of their relationship, he'd treated her more like a wounded animal, fearful he'd trigger something that would remind her of her rape; they'd both had to learn how to get past it. They had, but the journey wasn't easy. She would always love him for that. She'd hoped to build a similar life with Nate, but sadly, he no longer seemed interested. John seemed attracted to the idea. Unfortunately, he lacked the constitution and common sense to see the detriment working for a soulless company had on forming a meaningful relationship.

"Sorry to disturb you," John said, shifting behind her and lifting her gently off his chest, "but I have to see a man about a horse." Mony moved over to let him up and stood to stretch her legs. She'd become stiff from sitting after using muscle groups she'd long forsaken. A gust of wind blew across the water. She shivered, bereft of John's body heat, and joined him below.

John stood in front of the kitchen sink drying his hands; he looked contented, in his element. She crossed her arms, appreciating the view. John was a man who'd clearly taken care of himself. His well-defined muscles corded through his arms, indicative of the strength it required to manage his boat. He said, "Ready to head back to the mainland?"

Mony walked to him wrapping her arms around his waist. "I got chilled when you left. I just need to warm up."

"I can help with that."

He took her in his arms, rubbing his hands up and down her back. It felt good. She wondered how humans could go so long without being touched. She brushed the back of her fingers across his cheek. He took her hand and began swaying to the soulful voices of Ella Fitzgerald and Louis Armstrong singing "The Nearness of You." The way his citrusy scent mingled with the freshwater air and the cabin's musky odor of wood aroused her. Mony laid the side of her head against his chest and heard the steady rhythm of his heartbeat kick up a notch.

"Stay with me tonight," he murmured.

She was tempted. John had not only shown her a good time; he'd extended his kindness by giving her a glimpse into his personal life. It was a trusting gesture. She found it ironic that family would be a central theme in both of their lives. Their greatest difference seemed to be that John's heart beat with the rhythm of the city, whereas she was rooted in the country. Fragments of a past conversation came to mind.

"I'll be all right," she assured her surrogate brother. *"I promise I'll call you at the first hint of trouble. No, that won't be necessary. Yes, we're still on for dinner. I'll notify you before takeoff and when I land. Don't worry, I know what I'm doing."*

She could tell by the tone of Massey's voice he wasn't at all placated, but he respected her boundaries. Tonight, he left to her discretion. Tomorrow was soon enough for her and John to resume the role of adversaries. She kissed John gently on the cheek. "I have until sunrise before my coach turns into a pumpkin."

He undressed her slowly, peeling back each layer of clothing in deliberate seduction. She stood naked in the glow of the dimly lit cabin as John's gaze glided over her body. Mony wrapped her arms around her middle, an instinctive reflex. John had anticipated the response and took her hands, redirecting them to his shirt. She began unbuttoning, resisting the urge to claw and tear—she had to savor the moment. It was uncertain when the next opportunity would occur. She willed her hands to be steady as she worked at undoing the fly of his pants. John had incredible control and savored the anticipation building. He took her in a closed dance position, clasping her right hand next to his chest and placing his right hand on her left shoulder blade. He moved in a foxtrot rhythm, the steps smooth and subtle, as if they were on a crowded dance floor. He inched them toward the stem of the boat. He was a consummate dancer, with an inherent sensuality in each step. His adept skill compensated for the natural fluidity she felt dancing with Nate. He wasn't Nate.

The temperature became sweltering in the cabin. Sweat beaded along her hairline, between her breasts, and along her spine. *Was it nerves or anticipation?*

He lifted her up onto the bunk in the bow of the boat, and she trembled when her back touched the mattress. The quarters were tight for a tall man, the width not much more than a double bed. John stood in the doorway of the small sleeping space and pulled the V-berth cushion, filling the open area in the mattress. He guided her hips toward the foot of the bed and spread her legs as he settled on his knees between her thighs.

"I'll take care of you first." He'd said the same the first time they'd made love. Was it insight, experience, or both?

Her butt rested on the mattress edge, leaving no place for her feet to gain purchase; she draped her legs over his shoulders, completely at his mercy. He needed the control, an assurance he gave as good as he'd received. She stroked the silken strands of his raven hair, delighting in his sinful mouth as he fluttered his wicked tongue over her clit and rimmed along her cleft. She writhed at the onslaught, moaning with pleasure.

"You are so greedy," he said, gazing up from between her legs.

She looked down her torso with hooded eyes. "How long do you plan to torture me this time?"

"Foreplay," he corrected her with a playful grin, "and not long. You're much too ready for me."

She was ready. Maybe it was because she'd been

thinking about his touch all afternoon, perhaps from the moment John had followed her outside the restaurant. This was why she'd refused to heed Massey's warnings traveling to Chicago. Deep down, she'd hoped John would find her. He'd awakened something inside her the night they'd shared on the train, something she thought died with her husband. Nate's unexpected departure had made her acutely aware she didn't want to spend the rest of her life alone.

He stood when he took her—no coincidence that the height of the bed was perfect for him to dominate the pace. She should have been affronted, having sex in a place where he'd had other women. She tried not to think about it. It was foolish to consider the intimacy they shared as anything more than temporary.

Mony wrapped her legs around his waist, opening to his powerful thrusts. She wanted to hold him against her body, feeling the heat of his passion rise toward climax, but this round was his, and he took what he wanted. She let him. The rhythmic pulsing of his orgasm pushed her into another one of her own and she cried his name as tears of ecstasy streamed down her cheek. She flung her arm over her eyes. When his orgasm was complete, he climbed onto the bunk and blanketed her with his body. She coiled her legs around him like a snake.

"Did I hurt you?" he asked in a gentle whisper.

Mony brushed away the tears, trying to rein in the torrent of emotion. "Yes, just not in the way you think."

John replaced the cushion and slid alongside her. Spooning against her back, he cradled her in his arms. "It is in the way I'm thinking. I want to ruin other men for you, show you that a life is possible between us. I want your heart to belong to me."

So had her late husband. Like Bob, John had found her vulnerable and confused. It had taken years for Bob to build the sort of relationship he envisioned.

The morning air was brisk but became warmer, more humid as they drew nearer to the city. They spoke very little on the drive from the marina back to her hotel. John let go of her hand only to shift gears. The city glowed as if it were daytime, the traffic undiminished. Mony wondered how anyone could sleep in such a place.

A light mist began to fall against the windshield, though not enough to keep the wipers going. John pulled in front of the hotel's main lobby doors and shut off the car engine. Taking her hand, he turned to face her, "When will I see you again, Ramona?"

He knew the answer.

Mony looked down to where their hands joined and began fiddling with the titanium ring on his hand. It was handsome, simple yet elegant. It spoke of the man who wore it. She could have done so much worse her first time back in the dating pool. She looked into his warm, assessing eyes, darkened in the shaded light around them. An image came to mind—those would be the same eyes staring at her from across the courtroom, callous, calculating, implacable.

"I'm afraid of the next time," Mony said honesty. "We are on such opposite sides of the spectrum. My brother told me you're dangling something over his head. Surely you don't think—"

"He's not your brother," John said with a tone of exasperation, "and I am not hanging anything over his head."

Mony sighed. "John, if you can't see past that fact the Fergusons are as much a family to me as your sister is by flesh and blood to you, then we're already at an impasse." She let go of his hand and reached for the car door handle.

John reached across the console to halt her escape. "Does that brotherhood include the rock star?"

She had no answer for that, at least not one he would understand. The term "brother" was something she used to pass Nate off as family when the moment required it. Since she had never been wife to either Ferguson, it was the closest term she had for defining the relationship between them, until sex came into play. Nate was an enigma.

John released her hand and got out of the car. Rounding the hood quickly, he then pinned her between the door and the car.

"Ramona, please, I don't want to fight, and I don't want us to end like this. Tell me what I have to do to make us work." John took her into his arms, desperation in his grip; it terrified her. Mony leaned her head against his shoulder and felt his arms relax.

"John, I honestly don't know that there can be a future for us. I don't expect you to change your life for me, because the truth of it is, there is no future for me without Nate in it. I am bound to him." She pulled away and looked up into John's sad, confused expression. "I wish I could explain it to you in a way that you could understand, but even if that were possible, it wouldn't change the outcome." She lifted on her tiptoes and kissed him gently on the cheek. "I had the most exhilarating day, and I can't thank you enough for the kindness you've shown me. You are a wonderful man and a magnificent lover." She cupped the side of his cheek. "There is someone in this world who will love you as you deserve."

She stepped around him. He let her pass. Before she entered the hotel, John said to her, "Ramona, I've already found that special person. I want you to know that I will fight for you, and your love, until the last shred of hope is gone."

Mony looked back and saw the determination etched on his face. She knew he believed the words he spoke were sincere. But he didn't know her, not really, only how her body responded to physical loneliness. He saw what she wanted him to see, and in that moment, she realized fulfilling his sister's request would be impossible.

CHAPTER 7

MASSEY

Massey sat in the back seat of the SUV as it bumped along the familiar landscape. After Nate left home, there hadn't been much of a reason to maintain the minimum maintenance road that ended at the Altman place. Kip paid good money to have the county grader smooth a single-lane path. With neither Mony nor Nate on-site, Massey had asked Mony to call the sheriff, granting verbal permission—a formality. During their conversation, she told him about her sailing venture with Finch. He didn't like it, but what could he do about it, except curse his dumbass brother for leaving her alone and lonely.

The sheriff drove his vehicle, keeping up appearances out of respect for the property owner's absence. He didn't want to give Monroe further ammunition in his court case. Massey remembered the last time Monroe thought a Ferguson was trespassing on the Altman property—he'd confronted a group of their friends gathered on the lake for hockey practice, a longstanding tradition. Jason Monroe and his attorney John Finch had been on an aerial survey and landed on the lake thinking they could strong-arm the group into leaving. It was there that Massey had learned just how dangerous Monroe could be. Mony had accused him of carrying a concealed weapon; unfortunately, no one else had seen it. Even though several months had passed and the gun was probably lying at the bottom of the lake, Massey was determined to look for it.

Since it was along the way, they stopped by the family farm. Something or someone had been randomly setting off the motion sensors over the past few weeks. It was getting expensive having a security team dispatched for a false alarm; he wanted to check it out.

"Any ideas on what's triggering the sensor?" the sheriff asked, making conversation.

"Out here, could be anything," Kip said, disarming the security alarm to the house.

"It would be a free place for squatters," the sheriff said warily. "What sort of security system do you have on the place?"

"Military grade," Kip replied, mildly offended. "You'd have to have significant skill and equipment to get around it."

The three men canvassed the house quickly. Massey hadn't been back to the family farm since the day Nate had left. It seemed to be exactly the way he remembered, right down to the pile of clothes left on the closet floor in the upstairs hallway; yet something felt off. He did a walk-through of Nate's room, searching the drawers, desk, and the nightstand. Everything seemed in place. Nate's cell and credit cards sat in a neat pile inside the nightstand.

Inside—that wasn't right. In Nate's hasty departure, he'd left everything in a disheveled pile on top of the nightstand. Who straightened it?

Kip shouted up the stairs to let Massey know that he and the sheriff were heading out to the truck. Massey picked up Nate's phone, charger, and credit cards before joining them. Outside, he suggested they look around.

While his dad and the sheriff checked the outbuildings, Massey walked around the perimeter of the house. He wasn't sure what he thought he'd find. Evidence of numerous tracks marred Poppy's flower beds along the foundation, and many of the tulips were half eaten. The deer left the daffodils alone, but something was going after the hyacinth, crocus, and lily bulbs. Massey bent down for a closer look and was startled when a fat squirrel hiding in the underbrush of a bleeding heart scarpered away, an iris root in its mouth. He'd stumbled back, laughing at his own jitteriness. The laughter stopped when he spotted a boot print embedded in the muddy earth next to the old coal chute.

For the next half hour, the three men combed around the foundation of the house but found no other footprints. Massey said, "Nate could have easily left the footprint when he was winterizing the house. The ground never freezes along the foundation. And the sensors going off were probably triggered by the deer making a meal out of Poppy's flower beds." It sounded logical, but the boot mark niggled at him.

The sheriff said, "We'd better take a look at Buddy's

place."

Massey unlocked the security box on the kitchen door, and he and the sheriff went inside. Kip stood at the bottom of the porch steps and said, "I'm going out to the hangar to have a look around," before taking off in that direction.

Massey walked through the familiar farmhouse with a heavy heart. He hadn't spent as much time there as Nate, but he still had fond memories of the place. It was a warm, friendly, inviting space, always filled with boisterous laughter. Now it felt like the century-old building that it was. He turned to the sheriff. "If you don't mind starting in the kitchen, I'll go through the rest of the main floor."

The great room was a combination living and formal dining area, except the space where a dining table would have stood was occupied by a baby grand piano. It was the kitchen that had been the hub in this household, unless Mony or Nate were playing the piano. Mony had covered all the furniture, which was minimal, when she left. It took Massey all of five minutes to rifle through the two end-table drawers, the small bookcase, and the TV stand. He found nothing. Lifting the piano bench seat, he checked through the sheet music and found nothing remarkable.

The sheriff hollered from the kitchen. "Nothing here, Massey—where else do you want me to check?"

Massey shouted back, "Why don't you head upstairs. I'll check the basement and then join you." He heard the weight of the sheriff's footsteps climbing the stairs as he went to check the bedroom on the main floor.

Buddy's room was stark as well. Mony had left nothing

in the drawers and had tossed out the old mattress and box spring, leaving an empty frame. Massey checked the walk-in closet, which held a few empty hangers. There was nothing on the top shelf. In the floorboards, he noticed a concealed trapdoor and pried it open with his key. The space was empty. He guessed it may have been the space where Buddy kept the small fireproof safe Mony had taken back to Minnesota. He'd have to get after her about looking through it.

He was backtracking through the living room when an incoming text pinged. It was from Mony.

I'll be landing in Bismarck Friday around suppertime.

Massey texted back. *Good. Supper's at my place. We can fly to Williston the next day. Before you come, OPEN THE SAFE.*

She posted a thumbs-up. Looking at his phone sparked a thought.

Do you have Buddy's cell phone?

No.

He found a charger in the kitchen junk drawer and was about to look for a phone when the sheriff hollered, "Massey, you'd better come up here."

The sheriff was standing in the middle of Mony's bedroom with a forlorn expression on his face. "I know this sounds kind of weird," he said with a nervous laugh, "but I'm not entirely comfortable going through Mony's drawers."

Massey understood. "I'll take the dressers; you check the closet and cedar chest."

The drawers were empty—the chest was not. It was like a time capsule filled with items given to her by Nate.

Massey recognized the well-loved stuffed toy Nate had won at the county fair. Another item was a rolled-up blacklight poster of two buzzards sitting on a dead tree branch over a longhorn skull. The caption read, "Patience, my ass. I'm going to kill something." *It's so Mony.* The sheriff said over his shoulder, "Let's hope Kip is having better luck out in the hangar."

Before locking up, Massey searched the furniture again. Sliding his hands deep into the cushion of Buddy's favorite recliner, he found the cell phone. It was incredible no one had found it. He slipped it into his pocket and went to the basement.

Built in 1892, the house had originally been a hunting cabin for a railroad tycoon out of Calgary. A local farmer purchased it in the early 1930s and added onto the structure using surrounding fieldstone for a foundation. He abandoned the site in 1939, after President Franklin D. Roosevelt established Lake Zahl National Wildlife Refuge and created a new farmstead closer to the township road, away from the lake. Kip parceled off the site when he purchased it in 1968, along with some acreage to Buddy. Buddy had made several home improvements over the years, but the stone foundation remained unchanged.

The one-room basement was old, dank, and musty. Standing on the steps, Massey could see daylight seeping in through cracks in the northeast wall. He walked closer and caught a whiff of something decaying, then noticed a dead rodent in the corner lying on a substantial pile of dirt. *That seems odd.* Not the dead mouse, but the dirt. He examined the crumbling grout between the spaces of stone. It almost looked like something was picking away at it. *But what?* He shook his head, trying to rein in his imaginative thoughts; then he saw the head of a six-inch-long chisel sticking out of the dirt pile. *What in the hell?*

Walking back upstairs, he found an old hand towel in a drawer, then went back into the basement. He carefully picked up the chisel using the towel and wrapped it before finishing his search of the basement. Finding nothing else out of place, he stowed the object in his jacket and joined his dad and the sheriff in the hangar. They were standing over a military footlocker when he entered.

Kip looked up and asked, "Any idea where the key might be?"

He hadn't the faintest idea.

They'd scoured the hangar for about half an hour and came up empty before the sheriff asked, "Any idea where Buddy keeps his bolt cutter?"

It took the three of them to load the trunk into the sheriff's SUV. Kip and the sheriff took a breather and leaned against the vehicle. Massey saw an opportunity and said, "I'm going to check the shabin."

The sheriff stopped him and pulled a Glock from his glove compartment. He handed it to Massey.

"Do you really think that's necessary?"

Kip pulled back the inside of his jacket, revealing his sidearm. He said, "Just in case."

Massey took the gun, checked the safety, and stuffed it into the belt at the small of his back, grateful he wasn't the only one feeling paranoid. He said, "Wait for me here. I won't be long."

The squawk of waterfowl grew deafening as he got closer to the lake. It was invigorating to hear life in such a desolate region; he had to empathize with Mony's hesitation to drill. The northwestern corner of his state was already dotted with enough methane burn-off stacks to be visible from outer space. He didn't want to think what the toxic waste from another drill site would do to the ground-water tables. There was no balance between conglomerates, local farmers, Native Americans, or the national parks in the region. The one that had the money held all the power.

The edge too soft to walk along, Massey stayed back several feet from the shoreline. He also didn't want to disrupt the nesting. The remnants of their makeshift hockey rink were already gone, the goalie nets stored in the warming house for another season. Several ducks had gathered on the raft where he, Nate, and Mony used to go swimming. The memory was bittersweet.

"What the hell did you think you were going to find?" Massey muttered to the noisy waterfowl. He headed toward the warming house. To call it a warming house was an understatement—the building, which started out as a simple one-room shack, expanded over the years to the dimensions of a ranch-style cabin, hence earning the name *shabin*. Furnished to the hilt, it was the ultimate man cave.

As he walked around the perimeter of the building, he noticed multiple footsteps imprinted in the ground. There were more surrounding the firepit, running between the lake and the shabin. Not a surprise—the Trouble Shooters had been there less than a month ago. There would have been plenty of foot traffic. What drew his attention was that some of the footprints were small, not made by the weight of a grown man's foot.

He stepped onto the porch and checked the door. The lock hung loose, clearly broken. Massey reached for the Glock at the small of his back, eased the door open, and stepped inside. The putrid odor of human habitation hit him first. The second blow came from behind.

CHAPTER 8

JOHN

John was working on a closing statement draft when he heard a familiar voice filter in from the hallway. He glanced up to see his sister Lyn and her wife, Heather, standing outside his office, chatting it up with Franklin. They were dressed for sailing. He couldn't help but notice the predatory glances both women were garnering from every male in the corridor.

They're wasting their time.

After a beat, the women proceeded through his office door, closed it, and made themselves comfortable in the client chairs in front of his desk. Without looking up from his document, he asked, "Is the package secured?"

Lyn leaned forward, resting her elbows on his desk.

"Of course," she said matter-of-factly, "but I don't know why you didn't give it to her on the boat."

"We had more pressing matters," John said quietly. He always spoke openly to his sister about his relationships and had told her about Ramona staying the night. It was like a romance novel for Lyn and her spouse—they'd eaten it up with a spoon. But, for him, it was more than a story recounting his male conquests. Both women offered female insight and advice, something he frequently found to be very useful.

"John Atticus Finch, what the hell are you up to now?" Lyn teased.

He'd been waiting for that question.

He laid out the next phase of his plan in the seduction of Ramona Strong. Both women conceded it was romantic and discussed details on what tactics to use. He then finagled them into hanging onto the package until he could make the appointed delivery. He thought the discussion had ended when Lyn said to him, "This is all fine and well, little brother, but are you sure this is the approach you want to take with her?"

"What do you mean?"

Lyn looked to her partner, then to John. "This all feels very manipulative, especially right before the probate hearing. It's possible she may perceive your intentions as insincere. From what I could tell during our picnic on the boat, she has a very suspicious nature. Maybe you should wait until after the probate hearing to execute your plan."

He didn't entirely disagree with his sister's train of thought, but after probate, there would be no reason for him to be hanging around. He needed to strike while the embers of their lovemaking were still burning. "Isn't it also possible she might think I'm gold digging if I wait until after?"

"Only if she wins," Heather said.

"She'll win," John said glumly. "Monroe doesn't stand a chance challenging her in a North Dakota courtroom, and the ruling will be final. There is no second opportunity."

"There's another option," Lyn offered. "Show her you have no stake in the outcome of her case by stepping away. No words speak louder than the actions of a man willing to make a sacrifice for love."

Another romantic thought, and one he'd entertained in the back of his mind as well. He had been willing to make concessions until Ramona shut him down before she left Chicago. He sighed. "I'm afraid stepping away now would leave her much more vulnerable. My replacement would exploit any skeletons that might be hiding in the proverbial closet."

"Are there any?" his sister asked.

"Nothing concrete, but she does have this weird relationship with the Fergusons. They're the ones you should be worried about exploiting her vulnerability, not me."

"Has she ever alluded to that?"

"Not in so many words, except to say I don't know or understand the relationship, but the attorney is extremely protective."

"So, what's wrong with that?"

"Nothing, I suppose. But it's still unsettling that her son should look so much like a Ferguson without actually being one. Plus, she has the behavior of a woman who may have been sexually abused."

Lyn bristled. "Why do you say that?"

"It's there when we have sex. She has a hesitation,

an uncertainty I've never experienced with any women before, even ones who were married."

"This is conjecture, counsel," Heather interjected. "You're going to need cold, hard evidence if you're going to pursue that course of thinking."

"You make a valid point, opposing counsel," he said to his sister-in-law. He shook his head. "I feel as though I'm taking all the risk. If Ramona would just meet me halfway."

At that comment, both women sighed audibly.

After Lyn and Heather left, John got back to his draft, only to be interrupted again when Franklin announced over the interoffice comm, "Mr. Finch, Norman Stapleton is on line one. It's the third call today. How would you like me to handle it?"

John considered a moment, then said, "I'll handle it."

Norman Stapleton was antagonistic from the jump; John immediately disliked the man. He dominated the conversation with wild accusatory statements about how the government had it in for him just because he didn't have a military background. They'd shot him down when he tried to prove his wife Charlene was entitled to Buddy Altman's military pension, which they'd already awarded to Ramona. John couldn't get a word in edgewise until he managed to say to Stapleton, "I need to see the original document before I take your case. I will be traveling to Minnesota day after next. Where would you like to meet?"

He'd just hung up with Stapleton when there was a

knock at his office door. Sporting his customary Armani casual jacket and woolen trousers, Ethan Rice leaned insolently against the doorframe and said, "Got a minute?"

John didn't have even a second for Ethan's bullshit today, but he'd been anticipating the ambush since he'd seen him at the taxi dock. John waved him in, thinking to himself, *Keep the enemy closer.*

Ethan took the seat his sister had vacated. "I hear Lyn and Heather stopped by," he said, looking around the room as if they might be hiding under a table. "You should have told me. I wanted to make a wager with your sister-in-law for the upcoming Mac race. I also wanted to congratulate you and Lyn together for qualifying for the Island Goats Sailing Society this year."

John nodded his thanks.

"Speaking of sailing," Ethan went on, "who was the lovely woman you were hiding in the Lambo? Was she the same piece of tail you were chasing out of the restaurant the other day?"

John gave a wry smile. Ethan already knew that answer, along with all the details of the probate case. He'd been trying to weasel his way into Jason's good graces ever since the old man kicked him off the Altman-Ferguson land acquisition. Jason had been bitching to him for the past couple of months. Ethan empathized with Jason's position, offering support in the event John was unable to continue with the case. John said, "Ramona Strong, owner of F&A Oil from Williston, North Dakota."

Ethan sneered. "Only part owner to hear my brother-in-law tell it, and she's a real bitch."

John's jaw tightened. He wanted to punch the vulgar bastard in the teeth but kept his composure. "You're a little behind the times, my friend. Jason's been off the project for months now after that little embarrassment with Strong and the Fergusons. It's old news."

Ethan continued baiting him.

"So, you're fucking the opposition before the big probate hearing," he said, waggling his eyebrows. "Nice."

Now John wanted to kill him. Instead, he gave a haughty laugh and ignored the remark. "I've actually been waiting for old man Monroe to put Tia in charge of the family business. Wouldn't that be a kick in the ass?"

The cocky smirk on Ethan's face faltered. His wife, Tiffany Monroe, already wielded more money and power than Ethan ever dreamed. And since he'd signed a prenup, there wasn't a chance he'd ever get his hands on it. John wasn't sure if his former college roommate had knowledge of John's friends-with-benefits relationship with Tia, but he certainly had knowledge of Ethan's infidelities. The man couldn't keep his pants, or his mouth, zipped.

"At least she wouldn't piss herself," Ethan said with a forced laugh. Slapping the arms of the leather chair, he stood and headed for the door. "Well, I'd better let you get back to work. Let the dyke know I'm ready to take her money whenever she's ready to place her bet."

John stood and followed him to the door. "Heather has been a tremendous asset to our team. We're favored to place in the top ten again this year," he said coolly. "It's highly unlikely you'll be taking anyone's money."

"Wanna bet?" Ethan countered, and made an awkward jabbing motion at John's gut.

John didn't flinch, and Ethan left.

John and Franklin spent the rest of the afternoon prepping for a divorce hearing the following morning. If all went according to plan, his client stood to do well in the settlement—if she remained quiet during the proceedings. The woman had a big mouth, with a temper to match. *Just another spoiled rich kid who grew into an adult with an overinflated conception of entitlement,* he thought uncharitably. She was the opposite of Ramona. John took off his reading glasses; rubbed his eyes and sneezed. His seasonal allergies seemed to be flaring.

"Gesundheit," Franklin said.

He sneezed again and pulled a bottle of hand sanitizer from his desk. Squeezing a liberal amount into his palms, John said with a nasally whistle in his voice, "I need to bring you up to speed on my trip to Minnesota."

He would kill two birds with one stone. Norman and Charlene Stapleton had agreed to meet with him to discuss their claim and show proof of the letter. He doubted very much the letter existed, and even if it did, any codicils to Altman's final will and testament would render it invalid. Attorney Ferguson would have made sure of it. Next, he would visit Ramona. He was placing an enormous amount of faith in his plan to win her over. It was a mission in direct contrast with the Stapleton meeting. John considered letting Ferguson deal with it. Stapleton surely would have already approached Ramona with his cockamamie claim, and it wouldn't be the first time a greedy relative came crawling out from the woodwork. Still, he convinced himself it was best to keep the enemy closer. He hoped Ramona would view it that way. He also had to warn her. She would be facing confrontation from all sides, with Ethan throwing in with Jason and Stapleton looking for a handout. John felt a growing volatility to the situation. He had to do what he could to defuse it.

"I'll be gone for a couple of days, so take the time off," he told Franklin. "It'll be your last opportunity before the probate hearing."

Franklin gathered the loose papers from the desk. "No problem. I've been promising to join Miguel at his exhibit on the south side before he goes to Toronto. He'll be gone a month after that." Miguel Roseau was Franklin's partner, an independent contractor developing single-family homes out of repurposed materials. "By the way, which one did you decide on?"

John pulled a handkerchief from his pocket and blew his nose. "Decide on what?"

Franklin lifted a brow. "Don't be coy, you know what I'm talking about. The pot's nearly five grand. I have three hundred dollars of my own money riding on this one. So what did you choose?"

John stuffed the soiled cloth into a ziplock baggie. "Really, that much? Why isn't the pot that good when I'm in on the action?"

Franklin shoved the loose papers in a folder and said, "When you're in on the action, nobody bets, because you always win."

CHAPTER 9
MASSEY

Sheriff Wagner sped down the pothole-riddled road, nearly losing his rear axle. Massey sat on the porch of the warming house, holding a dirty chunk of ice he'd dug up on the north side of the building against the back of his head. He stood as the SUV approached, walking out to meet them.

"What the hell happened?" the sheriff shouted. Both he and Kip exited the vehicle, weapons drawn and ready to shoot anything that moved.

"I'm okay, I'm okay," Massey hollered back over the deafening sound of the disturbed waterfowl. The effort made his head ache. "Put your guns away, you'll scare 'em off."

The sheriff and Massey's dad gave him an incredulous look. Neither man holstered his weapon.

Kip asked, "Did you fire the shot?"

Massey held up the Glock still in his hand. "Yeah, I figured it was the best way to get your attention."

"Well, you sure as shit got it." The sheriff barked out a

humorless laugh. "Christ, Massey, what happened?"

"I opened the door to the shabin and the smell of human filth and garbage slammed me in the face, then someone hit me from behind." He pointed to a cast-iron frying pan in the doorway. "With that, I think. Next thing I knew, a pair of legs jumped over me and ran out the door. I didn't get a good look at 'em, but I imagine they haven't gone far."

"We didn't see anyone coming up the driveway," Kip said, "must still be around here somewhere."

Massey pointed out the footprints between the shabin and the firepit, and the three men worked out from there in a widening circle to see where else they would lead. When the tracks reached the shoreline, they walked as close as to the water's edge as they could, putting the waterfowl roosting there in a seriously foul mood. The squabbling was so loud that it was impossible to listen for human movement of any kind hiding out among the weeds. Massey tried to find where the smaller set of prints may have led, but they were lost among the larger prints.

After twenty minutes, shoes soaked, they returned to the shabin, Kip standing by the doorway while Massey and the sheriff examined the interior. Ragtag blankets and sleeping bags were scattered around the floor, along with empty bags of junk food, candy wrappers, apple cores, drug paraphernalia, used condoms, and cigarette butts. The sheriff pulled two pairs of latex gloves from his pocket and handed a set to Massey. "Touch things as little as possible," he cautioned. "We might get lucky and be able to lift some prints."

Massey slapped on the gloves. "What a mess," he said, glad for the barrier. "How long do you suppose they've been hiding out here?"

Kip answered, "If the Trouble Shooters were out here three weeks ago, it's less than that." He pointed to a patch of flattened grass along the shoreline. "I can see where someone may have cut across the lake from the township road, either on a snowmobile if there was still solid ice or in a small boat or canoe. It would be easier to tell if I had my waders along—Massey, I think your head is bleeding."

Massey placed a hand where the blunt object connected with his head; grit from the dirty ice mixed with a red tinge marred his fingertips. "Shit."

The sheriff said to Kip, "Get the first aid kit out of my truck."

Massey sat on the front porch step while the sheriff dabbed antiseptic on his wound. "You may need a stitch or two," the sheriff said. "You'll definitely have a goose egg."

Massey sighed inwardly. His wife was going to have a major conniption. He couldn't worry about that right now. "What do you think we're dealing with?"

"As I said before, with both homesteads sitting empty, it's a prime location to set up shop." The sheriff held up his hand to cut Kip off. "And I don't care what sort of security system you have. These people are desperate and devious. All they need is a cell phone and internet access and they can look up anything. It's no secret Nate and Mony aren't here."

Kip said, "Could we just be dealing with some local high school kids looking for a place to party?"

"Not likely."

Massey asked, "What about a runaway hiding out?"

"None reported, and around here, runaways are typically abductions. There is more than one person involved here. I'm more inclined to lean toward a prostitution den or human trafficking."

Massey looked to his dad, a silent understanding passing between them. *They would have to tell Mony.*

Three squad cars and a first-responder wagon pulled in the farmyard. Kip said angrily, "What the hell is this?"

The sheriff's jaw stiffened. "Backup."

An investigative team swept the shabin for prints, cordoned it off, and placed a new padlock on the door. As a team member walked by with the bagged cast-iron skillet, Massey reached into his coat pocket and pulled out the chisel he'd wrapped with cloth. "Here, you may as well take this too. I have a sneaking suspicion they may be related." One of the investigators held open a clean bag.

"Where did you get that?" Kip asked. Massey explained what he'd found in the basement, as well as the stacked credit cards in Nate's bedroom.

"This is something bigger than some hoodlums looking for a place to hold up, that we're dealing with," Massey said grimly. "This is organized."

Kip merely nodded.

Back in town, they were surprised to see a small cluster of people in front of the law enforcement main entrance. One person was holding a news camera. Massey muttered,

"This day just keeps getting weirder."

The sheriff glanced up into the rearview mirror with a sheepish expression. "I may have overreacted after you fired off the gun."

Along with the local newspaper and a TV reporter from Dickenson was a freelance reporter whom Massey recognized—Cayden Peckersch stood in the front, agitating the small gathering in typical anarchic fashion. Cayden, a self-proclaimed investigative journalist, came to the region two years ago with a flock of documentarians trying to uncover the "behind the scenes" look of the oil industry. Massey didn't necessarily disagree with reporting the truth about the oil industry. Everything had its good and bad points. It was the manipulative way Cayden went about gathering the truth which Massey found disturbing.

The investigative journalist had become something of a local personality after he'd gotten the exclusive on the explosion on an oil rig north of Watford City that killed two oil workers. He was hailed as a journalist with integrity, but his fifteen minutes of fame were short-lived after the wife of one of the deceased workers alleged that he'd given candy to her seven-year-old daughter in exchange for the families' man camp trailer number. The allegations were never substantiated, but the incident earned Cayden the nickname Candy Man—or Peckerhead from the less generous.

He was nothing more than a paparazzi reporter trying to sensationalize other people's misery. He lost all credibility after that.

As they approached the group, the sheriff said, "What's

going on here, folks?"

Cayden stepped out front and center, keeping one eye on the camera. "We hear there were shots fired out at the Altman farm. Will you corroborate?" Candy Man had obviously been monitoring the police scanner.

The sheriff chuckled. "It wouldn't surprise me, Cayden, since Altman's property is in a wildlife management area." The remark drew a few snickers from the crowd. Candy Man wasn't part of them.

"Then you won't mind telling us why three squad cars and a rescue unit were dispatched to the location?"

The sheriff went on with vague remarks, using words like *routine response* and *false alarms* to appease the crowd. Candy Man pressed the issue.

"A routine check that requires two non-owners and a county sheriff? Doesn't sound right. Did Ms. Altman or Nathan Ferguson authorize access?"

Massey noticed his dad's posture bristle from the corner of his eye. It was common knowledge that Nate held a share of Buddy's property as well as the oil business. It was also evident that Nate had been gone for months. What the locals really wanted to know was whether their favorite hometown boy had returned. What Candy Man was after was anyone's guess.

"Senator Ferguson doesn't need permission to check his own property or to run his business," the sheriff interjected. "F&A Crop Dusting Company is headquartered on the Altman property."

Someone spoke up in the crowd. "We know that. What did he need you for?"

"I'm part of the department, aren't I?" the sheriff retorted.

The banter went back and forth a while as the sheriff gave the crowd the usual evasive responses. He held up his hand to indicate no further questions and started walking toward the main door when Candy Man shouted, "Does your involvement on this call have anything to do with the drunk Indian girl passed out behind the Lake Zahl bar a few weeks back?"

The sheriff's steps faltered. "Are you saying it does, Cayden?"

The question reignited the crowd in a barrage of speculation involving both events. Massey hadn't known about the teen girl, but it was clearly a hot-button topic in the community. Conspiracy theories volleyed back and forth, trying to tie the two events together. Massey listened, trying to untangle any threads of truth from conjecture. In the end, nothing significant filtered out.

"I've wasted enough of the taxpayers' hard-earned money on this pointless discussion. I need to get back to work."

As the sheriff, Massey, and Kip walked into the station, Cayden called out, "Attorney Ferguson, is that dried blood on the back of your shirt?"

Unable to avoid the direct question, the sheriff again stepped in with a response. Over his shoulder, he said, "Yes, it's what happens when you don't duck while walking under a propeller."

With the sham press conference out of the way, the sheriff went about the unpleasant task of calling in the members of the Trouble Shooter hockey team. They were hoping someone might have seen something unusual while closing the shabin and storing the hockey equipment for the winter; if not, at least it would narrow the timeframe as well as the mode of access and the route to the location. At the end of the day, they'd learned the ice hadn't been solid enough to support the weight of an ATV or snowmobile, opening the possibility for access by boat or canoe. "The lake has been open a little over a week," the sheriff said. "Kip, when did the security alarms start giving you trouble?"

Massey answered, "Eight days ago."

Later that evening, Massey sat at his parent's kitchen table, eating a slice of rhubarb dessert and telling Poppy the story. Topping off Kip and Massey's coffee, Poppy asked, "Have you told Mony?"

Poppy disagreed with Kip's decision to let the sheriff conduct a more extensive investigation before bringing Mony in on the situation. "If Candy Man tweets some twisted version of the truth on the internet or whatever, Mony will be furious she hadn't heard the story from us first."

His stepmom's logic made perfect sense, but Massey supported his dad's decision—the delay dovetailed nicely with keeping Mony's trip to Chicago out of the conversation for now. To appease his stepmom, he informed both his parents of Mony's flight to Bismarck the day after next. In addition to the immediate problems, he needed to discuss another matter: what to do with Buddy's cremated remains. Between the missing deed, running two business, and Nate's disappearance, the matter had fallen off his radar. There was no stipulation made in the will, but over beers a couple of months prior to his death, Buddy had informed Massey he'd wanted his ashes strewn over a village located somewhere in the Hoang Lien Son Mountain Range, in Vietnam. It was an absurd notion. Massey couldn't even find the village on a map, let alone begin wading through the red tape, government regulations, and legal procedures for transporting human remains out of the country. He hoped Mony would shut down the whole idea. It was highly doubtful Buddy's wish would ever come to fruition.

Poppy nodded. "Good. Now, let's go have a look at that footlocker."

The sheriff had stopped by earlier with a bolt cutter and removed the lock. He was curious about the content, but since Buddy had stipulated everything inside the hangar was all part of the F&A crop-dusting business, he didn't have a legal reason to stick around. Poppy watched from the doorway as Kip lifted the lid to the locker. His dad no doubt was hoping he would find the missing title and deed. When he lifted an old Brownie camera, a woman's hat, and a string of pearl beads, he said, "What the hell is this?"

Massey laughed. "Looks like the kind of stuff the sheriff and I found in Mony's hope chest."

Poppy stepped into the garage and knelt next to the locker. "There's where all that stuff ended up," she said with excitement.

Oodles of pictures had been jammed into a couple of boxes along with various holiday greeting cards. She lifted a cardboard cylinder of Tinkertoys and a harmonica. "It's the stuff Buddy had in an old steamer trunk he kept in the attic."

Kip wasn't amused. "How would you know that?"

Poppy opened one of the boxes of greeting cards and began thumbing through them. "Don't be jealous," she admonished. "I helped Nathan move a bunch of this stuff over a year ago when Buddy had decided to give it to Kat. I suppose he thought his footlocker was the next best place to store his mementos."

Kip leaned over and investigated the locker. "Is this everything from the trunk?"

Poppy kept flipping through the stack of cards. "Heavens, no. He was buried in his uniform, so that's out, and Mony has all his ribbons and metals. Plus, I don't see—"

An old photo slipped out of one of the cards and fell into her lap. She picked it up. Her face went pale.

"Poppy, are you all right?"

Both men knelt next to her and looked at the glossy photograph she was staring at in her hand.

Captured against the backdrop of a brilliant blue ocean on a bright sunny day, his parents looked like a happy young couple with a growing family. His dad stood in his swimming trunks and a squadron T-shirt pulled over a well-defined, muscular physique. Nate, who was four, perched on Kip's shoulder, his dad's other arm had wrapped around his mother's waist. His mother wore a brightly colored two-piece bathing suit that showed off a bombshell figure, and her head sported a wide-brimmed, floppy hat. Massey stood in front of his parents, his mother's hands resting on his shoulders. He wore swimming shorts, a crew cut, and a silly grin. He was eight at the time. His mother had made a hundred copies of that photo and used them for Christmas cards.

It was a long time before anyone spoke.

"Such a beautiful family," Poppy said finally, and reverently handed off the picture to Kip.

Kip angled the glossy photo under the dim garage lighting. "Wasn't this taken the same summer you and Nathan almost set the barn on fire burning the rubbish?"

"No, it was taken the year before," Massey said. "The burn barrel fiasco happened the year you'd gone to Cooperstown and brought us back a couple of hardhats. We were pretending to be nuclear missile technicians."

Massey had almost forgotten about the incident. He and Nate had spent the whole afternoon scrounging up fuel for the fire, everything from a Popsicle stick project to some homemade Christmas decorations held together with enamel and epoxy—nothing was sacred. Massey laughed recalling the scene.

"We used some old cattails Mom sprayed with glitter paint for fuses. When the aerosol cans exploded—whoosh." He lifted his arms over his head. "It looked like a nuclear mushroom cloud from one of those old movies in science class."

Kip and Poppy laughed so hard that tears filled their eyes, handing off the picture to Massey. Accepting it, he said, "That happened the summer Mom took us to Yellowstone. Me and Nate wondered if the geysers were actually nuclear silos, and we—"

He fell silent, and the laughter faded.

His parents had invited him to stay the night—he declined. Tonight, Massey needed his own bed and the emotional support and comfort of his loving wife. Memories of his mother always exhausted him, and Michelle had a delightful way of helping him forget about painful things. Poppy tried to smooth over the awkwardness by encouraging them both to remember the good times as a family. She was right, of course. Their family life hadn't been all bad—it had just ended that way.

Kip went to bed early. Massey could feel the inner turmoil of his father's greatest failure. In a moment of weakness, Kip had shared with him his remorse for not having tried harder to save his first marriage. Although logic finalized the past, it was difficult sometimes not to fall into the quagmire of the "shoulda, woulda, coulda" thinking. It was inescapable, wondering where his mom was today.

Massey's wife strolled into their bedroom wearing a tank top and boy-short bottoms. Even in a simple ensemble, she managed to look sexy. The woman took care of herself in all ways, mind, body, and spirit. She slid between the sheets, snuggled up beside him, and began kissing his neck. He was immediately aroused. This was what he needed at the end of a roller-coaster day. Despite their age difference, his younger wife still found him desirable. It was a blessing. She moved over him, straddling his hips and began a slow, steady rocking motion against his pelvis. Massey stilled her movement. "Where are the boys?"

Michelle lifted his hands off her hips and gently pinned them above his shoulders, "Amy and Stan Harkenrider invited the boy's hockey team to her parents' campsite for an overnight." She leaned forward, nipped his jaw, and then took his mouth. Massey had a full-on erection. God, how he loved her lips, the curve of her hips, the swell of her breasts. She was sensual, confident. Michelle combed his hair with her fingers, the tactile stimulation soothing—until she ran her fingers over the goose egg on the back of his head and he winced.

"What's this?" she asked, parting the strands to expose the injury.

Shit.

CHAPTER 10
NATE

Trevor St. James had done extremely well for himself after the band split. Investing in several casinos just off the Vegas strip, he'd built his capital, then sold it off to create his nightclub. In no time, the club had become a premiere spot for new artists clawing their way toward recognition and a clearinghouse for major recording companies searching for their next big act.

The club looked out of place in the neighborhood. It was a deception. To compete with the more famous rock clubs along the Vegas Strip, Trevor had bought up an old, rundown, single-story warehouse building in a revitalizing district and created an outdoor theater club. He'd reinforced the interior of the building and made the entire rooftop one big party room. It had an eight-foot-high, ornate rod-iron rail around the perimeter, complete with party lights to keep drunken patrons from falling or jumping off.

If you didn't make it into the club, no worries. You could always enjoy the music while you waited. Adopting the open roof idea, many of the eateries and bars pulled in foot traffic off the streets; patrons could enjoy whatever artist was performing while they ate or boozed it up with friends. When a popular rock band was scheduled, it became one gigantic block party, drawing crowds from the Strip and downtown Vegas.

Staying true to his roots, Trevor named the place the Mile High Club. It had a steampunk atmosphere, taking on an aerospace theme evolved from popular space-fantasy and science-fiction films, along with a liberal sprinkle of the Old West. The rooftop light show was worthy of something created by George Lucas's Industrial Light & Magic. It was like going to a theme park, complete with pyrotechnics.

"Make yourself comfortable," Trevor said, entering the door's security code. "There's a couple of guest rooms and a private bath behind the VIP deck. Get some rest—the club won't be open for a couple of hours."

"Yeah, sure," Nate said. "I could use a nap. Got a whiskey sedative to go with it?"

"I'll have Gem grab a bottle for you. But don't go too heavy on booze," Trevor warned. "Save your partying for tonight. I'm letting everyone know the Fergmeister's come out of retirement."

"Don't worry, Mom. I'll be ready." Nate smirked and headed for the guest room. Yanking off his shitkickers, he flopped face-first onto the bed. He was nowhere near ready but told himself he'd get there.

Gem sashayed into the room a few minutes later, her lips wrapped around an expensive bottle of booze.

Uninvited, she sat down on the bed next to him. She wore a short, kimono-style bathrobe, like the one she'd worn at the house, and had evidently taken a quick shower. She smelled divine. Nate had been feeling a come-on vibe from Gem for days now. It was uncomfortable. Trevor assured him they had an "open relationship," whatever that meant. Even when Trevor explained, it made no sense. Being able to fuck around without repercussion was plain bullshit. Nate didn't claim to be an expert in relationships, but in his experience, women got pissed off at that sort of arrangement.

Gem leaned her lips next to his ear and whispered, "Want a backrub?"

She didn't wait for an answer and started pulling off his T-shirt. He sat up and grabbed the bottle of liquor, needing to numb himself for what was about to happen. Gem crawled onto the bed and kneeled behind the small of his back as she worked her fingers deep into his shoulders. It felt good. His head bobbed with each satisfying stroke, and he closed his eyes letting his body relax. Making conversation, he asked Gem, "You said you moved to Vegas. Where are you from originally?"

She came from the silver-mining country of southern Colorado, a small town nestled between the Pine River Valley and the Los Piños River. When the silver mines of the region had played out, she'd been among the poor folk living in trailer parks. Her daddy, a rodeo cowboy, hadn't been around much. One day he didn't come back at all.

"Mom worked for the Durango & Silverton Narrow

Gauge Railroad, which lay along the remnants of the old Silverton railway. She was a tour guide. When Hollywood came to town, she was an extra for *Butch Cassidy and the Sundance Kid.*"

"That must have been pretty cool," Nate said.

"Yeah, I guess, until a sweet-talking charlatan said she ought to be in showbiz and promised an audition. He told her, 'A pretty woman should take advantage of her looks before age and hard work rob it from her,'" Gem quoted with disdain. "So we packed our bags for California. Somehow, we ended up in Las Vegas, where Sin City robbed Mom of her assets instead. Give me your arm; I need to work on your range of motion."

Nate did as told, as Gem rotated one arm and then the other.

"Enough about me," she said, changing the subject. "Tell me about North Dakota."

"Not much to tell. My family has a large farm north of Williston, but I sold off the cattle a couple of years ago. I just have cash crops now—winter wheat, about 180 acres of dried beans, 440 in sunflowers along the backside of the wildlife refuge, and a shared bee colony."

"Honey bees."

"Yup. Did you know North Dakota has led the nation in honey production nine years running? We produced 34.2 million pounds in 2012 alone. Me and Buddy had been seeding wildflowers along the ditches as part of the North Dakota Agriculture Association Apiary Program for sustainability the past decade. We'd hoped to go organic someday."

"What does apiary mean?"

Nate corrected her pronunciation. "It means the site at which one or more bee colonies are kept, that's all."

"So you're a beekeeper?"

"Well, I'm not sure. Buddy took care of shipping the hives down south for the winter and brought them back in the spring. I'm hoping he told my brother their location and who's keeping them. They're probably wondering what the hell happened." Nate suddenly became aware of how many life projects he'd left hanging up in the air.

"So you've been living on a big farm place out in the boonies—sounds boring and lonely," Gem said in a tone tinged with pity.

It was neither of those things, Nate thought. He'd been happy, content, enjoying a bachelor's life. Until Buddy died and Mony came back into his life—until he let it all go to shit.

"Turn around, I've got some more work to do on your shoulders."

He did that. Gem sat in his lap, straddling his hips to face him. Her robe fell open, exposing her voluptuous breast. She grazed her lips across his cheek and forehead as she worked his shoulders from the front. He felt the softness of her breast against his skin. Running her hands across his chest, she kneaded his pectoral with such vigor that he had to brace himself, propping his arms behind him. She began to kiss lightly over his breastbone, working down, down, downward. She was seducing him. He let her.

Nate chugged the bottle of booze and mindlessly lifted his hips to let her peel off his jeans. She settled her head in his lap, took his cock in her mouth. He was already hard. The liquor was working fast, Gem faster. With the power of a vacuum hose, her mouth was wet and hot, and she took him deep. He gave no resistance, had no power to thrust. She did the work for him. He came quickly, and she swallowed him voraciously.

When she'd finished, she began to leave. Nate caught her by the arm. "What's your hurry? Stay a while."

She seemed confused by the request but obliged, sitting on the edge of the bed, her robe no longer covering her body. Nate tucked a loose strand of hair behind her ear. An awkward silence passed between them. He finally said, "Gem, is that your real name?"

Gem reached over to the bedside table and took a long drink from the bottle. "Yes, short for Gemini. I was a fraternal twin."

"Was?"

She winced on a swallow. "Yes, my brother died shortly before me and my mom moved to Vegas. I don't talk about it much."

"Christ, I'm sorry. I didn't mean—"

"It's hard to explain so people will understand, but I feel like a part of me is missing. You know? Like the phantom pain vets feel after an amputation. Weird, huh?"

"No," Nate said quietly. He understood. It was how he felt being away from Mony and Massey. Of all the things to have in common.

"How did you and Trevor meet up?"

Her eyes skidded away, "Tending bar at one of his clubs. Listen, I have a few things I need to do before tonight's performance." Gem picked up her robe off the floor, leaned over, and kissed him on the mouth. "This was fun. We should do it again later."

As she strolled out of the room, Nate felt a sudden urge to take a shower. He pulled the sheet over his naked groin and took a swallow of liquor instead.

Being in the club would bring it all back—at least he'd hoped. It would be good to be among old friends, to maybe drown the memory of Mony from the forefront of his mind for a little while. He wasn't ready to go back to her, not yet. There was too much he had to rectify. He had to explain his actions, had to apologize to his brother. He needed a plan to win her over.

CHAPTER 11

MONY

Mony grabbed her lunch bag out of the employee fridge. She was in a hurry to get home. For one, a storm front was blowing in, carrying a threat of damaging hail. For another, she'd promised Massey she would open the safe before she flew out to Bismarck. She'd been stalling long enough—it was time to face certain finalities. Her dad's life was in that safe, and once she opened it and knew all the intimate content, it would be like burying him all over again.

She headed for the main desk to remind her staff she'd be out of town for the rest of the week. Soprano-pitched shrills of delight followed by soft cooing and gentle voices were coming from the reception area. It was a sound a woman reserved for one of two things: babies and romantic overtures.

Her staff was huddled around what she suspected was a small dog or cat. *So much for beating the storm.* She considered charging the owner her after-hours fee. As she drew near, she recognized the pet owner's silhouette. "It can't be," she muttered. Then she heard his rich, warm laugh and knew her eyes hadn't deceived her. One of the lab techs looked up and saw Mony standing in the hallway.

"Oh, Dr. Strong, you've got to see this little beauty. She's simply adorable."

John turned to face her, his grin widening at the surprised expression on her face. Voices that had been eager to go home moments ago fell silent, wanting to check out the handsome new client with the sweet puppy. While John continued to flirt with her staff, Mony looked out the window to see the sports car he'd driven in Chicago sitting in the parking lot. This was the third time he'd shown up unexpectedly—this time unwanted. It was a bold move coming to her turf. It felt desperate.

Mony sent the staff home, much to their dismay, and took the pup inside the small exam room. John stood quietly in the corner while she performed her exam. She had to admit, the mini dachshund was adorable. With a classic tan coat, deep brown eyes, and long silky hair, she had a playful, friendly disposition. Mony rewarded the puppy with a treat and looked over at John. "I hadn't pegged you for a dog person."

He lifted a shoulder in nonchalance. "Yeah, well, I was helping out a friend. I guess I'm in a little over my head on this one. You're the only vet I know, and I was really hoping you could take her off my hands."

"You drove five hours in your little hot rod to dump a dog?"

"Not dump," he said in a defensive tone. "And her name is Eva—you know, like one of the Gabor sisters."

"Clever."

Mony doubted John had ever been in over his head, at least not without motive. She'd done her research on Temple, Rice, and Goldman's golden boy. He had a stellar reputation as a divorce lawyer with a high success rate representing high-profile women. She wasn't surprised. What disappointed her was his infamous reputation as a womanizer.

The puppy let out a squeak.

"You couldn't sweet-talk one of your rich female clients into taking her?" Mony said, softening her touch. "She's not a hard sell. Hell, you could give her away as a present. She must be a purebred and would make an excellent apartment dog. Mini dachshunds are very popular in the city. But you'd have to make sure she doesn't get lazy or fat. Obesity can be very hard on their short, stubby legs and long back."

John appeared affronted by the remark. "I'd hoped I'd already found her a home."

It occurred to her—*I'm the rich female gifted with a puppy*. She sighed inwardly. "Okay, okay, don't break my arm. I'll take her off your hands." She placed Eva on the floor and observed as the puppy began to explore. Eva sniffed at the array of odors left by previous patients and gave a vigorous sneeze before leaving her mark.

John scrunched his nose. "Geesh, sorry about that. Do you want—?"

She grabbed a paper towel and wiped the pee off the floor before John finished his sentence. "No problem, it happens all the time around here." She walked to the sink in the hallway, Eva and John trailing behind. As she washed her hands, she said over her shoulder, "Why are you really here, John?"

When he didn't answer, she turned to face him. Christ, why did he have to be so damn handsome while she stood there in her scrubs, the pungent odor of animal perfume clinging to her body? His lust-filled gaze was completely unwarranted. It made her feel uncomfortable, vulnerable, the way she had when he picked her up out of the snow. She reminded herself he was on her turf now.

"I was driving back from a client meeting in Rochester. I knew you were somewhere along the route, so I decided to look you up."

Eva began sniffing around the wastebasket. Mony tossed the used paper towel, startling the pup, and snorted. "You always take a dog along to your client visits?" She held up her hand. The lie was so apparent, she didn't want him embarrassing himself. "I hope your travel plans included an overnight somewhere with a garage or an overpass above you." She pointed out the window. "Those clouds are carrying hail, and I doubt your little hot rod can beat this storm."

John grinned wickedly. "Is that an invitation?"

Here we go. She'd closed that door before leaving Chicago, yet here was John, blowing right through it. He was charming, fun, smart, and sexy as hell, and she enjoyed his company, but the guy needed to get a grip. She sensed a guardedness in his demeanor. The lack of his usual self-assured, cocky swagger put her on edge. He was hiding something. She reached down and scooped up Eva.

"Come on. It looks like it's my night for taking in strays."
They made their way toward the employee exit. She
paused—and gave a sharp whistle. "Come on, Shep, it's
time to go home."

John's eyes widened registering the heavy footfalls and
toenails clicking on the vinyl floor. Shep rounded the
corner, paused, and canted his head at John. "Don't make
any sudden moves," Mony teased. "Shep's a trained killer."

John took a deep swallow. From the side of his mouth,
he said, "No problem, but can I change my shorts first? I
may have soiled myself."

Mony drove a steady speed through the deluge of rain
and hail. No small feat, towing a horse trailer. It was a
good thing she'd let John park the Lamborghini in the
small garage back at the clinic; the hail would have ruined
his paint detail. The road they traveled snaked parallel
to a small stream that was spilling over its bank. She
hydroplaned a couple of times, reacting quickly when
small rocks tumbled off the side of the bluff. A full-blown
rockslide was not uncommon in the valley. John sat rigid
against the door, hanging white-knuckled onto the *oh shit*
handle. Shep sat in the middle. It felt comfortable having
the barrier between them. The dog seemed indifferent
to John's presence, looking attentively out the front
windshield. The puppy cried relentlessly at his feet.

Mony shifted gear to accommodate the incline in her
driveway and said, "I have to park the trailer next to the
barn. I don't suppose you have boots along?"

He didn't.

She smirked and pulled truck and trailer as close to her front porch as the extended length allowed, then said, "Tuck and roll, Your Majesty. The front door's open."

John opened the passenger door—Shep immediately leaped over his lap exiting first. Startled, he asked, "Do you want me to take the pup?" Mony shook her head. With no further comment, he quietly got out of the truck. As she backed the trailer into a narrow space between the barn and a shed, she noticed him standing in the rain, watching. It seemed odd.

When she entered the house twenty minutes later, she found John standing in the living room, reading the back of a book lying pages down on the end table. "*The Breedling and the City in the Garden,* by Kimberlee Ann Bastian," he read aloud. "Do you know *The City in the Garden* is the Latin phrase written on the great seal of Chicago?"

She did not.

They sat down to a simple affair her family called end-of-the-garden soup with a hearty loaf of whole grain bread. The conversation was pleasant. John asked questions about the farm and her veterinary business, never once mentioning the probate hearing. She appreciated that.

"We've tried to create a self-sustainable farm," she said, ladling another serving of soup into his bowl. "I can't even remember the last time I was in a grocery store." They carried on like that for a while, until the underlying tension got the best of her. She repeated her earlier question.

"John, why are you here?" He seemed to be waiting for the question.

John opened his mouth, but she cut him off. "And don't give me that rehearsed bullshit about passing through. You picked a dot on the map that was marginally plausible. I don't need to know your business, but you told me yourself you didn't like to travel for work, remember? Just give me the truth, or I'll have to sic Shep on you."

The dog at her feet perked up his ears at the sound of his name. John looked at the dog, weighing his options. He went with, "As I said, I had a client in Rochester and—"

Mony frowned and looked at the dog. "Well?" Shep got to his feet, sat next to John's chair, and gave a low growl. She nodded. "I thought so." To John, "I should warn you, Shep has the best bullshit-o-meter of any mammal, two- or four-legged. Bob used to take him on jobsites when people tried to finagle out of paying him. Shep has quite a reputation for being an equalizer. So I'll ask you again. Why—"

John held up his hands in defeat. "All right, all right. I needed to see you, Ramona—wanted to see where you worked, how you lived. I wanted to be near you again. I wanted to warn you."

She stiffened. "Is that a threat?"

Shep emitted another low growl. "Not a threat," John said, keeping his eye on the dog. "Just inside knowledge. I've worked with Monroe Oil Company since I graduated from law school. One of the first accounts I brought into the firm. I know how they operate, and that hysteria you saw at your little military headquarters back in North Dakota this past winter was kid stuff."

She rolled her eyes. "I'll say."

The rise in his voice brought the dog to his feet. "Goddamn it, Ramona, I'm serious. Jason is a ruthless little bastard, and his old man is worse. For Christ's sake, you don't even lock your doors. You're a woman with wealth and power, and you live out here alone in the backwoods like nobody knows it. It's not safe. If I can find you, so can they, and they won't come bringing cute puppies."

Mony pushed away from the table. It was the same lecture Massey had been giving her for months. Eva scampered out of the box near the counter and started to whimper. Mony scooped the puppy up, headed to the door off the kitchen, and put her outside.

Standing in the doorway, she looked up into the bluff side and noticed the rain had stopped. Heat from the ground collided with the cold air in a test of will, creating a smoky haze. She finally said, "So what's his plan? Is he going to break into my house steal my flat-screen, trash the place, or something? This is my life, John. I'm not going to change who I am and how I live because of some spoiled rich boy."

John walked up behind her, putting his arms around her waist. She didn't pull away, but she didn't soften. He rested his chin on her shoulder.

"I'm not trying to scare you, Ramona," he said softly. "I just want to be honest, and I don't want to see you get hurt."

She believed he didn't wish her harm, and that Monroe was a ruthless asshole. It was the word *honest* that rang hollow in her ear. She waited for further explanation of

Monroe's threat and was disappointed. It seemed John was losing his control over her enemy, diminishing the need for keeping him closer. What he told her was nothing new. She'd felt the disquieting sensation of being watched, a prickling at the back of her neck, ever since her return from Chicago. What she needed to know was, were his eyes watching—or Monroe's?

"I need to do chores," she said, pushing the thought aside. "You can stay here and snoop around the house to learn more about me, or"—she leaned into his chest—"if you really want to see how I live, you can join me in the barn." His shoulders lifted in a cringe.

The puppy sniffed around, picked a spot, squatted, then wobbled back to the door. "Good girl," Mony praised. She helped the little dog over the threshold, then turned to face John. "Have I ever told you that I love the way you smell?" she said seductively. "I'm afraid it won't be so after your trip to the barn." Leaving a kiss on his cheek, she broke away and got dressed for chores.

Her hair damp from the shower, she stood in the kitchen wearing a bathrobe, her hip leaning against the sink and her head canted to the side, working a Q-tip in her ear. *What in the hell am I thinking?* His sneezing unabated, John had lasted less than ten minutes in the barn. Mony absolved him from chore duty and he left obligingly. She gave him credit for trying, at least, but his valiant effort couldn't disguise the cold fact he would never fully be a part of her world.

"Christ," he muttered behind her.

She turned slowly to face him. He'd slipped into the well-worn sweats and T-shirt she'd laid out. The look suited him. With a moan she said, "God, what is it about a cotton swab in your ear that feels so good? It's almost as good as sex."

John wasted no time crossing the room and reached for the knot that held her bathrobe together. She let it slip from her body, letting the waft of lavender seduce his senses. He ran his hand along her naked ribs to her hips and back up to her breasts. Leaning his forehead against hers he said, "Hmm, it's like opening a present. I love the way you smell."

She didn't deny his advance, but she didn't encourage him. It felt unnatural in their present setting. Easing her toward the table, he cupped her butt and lifted her onto the wooden surface, leaning her back. She flinched at the bit of cold against her bare skin, causing her body to stiffen. John put his faith in the quality wood construction and crawled onto the table. The way he took her mouth lacked his usual finesse, and she pulled him to her, grappling at his shirt. He lifted away long enough for her to finish the task. When she started for his sweatpants, he had to stand and finish undressing.

Standing naked, he grasped the inside of her thighs, pulled her legs apart, and slid her butt to the edge of the table. It wasn't quite the right height, like in his boat, but he'd make it work. Parting the lips of her sex, he glided his tongue along her cleft and fluttered over her clit. She shivered, denying him her sound of pleasure. John slung her leg over his shoulder and let her rest her heel between his shoulder blades. He responded to the pressure against his spine as he made another pass. Her body flushed, and her skin grew hot.

This was how she knew him. A sexy beast of a man with extraordinary skill. It was all they had. It had taken years for her and her deceased husband to find this kind of pleasure sexually, yet what they did share from the start was an intimacy deeper than the physical. It was the sort of relationship she no longer had the energy or desire to nurture with John.

John suckled and licked along the tender flesh until she came—her intensity unexpected. When the last tremor subsided, he crawled back onto the table.

"I'm going to fuck you hard and fast," he said darkly. "Then, I'm going to carry your naked ass over to that fireplace and fuck you again."

Her eyes widened at the carnal threat and she wrapped her legs around his hips, thrusting as he plunged. The urgency of her next orgasm caught them both unprepared, her erotic cry taking him over the edge. Their passion spent, he collapsed into the table as each recovered their breathing.

Abruptly, Mony said, "John, you need to let me up."

He lingered, seemingly enjoying the way she lay spread out sated and replete before, granting her request. Something felt . . . off—dirty, emotionally disconcerting. Finding no elegant way for either of them to get up off the table, they each rolled to the side and slid onto their feet. Mony hung onto the table's edge and closed her eyes, breathing purposefully. John caught her by the waist.

She leaned her head back against his shoulder. There were tears. "Orthostatic hypotension," she said. "It's what happens when I stand up too fast."

Her legs began to tremble, and he held her closer. This afterglow response confused her. She'd cried after sex before, but it was an emotional release, soothed by cuddling. It was ineffective this time. His embrace lacked emotional support or tenderness. Maybe it was because she felt worn down, manipulated—a conquest.

"I'm getting cold," she said, pulling away, and gathered up the robe, walking out of the kitchen naked. John donned his clothes quickly and followed. She was standing in her bedroom, pulling her nightgown over her head, when he caught up with her. Without looking at him, she said, "Please don't come in."

He stood stone still in the doorway, his expression one of hurt and confusion. "I'm sorry Ramona. Did I hurt you?"

She walked to the mirrored bureau dresser, picked up a brush, and needlessly ran it through her short hair. She looked at him through the mirror. "No." Robotically, she made her way to the bed and turned down the coverlet. "I'm sure you will need to be on your way tomorrow. I need to get up early too, so I'm turning in for the night." Forcing a smile, she faced him. "The guest room is two doors down on the left. There's extra blankets at the foot of the bed—"

John spoke from the doorway, "Ramona, please, will you come here and talk to me?"

Shep brushed past him just then, with the little puppy

in tow. The older dog climbed comfortably into an oversized dog bed at the foot of Mony's bed. The little pup followed. John snatched Eva up as she passed; she began to whimper.

Mony breathed a heavy sigh and walked toward him. "There is a night-light in the hall to find your way to the bathroom if you need it, and I have the night lamp on next to your bed." She reached out her hands. "Eva can stay with me tonight. Shep will keep an eye on her."

John held onto the pup as if holding it for ransom, then finally handed it over. Mony set Eva on the floor; she scampered over to Shep and curled up in the bed beside him.

Mony cupped her hand around John's chin. "You have nothing to be sorry about, and you didn't hurt me. The truth is, I'm tired and confused, and I can't sort this out with you here right now. You need to understand, the only man I have ever made love to in this house was my husband. I feel like I've betrayed him." She leaned up on her tiptoes and kissed his cheek. John released his grip on the doorframe, his arms automatically reaching. She stepped away. "Maybe we can talk before we head into town. Right now, I need to go to bed. You should have everything you need for the night. Help yourself in the kitchen if you're hungry and—"

"For Christ's sake, Ramona, I don't need food," John said with frustration. "I need you. Can I just hold you?"

She averted her eyes. She didn't want physical comfort; she needed trust, and if John wouldn't talk to her about what was behind his warning of his own accord, they had nothing. "Will you close the door when you go?" she asked, turning her back to him. "I don't want Eva running around the house all night. Thanks."

The click of her bedroom door signified the finality of his resolve, leaving her alone in her sanctuary.

CHAPTER 12

NATE

A pillow tucked under his arm, Nate lay facedown on the bed. His head hurt, but it had been worth seeing the old gang last night. Everyone was there, except for Rocky. Trevor made his excuses—said Rocky had wanted to come, but his unforgiving schedule prohibited it. *We'll see*, Nate thought. Rocky Rhodes, former lead singer and front man for the band Mile High City was notorious for being late as well as being a first-rate asshole. Rocky and Trevor never got along, and Nate thought it weird Trevor would neatly cover for him.

Despite the band's volatile breakup decades earlier, they'd all managed to get along. Drummer Tim Thompson was in his usual cantankerous, drunken row, and even Brandon Cody, the oldest and most conservative member of the group, showed up, seemingly enjoying the reunion. Trevor made a big show of announcing he'd bought out their former record company, Shooting Star Records, and moved its headquarters out to Vegas. By night's end, he had them all agreeing to a jam session the following day, for old time's sake.

It was the alcohol talking. Nate rolled over onto his back and found Gem standing over his bed.

"Sober yet?"

He snatched a bedsheet, covering his groin—an unnecessary reaction, really, given their little sexcapade yesterday. "Jesus Christ, woman, you trying to scare the shit out of me?"

Gem placed her hands on her hips. "I don't smell anything foul. And, anyway, it's time to get up. We need to get to the studio."

Nate gave her a half-assed salute, a gesture which used to aggravate his old man, a former Air Force commander, to no end. It failed to provoke the same desired response.

Pointing to his crotch, Gem said, laughing as she walked out of the room, "Oh, and let me know if you need help taking down that oversized tent you're pitching."

He felt a sense of accomplishment when the band broke early from the recording session to grab a bite to eat. Plucking out chords with snappy rhythms and a driving beat, they'd put music to some of the lyrics Nate had been mulling around in his head since his exodus from North Dakota. They'd managed to scrape together a few songs that didn't sound too bad overall. Dressed in a three-piece suit, Rocky joined them about an hour later. Trevor was the first to shake his hand. Nate half expected a fistfight, given their last encounter—Tim was counting on it. Much to Tim's dismay, when the perfunctory pleasantries were out of the way, they all got back to work as if none of it had ever happened.

They walked the few blocks toward the Strip. Nate caught their reflection in a storefront window as they strolled past. They looked more like a pack of wolves on the prowl than a group of middle-aged musicians. Trevor and Rocky kept jockeying for the alpha position, each insisting he knew the perfect place to eat. Rocky finally conceded and said to Trevor, "It's your town, man. But wherever we go, it better have a vegan menu. I don't eat meat." Nate looked at Tim walking beside him and rolled his eyes. Tim snorted a laugh.

The sidewalks of Vegas were crowded with the usual tourists, drunks, hawkers, and hustlers. Nate could have sworn he heard his name shouted a couple of times and chalked it up to the frenetic energy of the city. Then Tim suddenly stopped and slapped his shoulder.

"Don't look now, man but you have a fan club heading your way, three o'clock."

Tim lifted his chin in the direction of two young women waving their arms wildly in the air across the street. Their shouts in unison garnered everyone's attention.

"Uncle Nate!"

He froze.

Mony's daughters crossed over the street stairway and parted through the crowd. He stared despondently. It always caught him off guard how much Mony's youngest daughter, Mindy, looked a carbon copy of her mother thirty years removed.

Tim said to Nate, "Uncle? I thought your brother only had boys."

His bandmates stepped aside as Kat and Mindy plowed right into him, each wrapping their arms around his waist and giving him a hug and kiss on the cheek. The Vegas foot traffic continued to flow around them, but some people stopped to stare at the public display. A couple people snapped pictures with their cell phones, probably thinking they had caught someone famous. *Shit*, Nate thought; his anonymity was over.

The rest of the band stood awkwardly and basked vicariously in the attention the two vivacious young women lavished on him. Gem, the central female attraction among the male posse, bristled at the intrusion. Pushing her way toward Nate, she held out a stiff hand to Mony's daughters and said, "Hi, I'm Gem. And you are?"

"As in Jem and the Holograms?" Kat asked.

The reference was lost on all of them.

"No, Gem as in Gemini, meaning twin," she responded unamused. She glanced between Mindy and Kat, then at Nate. "You two look like you could be twins. You say this guy's your uncle?"

Mindy and Kat burst into laughter. "People say that about us all the time," Kat said, not bothering to explain the irony—having the same father but different mothers. Kat took Gem's offered hand. "Sorry for my rudeness. I'm Kat Strong, and this is my sister Mindy. We've been calling Nate uncle for as long as I can remember. Old habit, I guess." Kat offered her hand to Trevor, who stood next to Nate, then to the rest of the band. Mindy maintained her proprietary hold around Nate's waist and did likewise. Introductions out of the way, Kat turned her attention back to Nate. "Mom didn't mention you'd be here in Vegas, or we'd have looked you up sooner."

Double shit.

Kat and Mindy fell in step with the group as they resumed walking. Kat was informing Nate how Vegas had been one of the stops on her book tour. She and Mindy were staying with a friend who lived not too far from Trevor's place. Rocky chimed in and said, "I hope you ladies will be joining us for lunch."

They sat around a large table and were handed menus—Kat and Mindy bookending Nate on each side. Rocky took the seat next to Kat. A sudden feeling of dread overwhelmed him. He didn't like Rocky giving his niece so much attention. Kat was an attractive, outgoing, energetic fireball who knew how to capture a room. He'd seen her in action at her book signings. She immediately began sharing that she'd published a children's book series loosely based on her mother and Nate's life growing up in North Dakota. It generated considerable conversation.

"Are you telling me our Fergmeister here stole a plane?" Trevor asked, a glint of mischief in his eye.

"Actually, my mom did. It was my grandpa's old crop-dusting plane. Uncle Nate was the reluctant copilot."

Tim asked, "Nate knows how to fly a plane?"

Kat shook her head. "No, my mom's the pilot. I use the term copilot loosely."

Amused laughter rounded the table. Nate felt the flush of heat in his cheeks.

"So your mom and Nate have known each other a long time," Trevor continued.

"Nearly all their life. Their dads are—were—partners in two businesses."

"Interesting," Gem said. "And your mom's name is?"

"Excuse me, miss," the waiter interrupted, "may I take your order?"

The interference saved Nate from further infamy. It pained him that his so-called friend was trying to spin his childhood innocence into a tabloid headline. He'd loved the telling of that story; it epitomized everything about Mony's spirit. Realizing the inquisition was far from over, Nate steered the focus of conversation back to his pseudo-nieces.

"Enough about your mom and me," he said, hugging Kat and forcing a lighthearted laugh. "Make them buy the book if they want to know the rest of the story. How about telling me what the two of you have been up to since Christmas?" He was hoping for new more about back home or the book tour; instead, Kat piped up and said, gesturing to her sister, "Mindy's been dating a captain of a frigate." She shielded her mouth in a scandalous fake whisper. "I think it's serious."

Mindy reached across Nate, attempting to punch her sister in jest.

Tim asked, "What the frick is a frigate?"

Ever enigmatic, Mindy had the same magnetism, charm, and manner of her mother. "He's currently on his way to Hawaii for RIMPAC exercises. We'll see where things go when he gets back." With that, she closed the discussion.

Rocky looked to Kat. "And what about you? Do you have a boyfriend?"

Nate couldn't tell who was jolted more by the audacious question, him or Kat. Her confident demeanor faltered a little when she said, "I'd rather not talk about that." Mindy pointed a finger at Kat in an unspoken exchange. Kat changed the subject.

He learned the two sisters had been traveling the entire time they'd left Williston and seemed to have no knowledge about the fight between him and Massey or his status with their mother. He would have liked to have kept it that way, but Mindy bumped his shoulder and said, "How about you? We'd love to hear what you've been up to lately." She wiggled her eyebrows at him. The gesture hadn't gone unnoticed.

"Yeah, Nate, I'd like to hear a little bit about that more myself," Gem said, provoking him. Nate gave her a dirty look.

"I've been doing a little traveling myself," he said, omitting the timeline. "I haven't been home for a while." He kept his comments vague, smiling and teasing, hoping to placate his niece. He felt like an ass. Mindy was the first to support him in his endeavor pursuing her mom—not an easy thing to do after recently losing her dad. Nate tried to steer the conversation back to Kat.

"Have you noticed how terrible she sounds?" Kat went on. "I called her twice last week. She says it's just a cold, but I think she has another upper respiratory infection. She'd gone to that conference in Chicago, had a presentation or something. Did you know about that, Nate? Anyway, she said she'd spent some of her free time at the Navy Pier and had gone sailing. Can you believe that? Mom. Sailing. As if piloting her own plane isn't enough, now she's trying to master the sea, or lake, or whatever. Did she mention anything to you?"

It was a question Nate could honestly answer. "No, she never mentioned it."

"Figures," Mindy said. "I hope she doesn't have walking pneumonia again. She's had an awful time fighting off infections since her cancer surgery last year."

TMI, he thought. They were sharing too much information. It astounded him how transparent young people were with their stories. Couldn't his nieces see there were vultures at the table, true detractors ready to devour their idealism? It made him sick.

Rocky made a sound of disgust. "I don't know why anyone would choose to live in the north. It has such a miserable climate."

Mindy agreed. "Our brother Dane has been working on her since Christmas, trying to get her to come out to California. Kat invited her out to Vegas too. I bet she'd have come if she'd known you were here, Uncle Nate."

He had no idea how to respond.

Their food came and the conversation died, providing a much-needed reprieve. Already up to his eyeballs in lies, half of him was grateful Mony's daughters were oblivious to his current situation; the other part felt like trash. His deception was deplorable, but what could he do? He'd have come clean if they hadn't been in a restaurant surrounded by people. The sort of conversation he needed to have with his nieces required privacy. It didn't help that Trevor and Gem kept stirring the pot. He tried to focus on his meal, but his appetite was nonexistent.

Tim asked, reaching across the table, "Are you going to eat your fries?"

He'd hoped that was the end of the Mony discussion. It was a foolhardy thought. Mindy said around a bit of her deluxe grilled cheese sandwich, "What are the odds we'd run into you, Nate?"

Tim said through his mouthful of fries, "It's Vegas," as if that explained it all.

Kat began conversing quietly with Rocky, explaining how she was finishing her most recent book tour promoting the latest installment in "The Adventures of Natty and Roman."

"You're quite the entrepreneur," Rocky said in a patronizing tone; then he turned the topic to himself. "You know, I'm writing a memoir about the band's rock and roll glory days and our rise to fame. Do you have any advice?"

Nate could feel his temperature rise, along with his blood pressure. Rocky was a known womanizer, and Nate felt compelled to punch the man in his phony, toothy smile—except he was having problems of his own.

Trevor said unexpectedly, "Why don't you ladies join us at my club tomorrow night for drinks, dinner, and music?" He handed them each a business card. "It's the Mile High Club, you can look us up online. Let your Uncle Nate know where you're staying, and I'll have a limo come over and pick you up."

Kat and Mindy leaned behind Nate's chair, conversing with one another. Kat whispered something to her sister. Mindy came back with a grin. "All right. How much is the cover?"

Trevor was mildly offended. "Don't say such things," he retorted. "You're family, and it's my treat. Just wear your hottest party dress and dancing shoes. Invite your friend if you want. Be ready, say—around nine o'clock?" Mindy and Kat each looked to Nate for confirmation. *How in the hell was he going to work the situation to his advantage?*

"I'd love for you to come and hang out with us," he said, smiling. It wasn't entirely a lie. He adored his nieces immensely and was grateful they even gave a shit about his opinion. After all, he wasn't their dad, though he'd always wanted to be. Now if he could only figure out how he was going to keep up the façade, especially with Trevor and Gem riding him. They seemed to derive some sort of sadistic pleasure from watching him squirm. He needed to nip that situation in the bud.

After lunch, Rocky insisted Kat and Mindy walk back to the studio, where he'd have his driver take them back to their friend's house. He kept putting his hand at the small of Kat's back, laughing and carrying on like they were the best of friends. The scene caused bile to bubble in the back of Nate's throat. Luckily, Kat caught on to Rocky's overture and kept pulling Mindy between them—smart woman.

Too tired to start anything new, they concluded their jam session for the day. Gem, Nate, and Trevor got into their own vehicle and headed back to the bungalow. The SUV rolled into Vegas traffic.

"Well, this turned out to be an interesting day," Gem said with a note of sarcasm in her voice. "Are you really their uncle?"

Trevor, who'd sat in the front, turned around and leaned his arms across the back of his seat. "Babe, haven't you figured it out yet?" Gem pursed her lips, responding with an irritated look. He grinned. "They belong to your muse, I presume?"

Nate didn't answer. He was too fixated on how he could have been so stupid as to confide his deepest secret to a known blackmailer. Trevor was his friend, always had been, but the guy navigated without a moral compass. He had no difficulty twisting a situation to his advantage no matter who got hurt in the process. It was what made him successful, something Nate admired. He wished at times he could behave so heartlessly and not lose any sleep over it.

Gem smacked Nate on the shoulder, hard. "You could have told me they were really your family. I—"

"What the hell do you think an uncle is?" Trevor snorted. He turned on the satellite radio and began whistling to Loggins and Messina's "Your Momma Don't Dance."

Nate kept his eyes focused out the window. The entire situation was one big clusterfuck. *How in the hell am I going to smooth over this mess?* There was a small voice inside his head that screamed, *Tell the truth.* He ignored it. What was the point? His opportunity for redemption was long past. He reached for a bottle of liquor sitting in the cup holder and took a long drink. The only thing left for him to do now was to delay the inevitable for as long as possible.

CHAPTER 13

MASSEY

Mony's Dakota Piper sat glistening on the Bismarck airport tarmac. It was a beautiful bird, the upper body painted white, the lower a royal blue with grey numbers to accent the exterior. The interior of the plane had blue velour seats and walls, with midnight-black carpet on the floor and room for six passengers. It was an older plane, given to Mony new on her high school graduation, but it looked nowhere near its thirty plus years. Nate, Buddy, and Dane had all kept the plane in premier condition, an advantage of having several mechanics in the family.

Mony was unloading a kennel too small to accommodate her German shepherd; as Massey approached, she introduced the occupant. The little wiener dog yipped and pawed at the door, jealous of the big dog's freedom. The German shepherd sat obediently next to Mony, oblivious to the protest.

"Hey there, fellow. You remember me?" Massey bent down to scratch behind the big dog's ears. "It's good to

see you again, Shep. Are you taking good care of Mony?"
Shep thumped his tail in a vigorous response and indulged
in the human's massage.

Massey grabbed a twenty-five-pound bag of dog food
and helped Mony finish unloading the plane. She slung
a duffle bag over her shoulder and took the puppy out of
the kennel, then stuffed it into her flight jacket.

"Come on," he said, "supper's waiting."

She spent the evening at his home, a rarity. It was good
to see his pseudo-sister relaxed and enjoying the role of
aunt, chatting it up with his sons. The boys adored her—
and the little puppy. His wife had a different view. Michelle
had a certain wariness around Mony. Even when she'd
been married, his wife seemed to consider her a rival.
She misjudged her. She didn't know the whole story. He
accepted that.

Early the next morning, Mony fired up the Piper while
Massey secured the big dog in his kennel. They'd both
agreed it would be good to have a third set of ears and
eyes along. As Mony went through her preflight ritual,
Massey buckled in and watched her from the corner of
his eye. There was something innately sexy about the
way she took command of her plane. She was confident,
in control, indomitable. It turned him on a little. Strong
women were his kryptonite. As the wheels left the
runway, a wisp of a smile graced Mony's lips. Leaving
the troubles of the earthbound behind, Mony Altman
controlled her destiny in the air. When she took to flight,
she was free.

As they passed over the countryside, it was difficult not to perceive the oil well and methane burners like a cancer on the landscape. The conundrum was that same cancer symbolized economic growth. But for whom? Aside from F&A Oil, there were no local, family-owned oil wells left in the region, a shame. His dad had spent his entire political career fighting to keep the revenue generated by the oil fields as an asset for his constituents. In the end, all the community got was the blowback of greed and destruction from outsider usurpers, a new rec center, a bigger airport, and few highway improvements.

He glanced over at Mony's profile. She was thousands of miles away.

"Where are you?"

"I was asking myself that very question," Mony said wistfully. "I feel conflicted, Massey. My house is empty and I've taken to investing my safety and sanity in a dog. It doesn't feel like home anymore. And if it weren't for you, Michelle, the boys, your parents, and the land we share to keep bringing me back, I wouldn't be here at all. I don't know what my role is in all this. You all have lives here. I'm just—a visitor." She breathed a heavy sigh. "I never saw myself running the oil business or the farm. Shit, I can't even keep up with the one I have in Minnesota. I'd have given it all to Nate if he hadn't left. Maybe he had the right idea leaving. Without him, it's as if none of this even belongs to me. It's just a wonderful memory, a place where I once lived."

"But it does belong to you," Massey said, unmoved. "You're just in a contemplative mood."

"True enough," she conceded. "It's what happens when I spend too much time alone."

"Then you need to stop spending your time alone."

Mony looked as though she were about to say something more. She didn't. He didn't pry; Massey wasn't always privy to her innermost thoughts.

He used the flight to fill her in on the details of the events at the farm the other day, excluding the footlocker and the photo. When he finished, Mony said, "I thought we had installed security on all the buildings."

"Everything but the shabin. I guess we figured we didn't need it since the hockey team practiced there twice a week."

"Will you press charges against the person who hit you?"

Massey snorted. "You mean if we ever find out who did it? Nah. I've been hit worse." He cringed, instantly regretting the remark. He'd been referring to his time playing hockey, not the fight with his brother.

Mony ignored it.

"We should consider a press release for damage control," he continued. "With those reporters waiting in ambush, we don't need idle gossip taking on a life of its own."

Mony waved it off. "We can handle the press. Everyone knows Candy Man's a pompous asshole, and the public will forget about the story by and large in a day or two. What I'm concerned about is what we're doing to find the person who attacked you."

"Until the forensics team has completed their sweep of the shabin, there's nothing much else we can do. Even if they manage to find decent prints, there's no guarantee they'll find a match in the database."

Mony pursed her lips unsatisfied and changed the subject. "I opened the safe."

It took him a beat. "Did you find anything?"

She reached into the inside pocket of her flight jacket, fished out a banded bundle of papers, and handed it to him. It appeared to be some sort of property abstract, and Massey's eyes lit with a smile. The glint was brief, however, dying as he read the paperwork. It was an abstract, but not the one they'd been looking for. It was a deed for a small ranch, located somewhere in the state of Arizona. Massey pored through the legal details. "It says here, the deed is in joint ownership with a G. R. Hernández, address Lake Havasu City, Arizona. Who's G. R. Hernández?"

"I was hoping you knew. From what I could see, there are only initials throughout the document, no first or middle name." Massey continued to shuffle through the pages. Mony said, "Do you think this G. R. Hernández knows my dad has passed away?"

Massey banded the papers back together and set them aside. "I honestly couldn't say. No one's called the business line inquiring about it that I'm aware of—plus, I've got nothing on this property in Arizona. This is new information."

Mony's shoulders slumped in a display of disappointment, and they lapsed into silence. Massey tried to recall if he'd ever heard Buddy or his dad mention owning joint property in Arizona.

Mony finally said, "Do you think it's where Dad might

have taken the bees for the winter?"

The bees. Why did he keep forgetting about the bees? He'd never had many dealings with the honey business. That had always been Nate and Buddy's project. But he knew the two of them had been part of the North Dakota apiary program for nearly ten years, and they'd established a lucrative income in the production of honey. "It's possible," he said. "I can check through the business contact, see what turns up. In the meantime, I can do some more investigating on this deed."

Mony pulled out a tattered notebook from her pocket and offered it to him. "Do you think this might help?"

He took the mini spiral from her and began flipping through the pages. This time she really had something— phone numbers, dates, and figures. It was the break he'd been looking for. "Geesh, Mony, you're a wealth of information. Makes me wish you would have opened the safe sooner."

"Yeah, well," Mony said, her voice repentant. "I dragged my feet, hoping I might hold onto Dad a little longer. You know, like he was still around or something. Stupid, I guess. But now that I've opened the safe, it makes Dad's passing seem more final."

It is. Dead is dead, Massey thought, but he kept the opinion to himself. He was no authority on grief but knew there were stages, and everyone dealt with it in their own time. "You know, I found Buddy's cell the other day at the house. This little notebook may be more valuable than that title. I'll cross-reference them with the office logs and Buddy's recent calls and see what I turn up."

"This would be a whole lot easier if Nate were around," Mony said quietly.

Maybe, Massey thought, but he doubted Mony was referring to the deed or finding the bees.

As Mony made her landing approach, they passed over the wildlife refuge. Massey said, "Let's walk over to our farm when we're done. I want to check out the place since we're out this way; we can take Nate's old truck back into town."

Shep leaped out of the kennel as soon as they'd landed and immediately began to sniff around. There would be all sorts of enticing odors being so close to the wildlife refuge, but Massey knew Shep's potential—Bob Strong used to bring the dog along on the hunting trips to Montana. German shepherds didn't have a reputation for their keen hunting skills, but Shep had an uncanny instinct for uncovering trouble.

They began with the outbuildings, examining the fortified locks and security sirens. Everything seemed in order. Still, Massey remained wary. It surprised him how having the family sanctuary violated had affected him; it was a disconcerting feeling.

The morning air was still cool, and there was with a distinct odor of burning wood. Odd. Trees of any kind in the prairie pothole region were a rarity.

Mony walked alongside him, glancing at the sidearm beneath his lightweight jacket. If it troubled her, she didn't say it—she was no stranger to firearms and an excellent shot in her own right. Next, they checked the hangar.

Massey flipped the switch, and the harsh fluorescent bulbs winked to life. It looked pretty much the way it had a couple days ago, minus the footlocker. Kip had already removed the chemical inventory in preparation to sell the business, a wise move. Storage in a remote, unsupervised location held too great a liability.

"If Buddy and Nate were here right now," Massey said, pointing at an old crop duster, "they'd probably be working on that old Ag Cat B-Plus."

"You mean *Grasshopper Two*," Mony corrected.

Grasshopper One was an original Grumman G-164, and it truly bore the nickname. Built in the late 1950s, it was the first aircraft built by a major aviation company purely for agricultural use. It sat prominently in the back of the hangar, a collector's item now. Buddy nicknamed all his Ag planes "grasshopper," and Nate worked on them all, learning through apprenticeship before passing along his passion to Dane. Mony's son made a handsome salary in aeronautical design and engineering out on the West Coast thanks to Buddy and Nate's mentoring.

"You and Nate used to spend a lot of time out here," Massey said.

"Not like Nate and Dane. I'm no mechanic."

She was being modest. Mony knew her way around an engine, but her destiny was to fly. "Every time I see this old grasshopper, it reminds me of that summer afternoon you stole it and took Nate up joyriding."

"Not *stole*," Mony protested with a sly smile. "We just took it out for a test flight, that's all."

The story of Nate and Mony's flight was infamous

and immortalized in her daughter's award-winning book series. Kat, however, put a more lighthearted spin on Mony buzzing old man Swanson's roofing crew and completely omitted the local authorities' reprimand. After promising she would never take the plane again without permission, Buddy took Mony and Nate into the house for frozen pizza and grape sodas and promptly forgot about the whole thing. While that part was true, it was liberally embellished in the children's version.

"Come on," Massey said throwing his arm over her shoulder. "We need to check the shabin."

Shep caught up with them from whatever he'd been investigating and trotted past as they followed the rutted dirt road. The sound of thousands of waterfowl grew louder, more intense, as they drew near. The air was pungent with the smell of wet grass and stale, muddy earth mixed with sand, and again he smelled a faint odor of burning wood. From somewhere out of sight, Shep began to bark frantically.

Instinctively, Massey pushed Mony behind him in a protective reflex. She bristled. He considered drawing his gun, then decided against it. It wasn't of much use if someone had a bead on them with a scope, hiding in the tall grass. Walking in the middle of the road like it was a Sunday stroll, they were sitting ducks. He'd let his guard down. Mony was immediately on alert, watching his back.

The big dog sat patiently at the water's edge. If it had been a human lurking in the weeds, Shep would have been in full-on siren mode, but something held his attention. They proceeded with caution. Massey stepped gingerly into the tall grass, trying not to get his boots wet. A couple of mallards squabbled at him, irritated by the disruption. It startled him. Mony lent him a hand, holding onto his belt loop to allow him a farther reach. "I think I see something," he said, parting the reeds, "but I can't reach it. Pull me back, and we'll get the old baling hook out of the shed."

She did that, then began taking off her shoes and rolling up her pants.

"What the hell are you doing?"

"We don't have time for that," she replied, and started wading into the cold water. She was standing knee-deep when she said, "What the hell?"

It took both of them to dislodge the small dugout canoe from the weeds and pull it ashore. Grunting, Mony complained, "Jesus, it's heavy."

"It's made of wood, not fiberglass," Massey replied.

They sat on the soggy shore, catching their breath. Shep came and sat beside Mony. "Good boy," she said, and scratched his ear. To Massey: "Where in the hell would you find wood to make a canoe around here?"

"My question would be, what's it doing on this lake? It looks very old, like something used in the days of Teddy Roosevelt. It should be on display in a museum or something."

"Maybe it was," Mony suggested.

Considerable craftsmanship had gone into fashioning the canoe. Carved out of a single piece of birch bark, there was no planking or elaborate prow piece separating the seating area. Some of the bark and root lashings were reinforced with modern-day putty over the spruce-gum waterproofing, but it was well disguised.

Mony said, "Who do you think it belongs to?"

Massey scratched his head. "Well, whoever it is, they must be around someplace. This is their only means in and out of here without being seen or caught." He scanned the shore, then looked in the direction of the fire pit. "We'd better check out the shabin."

The faint heat radiating from dying embers in the fire pit explained the odor of burning wood. It wasn't nearly as pungent as the stench of decay emanating from the garbage and empty beer cans scattered around the parameter.

He'd been to his share of frat parties, and he suspected Mony had been through her share of pigpens and barns, yet somehow animal feces never had the same abhorrence as human filth.

"I feel vile," she muttered, giving voice to his thoughts.

He poked at the embers with a long stick lying next to the pit and lifted a partially burned thong. Mony snorted. "Shit, did our end-of-the-summer parties look this bad?"

"Probably," he conceded. "It's a perfect spot. The place is empty, isolated. If it wasn't on your dad's property, we'd have had partied out here too. That's what this feels like, an underage beer party. Except for—"

"For what?"

Massey pointed to the partial deer carcass lying beneath the coals.

Mony squatted for a closer examination. At first glance,

it would have been easy to conclude the deer had died from natural causes, disease or old age, had it not been for the blade nicks on the ribcage.

"Well, ain't that a kick in the head," she exclaimed. "Someone has considerable butchering skill."

As soon as they stepped onto the porch, they could see the lock was broken, along with the security camera and the motion alarm. "So much for the upgrade in security," Mony said.

Massey motioned her away from the door and whispered, "Do you still keep your dad's gun in the Piper?"

She looked at him with surprise. "Now you're asking me?"

"Maybe we scared them off when we flew in," he muttered more to himself, "and maybe not."

"Who's *them*?"

"Whoever's hell-bent on trespassing?" Massey drew his weapon. "It's time we find out."

CHAPTER 14

MONY

Massey directed Mony to stand on the opposite side of the shabin entry as he eased the door open. She complied until Shep leapt inside and immediately began barking. Instinctively, she followed. Massey's arm shot out, blocking her entry.

"Goddamn it, Massey, you do that to me one more time and I'll—"

He held up a hand, silencing her, and continued blocking the doorway, surveying the scene. She could smell the refuse emanating from within. Shep continued barking, leaving no doubt someone was inside. Mony peeked around the mass of fur and saw nothing. She gave the big dog a shove and they both entered together.

"You better come out from wherever you're hiding, and do it slowly," she shouted, "or my dog will tear you apart." Shep added a menacing growl for good measure, but the trespasser made no response. Several seconds passed. Massey entered the cabin with his gun at the ready. She repeated the command.

A young female voice finally replied, "I can't. I'm stuck." Mony and Massey's eyes both lifted and saw a young Native girl held up in the cabin rafters.

She appeared in her early to midteens, with deep, copper-red skin, and straight, long, black hair. Her dark, almond-shaped eyes, heavily covered in ruined makeup, were sullen. She was very thin. Dressed in jeans torn by use rather than design, she had on a plunging V-neck T-shirt that revealed the beginnings of a budding chest and wore a tattered denim jacket. She couldn't be more than fifteen, Mony figured, and that was generous.

The young teen avoided eye contact with her captors, her facial expression one of resignation. In a flat voice she asked, "Are you going to beat me?"

Massey holstered his gun and righted the upended chair the youth had used to climb up to her current predicament. "No," he said calmly, "but you need to come down from there, now. We need to talk."

She hesitated a beat, then began shimmying herself off the crossbeam, allowing Massey to help extricate her from the rafter. The moment her feet hit the floor, she bolted toward the door. Shep cut off her escape, growling as he backed her toward an old recliner, and she promptly sat. Taking up a position in front of her, the dog kept a close guard.

"Are you going to give me over to those men?" The young girl directed the question at Mony.

The question took Mony by surprise. "What do you mean?"

The girl pointed at Massey. "Him, and those other two

men. Are they here for sex?"

It took every ounce of fortitude for Mony's voice not to break at the implication of the young girl's remark. "What other men? And why would I do something like that?"

The girl seemed affronted by the question. "I saw this man out here before with those other two fat, old men. Don't think I don't know Hitch gives the white bitches the choice marks and doles out the leftovers when their cunts get too sore."

Mony was accustomed to vulgar language, but hearing the word come from someone so young in a tone that suggested enduring unwanted sex was a punishment made her heartbreak. "Watch her," she instructed Shep, and motioned Massey toward the door. Stepping out onto the porch and out of hearing range, she whispered, "Does it still feel like an underage beer party?"

Massey shook his head. "I don't know what the hell this is," he said quietly. "The girl could be a runaway, she could be an abductee, or it could be both. She's probably the one who hit me over the head with the frying pan."

Mony glanced into the shabin to see the girl reaching to scratch Shep's ear. He let her. She smiled and said, "My little sis sure would like you."

The kid is so thin, she doesn't even look like she could lift a cast-iron pan, let alone wield it. Mony thought. She called to the child, "Are you hungry?"

The teen quickly retracted her hand and gave an insolent shrug. "I could eat."

Wanting some privacy to talk to the girl, Mony suggested Massey go back to the Piper to retrieve the cooler and some water. He gave her a skeptical look.

"Here." He shoved the gun at her. "Just in case."

She recoiled. "And do what? Shoot her if she tries to run?"

Massey grabbed Mony by the arm and walked them farther away from the door. "This kid isn't one of your cute little strays," he scolded.

Mony wrenched her arm free. "Are you holding that against her?"

"No. I'm saying, whatever is going on here, it's likely someone has hurt this child and she's not afraid to protect herself." They both turned their heads abruptly at the sound of Shep's playful bark—the girl had resumed scratching his ear. Massy sighed. "On second thought, offering food and hospitality would be a better way of earning her trust." He holstered his gun and said, "Be careful," then started jogging toward the Piper. Mony smiled at her brother retreating and rejoined Shep and their guest.

The young girl said nothing for a long time. Mony let the silence hang in the space between them, hoping it would motivate the teen to fill the vacuum. She was wrong. The girl was as still as a rabbit with a hawk circling above its head, an unusual discipline for a teen. Mony broke the standoff. "Can you at least tell me your name? I hate referring to you as *the trespasser*."

The young girl gave her an insolent gaze.

Mony tried a different approach. *"Tàku eniciyapi he? What is your name?"*

The girl sat up with interest. *"Makumidi."*

"*Makumidi, tuktél yatí he?* Where do you live?"

Makumidi looked at Mony with surprise and answered, "I live here." Then, "Are you Indian?"

Mony shook her head. "Not that I know of. I took a beginner's course in Lakota language when I was in college. I like to go to powwows, and I remember a few words and phrases. Is Makumidi your first or last name?"

The girl slumped back in her chair. "It's part of my last name. I don't know how to say the whole thing. Sissy is my first name."

An alias, Mony thought, but she went with it. "Why are you living here, Sissy?"

The young girl avoided the question and resumed petting Shep. "You have a nice dog," she said absently. "*Tàkeciyapi he?*"

"He is a good dog," Mony agreed, "and his name is Shep. My husband found him hurt and abandoned and brought him to me. I'm an animal doctor, and I nurtured him back to health."

"Is that man you sent away your husband?"

Mony thought a moment, "He's—um—*mihunkawanzi.* I think is how you say it. He's my brother and a good man too. He would never hurt you." She eased closer to join Sissy in petting Shep and segued into a different topic. "My mother abandoned me too when I was young. My *ate*—father—raised me, right here on this farm."

"I never saw him," Sissy said, her tone harsh. "Where is he?"

"He is with *Wakan Tanka,* the great mystery," Mony replied quietly.

Sissy's demeanor softened and nodded. "My father is dead too, and my mother left me."

"*Tuwá ksúyeya níye?* Is that who hurt you, Sissy?"

"*Wasicu*," she said with disdain, "white men who use me for sex. They like to—um—*amapa*. Beat me. Hitch says it's okay, as long as they pay extra."

Mony struggled to keep her composure. "This Hitch sound like a very evil person. Who is he?"

Massey ill-timed return ended the conversation. He set the cooler on the floor. Mony offered Sissy her sandwich, bag of chips, cookie, and the extra candy bar. Sissy attacked the food as if she were eating her last meal.

Mony munched on a carrot stick and said, "I'm sorry for the slim pickings. Did you have enough to eat?"

Sissy patted her tummy and said with a tone of gratitude, "*Imápi ksto*. I'm full."

They'd finished eating when the sheriff drove up. Mony gave Massey an accusatory look.

"What was I supposed to do?" he said defensively. "We need to get to the bottom of this mess, and for that, we need the law."

The sheriff stepped out of his truck, hitched up his pants, and said, "So where is the little perpetrator?"

His rapid-fire questioning of the teen proved ineffective. Mony wanted to slap him; the gesture would probably have been equally ineffective. After twenty minutes, the three of them sat on the porch while Shep stayed with Sissy inside. Massey reviewed the sequence of events. Mony remained silent. She didn't know why, but it felt like sharing her conversation with Sissy would be akin to betraying her trust.

The sheriff said, "It's not surprising she wouldn't talk. Indian kids are like that." He turned to Massey. "Do you think she's the one who hit you with the frying pan?"

Massey shrugged. "It's possible. She just admitted being out here a couple of days ago, but I didn't get a good look at who hit me."

The sheriff rubbed his chin. "Well, looks like I'll have to haul her in for questioning."

Mony protested, "Is that necessary? It seems wrong to threaten a child with incarceration when it's clear she is a victim. Why can't we just talk to her here?"

"You can see how well that's going," the sheriff said with a patronizing tone, "and it's uncertain whether she's a victim. Besides, I need to contact tribal social services. If this girl is a runaway, they'll be the best resource in getting her reunited with her family after we've questioned her."

Mony hated the arrangement, but she didn't have a better plan. "All right, but I'm staying with her, just in case it was a question."

The sheriff replied, "Of course you are."

They arrived at the sheriff's station. In Mony's mind, it should have been a straightforward matter—find out who this Hitch was and bring him in for questioning. Her idea was far from the truth; it was more like the shell game. The sheriff took the girl into custody for trespassing, the least incriminating charge, but Mony wasn't having it. She advocated for Sissy's claim about being involved in human trafficking and made it her mission to protect the child. She lost her say in the matter, however, when she refused to press charges, citing it as unjust punishment of a victim. The sheriff gave her the cold, hard facts.

"There's nothing more I can do," he said with exasperation. "The girl's not cooperating. It's a tribal matter."

Mony became livid at the response, but it did her no good. The sheriff eventually turned the teen over to a social worker and said, "That's the end of it."

Like hell, Mony thought.

"What are you going to do about this Hitch person?" she demanded.

"There's nothing I can do. The name isn't in the database. I—"

Mony was about to launch into another tirade when the sheriff added quickly, "I'm not saying this guy doesn't exist. There's a lot of criminal activity going on in the county that eludes the law."

Criminal activity happening right on my own property, Mony thought angrily.

The sheriff's resolution to Sissy's case was unacceptable in Mony's mind, one she was determined to rectify—even if it meant finding a solution on her own.

CHAPTER 15

JOHN

John hurried through the office corridor with Franklin half a step behind him. As if Monroe Oil Company hadn't taken up enough time and resources, the prick capped it off by scheduling a video conference at the end of the day. Franklin helped John prep for most of the afternoon, compiling information he hoped would convince Monroe of the futility of his quest. It was time to find a different project. Monroe Senior's tactical error in challenging Ramona's inheritance may have slowed down the complete acquisition of her estate and delayed drilling, but the outcome was as predictable as the sunrise. The local court would rule in her favor, with or without title or deed, ensuring the daughter of the community's most benevolent citizen a clear victory.

John rounded the corner to the conference room and stopped abruptly.

He was only marginally surprised to see both Monroes sitting together at the table. He'd heard rumors the two had reconciled, at least for their public image. Franklin had also overheard Quincy Goldman on the phone planning a meet-and-greet as soon as the Monroes got into town. Nor was he shocked to see Quincy and Fran Temple—two of the law firm's three owners—present, especially with their biggest client in town. What had him stopping in his tracks was Ethan Rice sitting all nice and cozy to the left of Jason like a part of the family.

Franklin was looking down and hadn't seen John stop, plowing right into him. Papers flew everywhere. Jason let out a Texan hoot, shouting, "Better than the Marx brothers."

His paralegal made a pitiful look, but he said nothing. John mouthed an apology and helped him gather up the folders. Goldman and Temple sat idly, hiding disappointment and donning their game faces, leaving John and Franklin to clean up the mess. Thomas Monroe clapped Jason on the shoulder in a poor display of self-contained amusement. Ethan launched his first volley of the meeting:

"A little nervous, John?"

He cursed inwardly at the knee-jerk reaction and took a moment to compose himself. Ignoring the remark, John said, "And for our next act, we'll be performing 'Who's on First?'"

Monroe Senior slapped his leg and let out a belly laugh. "That's what I love about you John, you're always quick with a joke." The exaggerated laughter made everyone uncomfortable; John wondered who exactly was making who nervous.

Goldman and Temple responded with grimaced smiles. Resuming her composure, Fran Temple, a tall, stately woman with an impeccable updo pulled so tight against her facelift it made her look like a Stepford wife brushed microscopic fiber off her pencil skirt and said, "Our apologies for not having notified you sooner, John." Unrepentant, she continued, "Mr. Thomas and Jason Monroe informed us only an hour ago that they were in Chicago and had invited Ethan to sit in on the meeting. He is representing his wife, who was unable to attend. I hope this is acceptable."

Acceptable? What a laugh. He could shoot from the hip better than most when it came to an ambush, but the situation royally pissed him off. He could accept Monroe Senior's loss of confidence. What he couldn't abide was being blindsided by his own people. Goldman wasn't a worry; the man would lean whichever way the wind was blowing strongest, that was a given. Fran, however, was the storm. The tempest he would have to navigate with extreme caution. As for Ethan's claim to represent his wife, John knew for a fact Tiffany would never agree to such an arrangement.

Nearly a quarter hour of pleasantries passed before Monroe rolled around to the agenda at hand.

"How did your meeting go with Ms. Strong in Chicago the other day? Have you made headway convincing her to sell?"

Temple and Goldman gave John an inquisitive look. He hadn't informed them of his rendezvous with Ramona on the yacht or his trip to her office. It wasn't unusual for him to entertain potential clients; in fact, it was encouraged, at least by the male members of the senior team. But this time things were different. John was flirting with the opposition, causing a great deal of tension. He was convinced, however, that the only way Monroe could win was for Ramona to sell, a goal he and Monroe shared.

"Very well," John responded, "and not quite."

Ethan sneered. "I'll bet."

Old man Monroe smiled at the quip. He'd suggested seducing Ramona several months ago. She was a widow, fatherless, and female; in his mind that equaled weak and vulnerable, a sentiment shared by his son. "Ms. Strong isn't the type of person to go behind her attorney's back in any secret meetings," John clarified. "She was in Chicago on business and agreed to meet with me out of convenience."

Fran's lips thinned into a hard line, "What sort of business?"

"Ms. Strong is a respected colleague among veterinary doctors. She had a conference presentation in the city. She agreed to meet with me to determine what she would be looking for in a business offer that would motivate her to sell."

Fran's rigid face marginally relaxed.

Monroe persisted, "What about your trip to Minnesota?"

John held his game face. "I was attending to another case."

"What sort of case?" Ethan challenged.

John wasn't about to share Norman and Charlene Stapleton's financial claim on Ramona's inheritance, even to a colleague. Stapleton's clear disdain for Ramona was too easily exploitable. "That information is not your business," he said shrewdly.

"Come on, we're all working on the same team, aren't we?" Ethan said with a smirk.

He was about to say more when Fran interrupted, "Of course it's confidential," and shot Ethan a look of irritation.

Steering things back on topic, John said, "Fran asked me to compile an in-depth review of Ms. Strong's personal assets." Franklin stood and began to distribute the folders. "I'm afraid you'll have to share. Had I known the Monroe team would be in attendance, I wouldn't have sent the documents electronically." It was a partial truth.

The room was quiet as Goldman read over Fran's shoulder and the Monroe team crowded around the single document. Monroe Senior said, "It says here she has a quarry. What sort of quarry?"

John reached for the water pitcher in the middle of the table and poured himself a glass. He felt a sense of betrayal sharing the data, but the information was a matter of public record any resourceful lawyer could find. "Limestone or sandstone, I presume. It's pervasive of the region."

Jason threw up his hands. "You jackass. Don't you know that's what's used in fracking?"

Fran's voice cracked like a whip. "Mr. Monroe, you will refrain from derogatory language in my presence."

Jason was gearing up for another smart remark. Ethan placed a hand subtly on his forearm, dissuading further comment. It was Monroe Senior's turn to reach for his water glass. "This is bad, this is bad. Even without the liquid assets from dear old daddy's inheritance, she has everything she needs to drill right now—land, money, and raw resources."

Bet he wishes it was bourbon in that glass, John thought uncharitably; out loud he said, "There's a moratorium in the county where Ms. Strong lives prohibiting the development of new commercially run frac quarries. That's not to say Ms. Strong couldn't actively mine if she chose. There is a grandfather clause attached to her ownership rights. She and her late husband have been selling the silt runoff for cattle bedding about every fourth or fifth year. She hasn't initiated removal because—"

"Because her inheritance is held up in probate," Ethan interjected.

John grinned. "No. The probate hearing has nothing to do with the quarry. I believe the delay may be out of respect for her late husband, who was a staunch opponent to frac mining."

Fran asked, "But you just said they sold the sand. How can it be both?"

"There's a subtle difference between actively tearing down an entire bluff side and pulverizing it into sand, and passively removing what has naturally been deposited due to erosion."

Speaking up for the first time, Quincy asked, "Is she an environmentalist?"

The question was irrelevant.

"Ms. Strong has a fervid devotion to and respect for family," John went on. "F&A Oil Company has a small fleet of semis on standby as soon as she gives the go-ahead."

"But they can't drill," Jason retorted. "The probate hasn't been settled yet. This information is worthless, and this meeting is a waste of time."

"F&A hasn't started drilling yet," John said evenly, "because one of the business partners is currently unavailable to authorize drilling."

The room fell silent. To John's amusement, Fran Temple didn't even bother to hide her irritation.

"If Ms. Strong is as wealthy as your figures indicate, John—and I've no doubt they are accurate—she has no reason to even consider Monroe Oil's paltry offer." She glared at father and son. "There are at least three known international conglomerates in the region alone that have the resources to outbid you. Things as they are, we are all wasting time." She turned her attention to Ethan.

"And you Ethan—you specifically asked Quincy and I to sit in on this meeting to ascertain whether there is evidence to support the claim that your colleague's loyalties are compromised by feeble allegations of his involvement with Ms. Strong. While I agree no one in this office is above examination for misconduct, or reproach if found liable, I find no indication of any such breach in this instance. I do, however, believe your approach to the matter to be amateur—and a gross representation of this firm's reputation."

Ethan squirmed visibly. "I merely bring the information forward at the behest of my wife, Tiffany, a vested stakeholder. She'd heard the rumor of John's—"

"Are you implying you've based your action on conjecture and blaming your wife?"

Jason made an ill-conceived attempt at intervening in the conversation. "I've had question for a long time as to whether John Finch is representing his own selfish endeavors or my company's best interest. I support my brother-in-law's actions."

Monroe Senior gave an indignant humph; Fran continued as if neither had spoken.

"I will save you from further embarrassment in front of your clients, Ethan, and discuss your misconduct privately."

John caught the ghost of a smile as it crossed her thin lips. Despite her adamant disapproval regarding his cavalier relationships with women, she had an unwavering respect for the facts and had done her research. He'd won this round. It also meant he owed her, a debt she would undoubtedly collect. He brought the conversation back on topic.

"Bottom line is, I believe Ms. Strong's only conflict is whether or not to use the sand from her quarry. A drilling company is already in place. She flew to Williston yesterday evening, most likely to meet with Attorney Ferguson and her business partner Senator Ferguson to finalize the decision."

Jason said critically, "How would you know that?"

John ignored him and addressed the senior member of the team. "I'd like to refer back to a conversation I had with Tom at the onset of this acquisition endeavor."

Monroe Senior, who'd been sitting slouched in his chair half-listening, straightened and said, "John, you'll have to remind me what conversation you're referencing."

He offered a patronizing smile. "In order for F&A to continue competing in the oil business, it's paramount they remain a united front. Otherwise, their company will collapse. Even if Ms. Strong transports the sand to North Dakota and the senator has a drilling team lined up, they still need Nathan Ferguson's stamp of approval on the project. Mr. Ferguson left Williston several months ago; his whereabouts at this point are still unknown."

Thomas Monroe's eyes brightened, "Yes, the younger Ferguson. Now there's a piece of low-hanging fruit."

Fran glanced down at her watch. "Quincy, if we're going to keep that after-dinner social for Westby and Lynch, we'll need to leave now." She turned to John. "I've heard enough; you can handle the rest of the meeting from here." She gave a terse smile and shook each Monroe's hand before exiting the room with Goldman hot on her Louboutin heels.

That went better than expected, John sighed inwardly. With his bosses out of the room, he turned, focusing on the Monroes. He steepled his fingers in front of his lips and placed his elbows on the table, garnering their attention.

"What?"

Leaning forward, John addressed Monroe Senior. "That's strike two, Thomas. Call me out in front of my company again, and we're finished. Do I make myself clear?"

"Sounds to me like a threat," Ethan said in poorly veiled contempt.

"You shut your mouth," Monroe Senior snapped. "That's

the last time I listen to your sorry-ass advice. Whatever in the grand state of Texas made my daughter think to send you as her mouthpiece is beyond reasoning."

"I didn't," a southern voice drawled from the doorway. All eyes turned to Tiffany Monroe as she entered the room. Walking to her father, she air-kissed his cheeks and said, "Hi, Daddy. I'm so sorry I'm late. My secretary told me this meeting was scheduled as a teleconference in your office. Can you imagine my shock when I learned I'd been misinformed? Thank goodness someone had the courtesy to call and inform me otherwise." She blew a kiss in Franklin's direction. "Thank you, Franklin, you are such a dear. Why, I don't know what I would have done had I missed something important."

Ethan walked to his wife to smooth things over. "You have nothing to be sorry about, my dear. It was an oversight. Besides, you didn't miss a thing." Tia bristled at the condescending remark and turned away just as Ethan attempted to kiss her mouth.

"Well, be that as it may," she said brushing an unruly strand of hair back into place, "it shan't happen again. Shall it?" Ethan stepped aside as Tia leveled her gaze at her brother. "Now, what is this nonsense about our dear, loyal friend John conspiring with the enemy?"

Excusing himself and Franklin from the current fireworks display, John let the Monroe clan have at it. Nathan Ferguson crawling out of whatever hole in the ground he was hiding in was the least of Monroe Senior's worries. If the man wasn't careful, the destruction of his company would come from within.

At twenty minutes after nine, John packed his briefcase and told Franklin to do the same. It had been a hell of a long day. He contemplated the ramifications of what he'd learned. Someone was monitoring him, but who? The obvious answer was Monroe, but it could also be Ethan. He'd known about the Chicago meeting but not the trip to Minnesota. A knot twisted in his gut. *She doesn't even lock her doors.* Franklin stuck his head through the office door.

"I'm taking off, boss—anything else I can do before I leave?"

"No, you've done enough today. Go home and get some sleep. We still have another long day of prep before I leave for Williston." They said their goodnights.

Alone with his thoughts, John began to realize what Ramona had already concluded. A relationship between them was never going to work. Not only were they from two entirely different paradigms, but their presence in one another's life made each susceptible to predators and extortion.

He was about to lock his office door when he noticed a manila envelope lying on the floor. He opened it. Inside were eight by ten glossies taken with a sophisticated zoom-lens camera. One was of him and Ramona on the Ferris wheel at the Navy Pier. Another was of two of them standing on the deck of *Lynnie Q* in an intimate embrace. The other was of them walking across the farmyard. There was a note attached to the last photo.

If you think this is over, think again.

CHAPTER 16

NATE

All eyes followed the two women escorted to the VIP section. Ready to dance and dressed to party, Mindy wore a sporty racerback-style jersey dress in black, with peep-toe heels in a sparkling sapphire. Kat was equally dazzling in a tailored halter dress of deep midnight blue, with classic sling back pumps in a black leopard, fuchsia print. *They're too gorgeous,* Nate thought, feeling protective. Watching them approach, it still blew his mind how much Mindy resembled Mony. He wondered if every man saw what he had seen in the woman he loved. Kat mirrored Mony too, but in a different way. It was there in her facial expressions and the way she moved through the crowd. The men at the table stood as the two women walked up to him and planted a kiss on his cheek.

"Hey, hey, why does the Fergmeister get all the action?" Trevor cajoled giving each of them a hug and kiss.

"Thanks for inviting us," Kat said, "and thank you for sending a car. I know my way around Seattle traffic, but this here is crazy."

His nieces took the seat on either side of him while Trevor positioned himself directly across the table, with Gem to his right. She'd become completely disengaged from the conversation. Trevor mostly ignored it; Nate felt uncomfortable. Gem brewed like a tempest on the horizon while Trevor entertained his two new female guests. Kat and Mindy were completely enthralled as he talked about the club décor.

Minutes passed before Nate blurted, "What do you two think of Vegas so far?" It was a weak opener, but he had to push his way into the conversation. He didn't like the way Trevor monopolized his nieces' attention, as if they were some conquest.

The warm-up band finished and the stage crew began setting up for the featured act when Rocky strolled in. Fashionably late, he came behind Trevor and leaned forward, whispering something in his ear. Trevor's eyebrows lifted and he stood. "If you'll excuse me, I need to check on business."

"Secrets don't make friends," Kat said to Rocky with a half smile.

Rocky was all smile and took Trevor's chair. "What are you drinking tonight?"

Mindy pointed to an expensive liquor bottle sitting on the table. Rocky picked it up, studied the label, and set it back down. He leaned into the table, garnering everyone's attention. "I just heard that the lead singer for the featured act had a seizure backstage."

"There goes tonight's entertainment," Brandon said in a gloomy voice.

Nate had noticed an edginess to his friend the moment his nieces arrived. He wondered if Brandon's papa bear instinct was kicking in. Nate was feeling it too. He didn't like the showy interest Rocky or Trevor were lavishing on Mindy and Kat, but there was nothing he could do about it. First off, they were both old enough to tell him to fuck off if he stuck his nose where it didn't belong. Second, he wasn't their papa.

Mindy flirted shamelessly with Trevor, unaware of Gem's status. Gem didn't even try to intervene, and Nate couldn't understand why. As if that weren't uncomfortable enough, Mindy ramped up the tension by bringing the topic back around to Mony. Mindy had been his greatest supporter during the holidays; the thought of shattering her heroic image of him was devastating. He dodged direct questions with quaint remarks and sly winks. Mindy may have bought it; he couldn't tell what Kat was thinking.

Trevor walked out onto the stage, drawing the crowd's attention. People were starting to get restless during the extra-long break, but Trevor reined them in quickly. "Is everyone having a great time or what?" he shouted, launching the club audience into a series of whoops, whistles and cheers. Mindy and Kat lent their own siren cheer, nearly blowing out Nate's eardrum. Trevor waited for things to settle, savoring the attention. "Let's give a Mile High Club hand to Needle's Highway for getting this party started." Another volley of cheer and applause. He kept priming the crowd before delivering his sobering news. "I regret to inform you the lead singer for our main act has suddenly become ill. They will not be able to perform this evening."

Someone from the audience shouted, "Must have had the food at the all-you-can-eat buffet next door." The audience roared with laughter.

Trevor played off the heckler and redirected the crowd. "Here under the beautiful skies of Las Vegas, the Mile High Club takes pride in supporting new talent. We all had to get a start somewhere. We charge a minimal cover to support these ambitious artists, but there wouldn't be an audience, without all of you. So, tonight, I'd like to take the opportunity to comp your cover cost with a round of beer and rail drinks, patron's choice, on the house."

The announcement threw the crowd into a frenzy. Mindy leaned toward Nate and said, "Isn't he going to lose money doing that?"

Nate was about to educate Mindy on the fine points of comping with cheap booze when Trevor said, "And since I'm breaking the norm tonight, perhaps we can take it a step further." The spotlight beamed directly at the VIP booth. "Many of you have noticed we have another band in the house with us tonight. They haven't been on the scene for a while, but maybe we can get them to play a couple of songs with a little encouragement."

Low murmurs rippled through the crowd as eyes followed the blinding spotlight to where Nate and the rest of the guys sat. Someone began chanting, "MHC, MHC."

"No fuckin' way," Brandon said, stunned. "He doesn't expect us to get up there and play? We've only played a couple of times together. Is he crazy?"

Yes, Nate thought, *and shrewd*. Rocky was the first to stand. He waved to the crowd, then turned to face the table. "He's calling us out, guys. Are we going to just pussy out, or are we going to get up there and play?"

Tim stood so fast he knocked over his chair, drawing cheers and laughter. Nate and Brandon rose to their feet simultaneously. They moved in unison toward the staging area. Trevor flashed a showmanship smile as the band joined him on the stage. Nate looked back at the booth, unable to see Kat and Mindy. It made him anxious.

The stagehands wheeled a piano out on the stage, and the crowd thrummed with excitement. Nate couldn't tell if the pulsating in his body was coming from the audience or behind his chest wall. As the four men gathered around Trevor, they shook hands and slapped one another on the back like reunited comrades who'd survived the war. Despite it being their first public appearance in over twenty years, the crowd cheered and screamed like they did back in their heyday. Nate found it hard to believe a crowd in attendance for a boy band from London would remember or even care about some '80s rock and roll has-beens, but the chants kept coming.

They huddled briefly, then took their positions at instruments and mikes. Tim taped down a four count while Brandon and Rocky opened with a familiar electric blues riff. Nate joined in with a signature keyboard accompaniment, and the drums and bass kicked in. Rocky stepped up to the mike, singing out in a bluesy voice, "Lie to me and tell me everything's all right."

An explosion of whistles and cheers filled the air; for

a moment, Nate could have sworn he heard Mindy and Kat's siren cheers all the way from the VIP booth. It was invigorating. When the song finished, a roar of cheers rose from the street level and cars blasted their horns. Nate was genuinely surprised. They all were, except Trevor.

Trevor acknowledged Jonny Lang for the original song, then shouted over the crowd, "Do you want more?" It was an unnecessary question, but the crowd answered anyway. Rocky stepped up to the mike and broke out into a familiar guitar riff with a driving beat as the band filled in the rocking rhythm.

I woke up in the morning, my head was a mess
We're in another city somewhere out in the West
A thousand miles from home, yet people seem to know us
Waiting in line for hours just to see us

It was the Mile High City touring anthem from their first album, *Shut Up and Color*. They'd opened every concert with "Crazy Bastards, That's Us," a song that got them banned from seven major cities in the south. The album received an explicit warning label for the word "Bastards." "Mother fuckers," became the live audience version.

We do it cuz we love it, livin' the life of a star
Women, whiskey and fame, driving fast cars
We don't do it for the money because it's already spent
There's not even enough to cover next month's rent
So we keep rollin' down the highway in a house set on wheels
Just a bunch of crazy bastards, that's us.

As the song rolled into the chorus, the crowd sang along with their chant. Nate felt a rush of adrenaline as the familiar scene created a natural rhythm and flow. They played six more songs before slowing down the pace. The house lights dimmed and a single spotlight fell on the piano. Nate looked out into the crowd for Kat and Mindy.

Brandon played a chord and Nate began to sing. It was the song that had catapulted them to fame. It was Mony's song. Absorbed in his music, the memory of his heartache began to reverberate in his chest. He hadn't sung the song in over twenty years, yet the emotion he'd felt back then rushed forward as if Mony had just left him.

I was seventeen when they told me you got married
I wish I could be happy for you, but my life's come to an end
For how can I live in a world without you by my side?
Didn't you know, you were supposed to be my bride?
So I got in my car and drove as far as I could
Away from all the things we shared and the places we once stood
Only to learn you'd stowed deep in my heart
That place where we'd promised one another we'd never part.

His voice began to strain, the sorrow unprotected by his acapella, exposing him to his nieces and the crowd, the depth of his heartache. It was as real to him now as it had been them. An awareness creeped in. Losing Mony had made him the star he had become, vulnerable, volatile every time he sang the refrain of the song. He told himself he would have traded it all not to have sung those words. He'd had his chance—he'd squandered it out of jealousy.

Now I'm on my own and there is nothing I can do
To stop feeling the pain from the love we once knew
Is it all we'll ever be, just friends and nothing more?
My forever childhood friend, you've cut me to my core.

He looked into the crowd again for Kat and Mindy, but the flash of cameras left him blinded. He would talk to them at the break, come clean with his deception. He couldn't take it anymore, the uncertainty of Gem or Trevor's betrayal. After six months of hiding, his recompense had come due, his anonymity spent the second he stepped onto the stage. He had to face the consequences of his behavior. Trevor would try to exploit his disgrace, empowering his silence. He'd let himself be fooled into thinking he didn't need his family. Seeing Kat and Mindy had opened his eyes. Was it a blessing or a curse that they'd had shown up in the middle of his plight? It didn't matter. He knew what he had to do.

At the break, Nate pushed his way toward the VIP section and a swarm of adoring fans mobbed him. Tim shouted over his shoulder, "I'll save you a drink." It wasn't what he needed.

When he finally did reach the VIP area, a waitress brought another round of drinks and the table was boisterous with laughter. Gem came up to him and handed him a glass. "I've heard your music before, but I've never seen you perform. I understand what Trevor was talking about saying your music is cathartic. That was beautiful, Nate."

He saw through the poison-laced compliment and snapped, "Where are Kat and Mindy, and what did you tell them, Gem?" The jovial voices at the table fell silent.

Gem took a swallow of the drink she'd offered to Nate. "I didn't tell them anything."

Trevor stepped in to cover and came up with some

cock-and-bull story about the girls having to catch an early flight; he said they'd taken Rocky's limo back to wherever they were staying. Nate called them both liars and started toward the nearest exit.

Rocky stepped in front of him, "Whoa, big guy, where in the hell do you think you're going? There's another set. You can't just up and leave."

Nate rounded on him. "Get out of my way or I'll beat you to a pulp."

Brandon intercepted. "Look, Nate, I don't know why your nieces left, but you'll have to call them after the show. You'll never get out of here with the traffic."

Nate looked at his bandmates and wondered if they were all in on the conspiracy. Tim sat in the corner with the waitresses on his lap, drinking from the expensive liquor bottle. He laughed and said, "Like old times."

In the end, Nate returned to the stage, though he'd lost all desire to perform. It was a familiar position: forced to play a role when his heart and mind were somewhere else. With unexpected clarity, he realized why he'd left all those years ago. Anxious to get through the set, he protected his small wick of hope and resolved to talk to Kat and Mindy before they left town. It was his own damn fault, the situation he was in. He needed to fix it.

CHAPTER 17

MASSEY

Massey caught a ride with his dad over to the Blarney Stone the next morning for coffee and gossip. Hopping into the cab, Kip asked, "Where's Mony?"

"Sleeping in," Massey told him. "She was up all night surfing the internet for information on tribal laws, must have turned in around five o'clock this morning."

Kip shook his head. "She's wasting her time."

Massey didn't disagree. Mony, however, had a different view.

Backing out of the driveway, they passed by Nate's truck parked on the street. Massey recalled the hopeful expression on his parents' face when he and Mony had pulled up. It had been heart-wrenching to watch it fade when they'd realized it wasn't Nate. He'd never considered himself a spiritual man, but he sent up a silent petition anyway on the remote chance divine intervention would intercede and bring Nate to his senses.

The breakfast rush hadn't quite started when they'd arrived at the Blarney Stone, a good thing. Massey wanted a conversation with co-owner Shannon McDonald. They hadn't spoken since the day she'd instigated the fight with his brother, and he believed she owed him. If "Hitch," really did exist, the knowledge would have passed through the Blarney Stone. Standing behind the counter, Shannon and her brother Shawn were looking up at the TV, with the sheriff on his customary barstool. They were so engrossed in the news headline that no one noticed Massey and Kip.

The aerial shot of the Vegas strip panned across a sea of pedestrians and vehicles clogging the streets around a popular nightclub. A closed-circuit camera zoomed in on a heartwarming reunion between the members of Mile High City as they shook hands in an ostentatious display of friendship. Various angled shots captured Nate at the piano, playing a familiar love ballad, then cut to an interview with the club owner. Massey clenched his teeth. *Why, that son of a bitch. Five months of hell and the little bastard waltzes into the spotlight like he's king shit.* His dad apparently shared his sentiment.

"Well, at least I know what my prodigal son has been up too," Kip said angrily. "Did you know about this?"

Shawn and Shannon turned simultaneously from the screen. Shawn lifted his chin in his customary greeting; Shannon avoided Massey's eyes.

"No," Massey said, irritated by the accusatory tone. "Trevor St. James was the first person I contacted. I've been checking in with him for months. Trevor told me he was out of the country and hadn't seen Nate. It appears he's been lying."

They returned their attention to the TV, but after a few minutes Massey looked away. *When did Nate become such a blatant asshole? How could he not know the agony he put us all through?*

"Well, I'd better let Poppy and Mony know what's going on," Kip said stepping away from the bar and pulling out his cell.

Massey nodded. Then: "Hey Shannon, can I talk to you a minute?"

Shannon tipped her head toward an empty booth, grabbed the coffee pot and two cups, and led the way. She pulled a whiskey flask from her apron, poured a healthy shot into her coffee and offered it to Massey. He declined. She propped her elbows on the table, took a sip, and finally looked at him and said, "Before you get started, I never got around to telling you I'm sorry for the trouble I caused between you and Nate this past winter. It was wrong of me, and I don't expect forgiveness—I just needed to get it off my chest."

"It hardly seems relevant at this point," he said flatly. Massey had always liked Shannon, but he wasn't going to let her off the hook that easy. Nor had he been opposed to her and Nate's friends-with-benefits relationship. They'd both seemed satisfied with the arrangement, so he was content in letting it be. He knew where his brother's heart truly belonged, and if Shannon had been paying attention, she'd have known it too. He cut to the chase. "Tell me, what you know about a fellow named Hitch?"

Shannon frowned. "Hitch? I don't know any fellow named Hitch."

It was hard to hide his disappointment.

"Why do you ask?"

He debated the wisdom in telling the town's biggest gossip privileged information. He did it anyway. "We found an Indian girl hiding out at Mony's farm yesterday. She's been camped out there for a while. The place looked like ground zero for a sex and drug ring."

"Really? Was it the same girl the sheriff turned over to social services?"

So much for privileged information.

"Yeah. Mony refused to press charges and there was nothing more the sheriff could do to keep her."

Shannon leaned back in the booth. "It reminds me of a call the Lake Zahl search-and-rescue responded to a few weeks back. There was a minor passed out behind the bar in town. She was Indian too."

"Oh, what happened?"

"Well, the kid was beat up pretty bad, so we hauled her to the ER for treatment and stitches. I don't know what happened to her after that. Sent home, I guess. No one did a follow-up since, well, she's Indian, not our concern."

Massey cringed at the sentiment. "Do you know if she was fingerprinted in the ER?"

"It's possible," Shannon said. "Do you want me to check it out?"

"I'll have the sheriff check it out. What else you can tell me about the call?"

The enthusiasm left her face; for a moment, Massey thought the exchange was over, but then she said, "Dispatch said the call came from the pay phone inside the bar, but no one at the scene owned up to it. The weather was still pretty cold. We'd just gotten a late March snowstorm. The kid was nowhere near properly dressed. It looked like someone dumped her. She already was showing symptoms of hypothermia. She wouldn't say how she got there or who beat her up. She refused to talk to any of us—even me, and I'm pretty good with kids. Anyway, they'd found traces of date-rape drug in her system. That was a terrible fight getting the blood sample. It took four of us to hold her down. She's quite a fighter."

"Was she sexually assaulted?"

"We don't know. Getting the blood sample was nothing compared to the attempt made for a rape exam. The kid went ballistic. No one got near her after that."

They sat in silence drinking their coffee. Shannon changed the subject. "The sheriff mentioned something about finding an old canoe?" Massey nodded. She looked around the bar, then leaned in close. "Dwight Mitchell was here the other night carrying on about some new acquisition."

Massey didn't hide his astonishment. "To what did you owe Mitchell's patronage?"

Shannon snorted. "He started coming around right after Nate left town. Acts like he owns the place too, or at least plans to; it's been bad for business. His family already owns half the downtown. You know what slumlords they are ever since taking over that defunct property management business. Anyway, he's offered to buy out our loan on the bar." She held up two fingers. "Twice."

Massey waved it off. "You know Kip won't let that happen."

Shannon didn't bother to disguise her relief, then filled him in on how Mitchell had been holding regular bragging and bullshit sessions at the bar. "He claimed he'd recently come upon a valuable artifact. He didn't share the details except to say it had been payment for an owed debt." An expression of realization crossed her face. "Jesus, Massey, I just remembered, I do know someone with the nickname Hitch, only it's not a guy. A bunch of us girls used to call Cindy Van Dyke that before she married Dwight. I didn't realize people still call her that. Do you think she's the Hitch the Indian girl is referring to?"

Massey couldn't see it. "How would an Indian girl know a white woman's nickname, and where would the connection be?"

"Well, Cindy took a new position with the William County social services department about six months back. Maybe they'd crossed paths."

Massey was about to caution Shannon on the hazards of speculation when Kip appeared beside the booth.

"She's gone."

"Who?" Shannon asked.

"Mony, of course," Kip snapped. "I just spoke with Poppy, told her to wake up Sleeping Beauty. Both she and Nathan's truck are gone. No note, no explanation, just gone."

Massey stood. He should have seen it coming. Mony had been too upset about the young girl's well-being to let the matter go. *Shit.* He tried her cell—it went straight to voicemail. "Maybe she went out to the farm. We'd better get out there."

The sheriff entered the conversation. "I doubt it."

"What do you mean?"

"I just spoke with Sophie from dispatch. Mony left the station about an hour ago. She'd read about the Jane Doe found behind Lake Zahl bar in the police blotter and asked for the girl's description."

"Do you think she's gone out to look for the kid?" Shannon asked.

Kip said to Massey, "The sheriff and I will handle this. You're taking the company jet out to Vegas. See if you can talk to your brother and—"

"Christ, Dad, this is no time to be thinking about oil. Nate's been gone for months, a few more hours won't topple the business. He's hardly going to pack his bags and follow me home anyway, just because I know where to find him."

"Don't be so naïve," Kip admonished. "It's always about oil. And did I say bring him home? I said talk to him. If you think we're the only ones who've been looking for your brother, you're not as smart as you think. The entire country knows where Nathan is, including our adversary. Christ, with everything going on out at the farm, it's probably a ploy to lure both him and Mony back to North Dakota. Mony may be walking into an ambush right now, and she's too blinded by her sense of righteousness to even realize it."

It sounded like some paranoid conspiracy theory, but his dad's logic held several threads of truth. A tightness gripped Massey's chest, torn between his promise to Mony and his instinct to protect her. He tried reasoning with his dad. "Nate's fine where he is. Mony's the one in real trouble, especially if she's going to the Rez alone. We need to get to her first."

Kip came up to him and placed a gentling hand on his shoulder, his demeanor restrained yet firm. "Listen to me, Matthew, the sheriff and I will look after Mony. Nathan may be at risk too, and you need to talk to your brother, now. This misunderstanding between the two of you has gone on long enough."

Massey could make no argument strong enough to stay, and he reluctantly made his way toward the door. "You call me the second you find her," he said to his dad.

Kip replied, "The same goes for you."

CHAPTER 18

MONY

Mony headed east on ND-1804 toward New Town, her big German shepherd riding shotgun. After talking with the dispatcher, she had a name, an address, and a mission. Crossing the Missouri River at the Garrison Dam, she backtracked a few miles west toward Four Bears Village, located on the southern shore of Lake Sakakawea—her destination.

The lake was a result of the Garrison Dam, constructed in the early1950s. Considered a feat in civil engineering, it was an earth-filled embankment dam, the fifth largest of its kind in the world. Built as part of a flood control and power generation project along the Missouri River, it had forced the Three Affiliated Tribes—a group of Native American's composed of the Mandan, Hidatsa, and Arikara nations—to relocate, most of them to New Town. The Tribes had lost nearly 95 percent of their ancestral land to eminent domain, shattering their way of life.

The small community she entered boasted a marina, a state park, and a casino. Her pursuit was not recreational.

She parked along a quiet street in front of a modest, rambler-style home surrounded by a chain-link fence. A beat-up car sat in the driveway, and a large kennel was next to the garage. Mony stared at the wheelchair ramp running parallel to the front door and thought, *What am I doing here?*

To Shep she said, "You stay here and cover my back." The dog canted his head as she rolled down the window to give him some air.

The German shepherd watched intently as she checked the yard before opening the gate. She had gotten halfway to the front stoop when a large mutt, a mix of Lab and some other hunting hound, came loping from around the house. Human and animal stopped in their tracks, along with Mony's heart. Making eye contact, the female canine lifted her head, assessing the intruder.

"Well, hello, pretty girl," Mony said as if cooing to a baby, reaching slowly into her coat pocket for the soup bone she'd picked up earlier. The dog caught the scent, and Mony set it on the ground. The canine approached cautiously before snatching the treat, and without a backward glance walked back in the direction from where she came, proving once again Maslow's theory.

Mony proceeded to the front door, knocked, and waited. Again she questioned the prudence of her actions. She wished she'd have brought along someone who was more familiar with American Indian customs to facilitate communication. She was relying on her personal belief that all women could relate to one another, regardless of ethnic background, when it came to the welfare of a child. It was a feeble plan. She knew nothing about the girl's life or her experiences. Maybe this was nothing out of the ordinary for the child, but it should be. Mony knew herself well enough to understand she'd made this a personal crusade, but she couldn't back out now. Turning her back on the child without offering help was inconceivable.

A young girl with long, black, braided hair in pigtails and wide, almond-shaped eyes answered the door. It was hard to tell her exact age. She possessed an aged wisdom to her expression; the body just hadn't caught up yet. The young girl pointed at Mony's face and asked, "What happened to you?"

Mony instinctively raised her hand to the injury she'd sustained a week ago sailing. She'd forgotten all about it, but at least she had the girl's attention. Before Mony could respond, an elderly female voice hollered from somewhere in the house, "Who's at the door, Lil Sis?" The girl pushed the door open wide and a woman in a wheelchair appeared at her side. She was a large woman and wore a loose, button-down blouse with a wraparound skirt. Her lower legs were visible, a deep, purplish-red with fluid weeping around the shins thick as tree trunks. The woman said, "Who are you, and what do you want?"

She cleared her throat. "Hello, I'm Mony Altman-Strong. I live over by Williston. Your daughter Sissy was on my property last night. I wondered if I could speak with you about that."

"She's not my daughter, and I don't have to talk to you.

Now go away." The woman started to close the door when Lil Sis pointed toward Nate's truck. The woman squinted her eyes. Shep stared back. She asked, "Is that your dog?"

The woman tried to lean forward in her wheelchair, but the seated position limited her field of vision. She turned her cold, dark gaze on Lil Sis. "Where is that good-for-nothing mutt of yours? She's supposed to be guarding the house."

The young teenager lifted her shoulder in an insolent shrug, ignoring the question. "Should we let her in, Grandmother? She doesn't look like a trespasser. She looks hurt."

"What do I look like, a hospital?" Mony thought the woman might have slapped the girl, if she hadn't been bearing witness. "I suppose you want to let your dog in too," Grandmother said in a caustic tone.

"No, he'll be fine in the truck."

Grandmother looked doubtful. "In this neighborhood? Better bring him in."

Not wanting to argue, Mony whistled for Shep. He leaped gracefully through the open window, then bounded over the gate and trotted up beside her. Lil Sis and Grandmother all but whistled, clearly impressed. "Aren't you going to go back and roll up your window?" Lil Sis asked.

She shook her head. "No, Shep will let me know if someone's bothering the truck." The two exchanged a look of skepticism and let her inside.

Mony wiped her feet on a well-worn but sturdy braided rug and made a quick survey. Clutter filled the small living space, and Mony tried to envision how the woman in a wheelchair managed to navigate the obstacle course. A savory aroma wafted from the kitchen, something gamey like a venison stew. It was a comforting smell, reminding her of the home she'd grown up in.

Not wanting to stand over the woman in the wheelchair, she took a seat on the edge of the sofa above which two pictures hung. One was of the Lil Sis, the other of Sissy, each dressed in a beautiful costume made of buckskin and bejeweled with colorful beading and tiny bells. They were three, maybe four years apart in age, Mony guessed. On a table, a picture of a handsome young man in a military uniform occupied a place of honor, with a shadowbox of medals and ribbons next to it. In front, a turtle shell filled with a sage roll smoldered. Lil Sis sat on the opposite side of the sofa, eyeing Shep with intent. Mony asked, "Is Sissy home?"

Affronted by the direct question, the woman in the wheelchair responded in kind. "No. What do you want?"

Embarrassed, Mony amended, "Please forgive me. I didn't mean to offend. I was worried after she left with social services. I thought she might have been hurt and wanted to know she was okay. I hoped she could tell me about—"

"Why would a white woman care about an Indian girl?" Grandmother countered.

Mony didn't understand the retort. What difference did the color of either of their skin have to do with Sissy's deplorable situation? She dabbed at the sweat above her injured eye. It was too warm in the house to be dressed in these layers, but it gave her an idea. "Look at my face, and you'll see the answer."

"Why should I care if some white woman gets smacked around?" Grandmother said with indifference. "You probably deserved it."

Mony was starting to feel discouraged when she noticed Lil Sis had inched her way closer to Shep. When she was near enough to touch him, Shep nuzzled at the girl's hand, and she patted the dog's head, then scratched behind his ear. Shep thumped his tail with approval. Heartened by the exchange, Mony said. "He is a good protector. He especially likes girls."

Grandmother watched the interaction between Lil Sis and Shep, pursed her lips, and wheeled herself closer to touch the dog. "Our dog should be so smart."

Shep tolerated the overabundant affection, and Mony was grateful she'd brought him along. Perhaps she had an interpreter after all. "I can help you with that," she said, joining in the pet fest. "Animals have good instincts; I trust them."

"Too bad people aren't that way," Grandmother said dryly.

"It is too bad," Mony agreed. "Animals know respect for the female gender." She was careful not to brush either of the two female's hands lest she break Shep's spell. The connection between dog, white woman, and Indian was fragile at best. She let her comment hang in the air and relied on the teenager's impetuous nature to fill in the gap. Lil Sis did not fail to disappoint.

"Are you going to take Sissy away?"

The heartfelt question had Mony choking on her response. "No." She directed her attention to Grandmother. "But I do believe she's mixed up with some very bad people. People who would hurt her to hurt me. It's those people I'm after."

Lil Sis looked like she was about to say something when Grandmother said, "Go outside and check on your mutt. It's a hot day, she needs water."

Before Lil Sis could protest, Mony added, "Would you mind taking Shep too? He could use some water."

Lil Sis looked to her grandmother for approval, then said, "Come on, Shep, I will introduce you to Rainstorm."

When the two women were alone, Grandmother said, "Are you using my Sissy to get to these people you seek?"

Mony shook her head. "No. She is the bait to hook me."

Grandmother considered this and said, "Ask your questions."

Nervous, Mony asked, "What do you know of a man named Hitch?"

"Who's Hitch?"

Shit. Without Shep, she'd lost all ability to communicate. She shook off the misstep and tried a different approach. "Can you tell me about Sissy?"

The old woman told the sad story of how she'd gained custody of her two granddaughters. "My son died on a rescue mission during his tour in the Middle East a year ago. He was a respected healer among our community. He'd began teaching his daughters the traditional ways of the people and our language. Sissy was a quick learner, and she held great potential." It explained why Sissy could interpret some of Mony's broken Lakota. "Those pictures on the wall were taken during the Powwow's Grand Entry, honoring their father and all veterans. She was such a good girl, dutiful and smart, until she dishonored her family, just like her mother."

"What happened?"

Grandmother's voice hardened. "Ran off, back to her people. She's Blackfoot from the Rez near Browning, Montana. Lil Sis told me a month ago about Sissy skipping out of school and meeting with a white man at the gas station near the casino. At first, I didn't believe her. I should have listened. I don't know this Hitch, or who he is. All I know is he stole my Sissy."

Mony empathized with the teen's desire to live her own life and pitied Grandmother's lament for raising a strong-willed child. It was the epitome of every youth's happiness, hopes, and dreams. Not very long ago, she'd been that girl, heading to the big city of Minneapolis to chase a dream, except she'd had the support of her family. Sissy had no one.

"One day she stopped coming home," Grandmother said with a tone of despair. "Maybe she's better off. What use am I to her, old and fat and can't even walk? I only have Lil Sis to take care of me. It won't be long and she'll run away too; then I will have nothing."

Mony wanted to shake the woman and tell her to stop feeling sorry for herself. Instead she said, "Why do you say Sissy is better off, when you know it isn't true? Have you given up?"

Grandmother wouldn't answer. She just rocked herself

back and forth in her wheelchair and hummed quietly. Mony lost her diplomacy.

"You must tell everyone Sissy is missing and that her life is in grave danger. Your son was a respected man in this community. Surely the people will want to honor him by helping you find your granddaughter. You must do this, now, before it's too late."

She bargained, beseeched, and berated, but her words had no effect. Thirty minutes passed, and all Mony could achieve was *maybe*. Leaving the woman sitting in the middle of the room rocking in the wheelchair, Mony showed herself out.

Lil Sis joined her on her walk back to the truck with Shep and the dog she called Rainstorm. She said, "Sissy never made it to tribal social services last night. She's been gone for weeks. No one knows where she's gone, not even her friends." It sounded like a cover story, a younger sibling covering for a sister, except the child's eyes conveyed the validity. Shep started licking Lil Sis's hand, and the girl began to cry. "What's going to happen to my big sister?"

Mony fought back her own tears, frustrated with the entire situation. Deep down, she believed Grandmother hadn't forsaken her granddaughter. Exhausted by her own physical needs, it was too much for the elderly woman to handle. But for Grandmother to say Sissy was better off, that was more than she could bear. Mony had seen the aftermath of the life the white man promised Sissy down by the shabin. Not for the first time, she felt gratitude for her lot in life. She could have been that child.

Her life wasn't without tribulations, but she'd always had support of her dad, her husband, and the Ferguson family. It was time to give something back. Before leaving, she promised Lil Sis she wouldn't give up looking for Sissy. As she pulled away, she heard a sorrowful chanting sound wafting from the house.

Mony and Shep entered the Williston sheriff's station a little past one o'clock, only for all hell to break loose. Even Sophie, who'd been so nice just that morning, scowled at her. Sheriff Wagner came to the lobby.

"Get your ass in my office, right now," he demanded. "And bring the dog too."

Begrudgingly, she took a seat in the unforgiving molded plastic chair in front of his desk. Shep lay obediently at her feet. The sheriff dug right in. "Do you know I have half the county department and an entire hockey team out looking for you?"

Mony blinked in surprise. "Why? You should be looking for Sissy Moonbeam."

A heated exchange ensued over the next fifteen minutes, scattering the entire office staff. No one seemed to want to be involved, especially dispatch. The sheriff stopped yelling long enough for Mony to tell him everything she knew about Sissy, her grandmother, and Lil Sis. The sheriff crossed his arms over his chest, unconcerned. It pissed her off.

"I told you, this is a tribal matter," Wagner snapped, signifying their argument had reached a stalemate. Mony disagreed and was about to lay into him when he said,

"While you were out looking for trouble, Nate showed up."

She immediately stopped talking.

He told her about the events at Blarney Stone, Nate's appearance on TV, and Massey's immediate departure for Vegas. She listened attentively, schooling her face into one of passivity. Behind the mask, a storm of emotions raged and her gut twisted with a torrent of guilt. It was a relief knowing Nate was okay, but why did he have to come out of hiding now? His life wasn't in danger, and she sure could use Massey's help right now searching for Sissy. Then she pictured what the two brother's first meeting might look like, and a wave of bile caught in her throat. She wanted to kick Nate in his ungrateful ass and wished Massey would have waited and taken her with him.

The sheriff finished his story and asked, "So what are you going to do?" He was trying to sidetrack her. She wasn't having it.

Mony circled back to Sissy. "I think this girl is in some deep trouble, probably her entire family. Someone's got her, or she's running, I'm not sure. She may be running to or away from danger. I don't think we did her any favors flushing her out of her hiding place yesterday."

"I'm not talking about that, I was referring to what you're going to do about Nate."

Mony stared, brooding out the window. The sun hadn't quite made its way around the west side of the building, but she could see the sunlight reflecting off the storm clouds rolling in from Montana. She said, "Massey will take care of Nate."

The sheriff exhaled noisily. "Kip thinks your girl is a pawn to lure you and Nate back to Williston."

Your girl. Mony appreciated the acknowledgment. "I said the same thing to the grandmother. If only I could have gotten a description of this Hitch fellow, maybe we'd have something more to go on."

"What makes you so sure Hitch is a man?"

His remark puzzled her, until the sheriff handed her a piece of paper with Massey's handwriting. Reading, she looked up at the sheriff in surprise.

"It looks like Sissy might not be the only one in trouble. I think it's time to pay a visit to your old friend Cindy Van Dyke."

CHAPTER 19

JOHN

A travel mug in hand, John melded into the brisk pace of the foot traffic along the Chicago Pedway. The overcast day reflected his current mood, fixated on the news streaming on his phone. As if being under surveillance wasn't enough, overnight, Nate Ferguson had resurfaced. The full-fledged news blitz dominated social media, every network this morning depicting the Fergmeister with his bandmates in a stunning reunion. It was overkill. John's thoughts went immediately to Ramona. Would she go to Ferguson now that he was back in the picture, or had he always been there and it was only John's whimsical thinking that said otherwise?

He had to put it aside. He had more urgent matters to contend with.

The day turned decidedly worse when he arrived at work to find Randall Rice standing in his office. It was difficult to know what he wanted, but John had a pretty good idea. Franklin stood at his approach.

"How long has he been waiting?" John asked.

"Ten minutes, boss."

"Hold my calls," John told him tersely, and closed the door.

Randall greeted him with the usual cordial fanfare and said, "Do you have a minute to talk?"

John set down his coffee. "Sure. Can I have Franklin bring you coffee?"

Randall lifted his coffee mug and took one of the visitor seats while John settled behind his desk. Hospitalities out of the way, Randall got straight to the point.

"John, I'm concerned about your involvement with Ms. Strong. Do you think it's wise, sleeping with the owner of a company your client is trying to acquire?"

John took a long drink of his coffee. He'd known Randall Rice the longest of the senior members. They were sailing rivals, and Ethan Rice was his friend, until yesterday. The whole Rice-Monroe association played out like an episode on a soap opera, complete with corruption and infidelity. John was privy to many of the Rice family's most egregious secrets—knowledge he'd kept in confidence, for the right price. He feigned nonchalance at the question. "I'm not sure where you're getting your information, Randall, nor do I understand your concern."

Randall handed him a manila envelope. "You were saying?"

John recognized the photos. He shoved them back into the envelope and laid it on his desk. "I must be missing something here. I thought you were implying I slept with Ms. Strong. It looks to me we're fully clothed in these photos."

"I'm concerned," Randall said, keeping his eye on the envelope, "that it looks incriminating. I found this lying on the floor in front of my office door this morning. If anyone else has received them, it would be very bad for you. You know what a barracuda Fran is when it comes to the reputation of the law firm."

John did know. Fran Temple never hid her disdain for his involvement with his clients. But this interrogation wasn't about Fran or appearances. This was blackmail. "Fran is aware of my negotiations with Ms. Strong. Are you aware of Monroe's recent low-balled bid? It would appear they don't have the liquid resources to even make a decent offer."

"Perhaps you could dial it back a bit with the widow until after the probate hearing?" Randall suggested. "You are still representing the Monroe account, correct?"

John played along with the charade. "I can see where you might think I have an attraction to Ms. Strong. She is an alluring woman with many appealing attributes, but my relationship with her is purely business. There's no mixing trade secrets with pillow talk." It was mostly true. He and Ramona never talked business over sex.

Randall leaned forward reaching for the envelope. "That's a relief. We wouldn't want our golden boy caught up in a web of deceit. And the Monroe account?"

John rested his elbows on the envelope and said with a haughty laugh, "We're lawyers, Randall. Why would there be any need for deceit?"

Randall sat back in his chair. "You are correct, the truth is what we make it."

Watching Randall's expression, John put the envelope in his drawer. "I assume you won't need these. A good blackmailer always has a backup."

Pretending shock, Randall said, "John, are you implying I'm the blackmailer? Why, you're like a second son to me. Your success is my success. I'm merely passing along potentially damaging information to give you time to build a defense."

"So, you're assuming I need to defend my practice?"

"I meant counterattack. I told you before, I don't care about your relationship with that woman. It's Ethan. He tells me Monroe is losing confidence in your competency representing his company."

"Father or son?"

Randall became indignant. "What difference does that make? You have a stellar reputation representing women. Is it because Monroe is male and not female that your actions aren't quite on par?"

John offered a patronizing grin. "I believe you've been misinformed. I am representing the female interest for Monroe Oil. Didn't Ethan tell you? Tiffany was at the meeting last night."

Randall's jaw tightened. "What do you mean? What about Ethan? He's her husband. He should be the one representing their family's interests."

"I don't know what is going on between Ethan and Tiffany," John said coolly. "All I can tell you is what I know and what I observed. I know Tia signed my standard retainer for legal services. She hasn't given me a specific task at this time. And what I saw was that she's quite unhappy with the way her father and Jason are handling the F&A Oil acquisition."

Red-faced, Randall muttered something obtuse under his breath, then said, "That is one messed-up family."

John couldn't argue with that.

They hashed over the dissension among the Monroe family members for a while; when Randall had nothing more to say, he finally left, offering a feeble apology for the misunderstanding. "I mean you no discredit, John. You understand, I'm just looking out for the company's best interests. There is an enormous amount of stress associated with this case. Monroe is our largest account, and I know it has taken a great deal of your time. Don't be afraid to ask for help if you need it."

John escorted him to the door.

"Thank you for the offer, but I assure you, my team has all manageable aspects of this case under control."

As Randall exited, John found Quincy Goldman waiting for him outside his office, a manila envelope in his hand.

It was after lunch before Franklin could bring John his messages. He laid them on his desk and said, "Before you read them, I have a tofu oriental salad for you in the fridge. Now, how do you want me to respond?"

John rubbed his temples as the throb of a massive headache began to build. His three least favorite people.

"Start with Monroe. Tell him I'm in court all day and that I'll talk to him during our scheduled pre-trial prep meeting, not before. Next, give Stapleton my retainer and double my fee. Inform him I will have no further discussion about his case until after the probate hearing and that all future meetings will be in Chicago, nonnegotiable. If he accepts the terms, set up a meeting for the following week. As for Fran—"

John paused, weighing his words. The pressure coming down from Temple and Goldman yesterday had been palpable. Despite Fran's clear insight into the futility of Monroe's case, she'd stopped by his condo after her dinner meeting and had given him explicit instructions to find a loophole—any sort of loophole—around, over, or under the missing title or deeds and their validity.

"Tell Ms. Temple I will do my best to meet with her before the end of the day. I have a couple of strategies I want to run past her before I leave for Williston."

"Got it," Franklin said, jotting down notes. "And what about the mystery call?"

John leaned back in his desk chair and rolled his neck from ear to ear, trying to release the tension. In less than a week, it would all be over and his life would resume some level of normalcy. He would do his best during the hearing, as always, even though he knew it was a hopeless case. Monroe would move on and find some other landowner to harass, and the senator would drill his well. The Fergmeister would cut a new album, and Ramona could go back to the business of caring for animals. *What a load of crap.*

"Were you able to do a reverse-call lookup?"

"Yes, the call came from the Blarney Stone in Williston, North Dakota."

Interesting. A public location.

"Male or female?"

"Female."

Even more interesting.

"Did she leave her name or say what she wanted?"

"It was hard to hear. There was a lot of background noise, but I think she said her name was . . . Sheri, Sharon—"

"Shannon?"

"Maybe, Shannon could be right. Shannon McDonald. Do you know her?"

This was beyond interesting. Why would the fiery, redheaded bartender who wouldn't give him the time of day during their last encounter suddenly want to talk to me?

"And the message?"

"Just the callback number there in front of you, boss. Do you want me to return the call?"

John put the note in his shirt pocket. "No, I'll take care of this one. Now let me bring you up to speed on what's going on."

When he'd finished, the look on Franklin's face was akin to shock. "What are you going to do, John?"

"Someone is trying to blackmail me, and I need to find out who. I want you to hire a private detective to do some reconnaissance work for me. But don't do it at the office, do it from home. I will compensate you for your time. I don't need you constantly looking over your shoulder or behaving in the work environment like it suddenly turned into a minefield. Let's start with the photos the senior partners all seem to have and see if they can tell us anything. Then—"

Franklin gasped. "Fran has them too?"

"Undoubtedly. Yet for some reason, she wasn't the one attacking me in my office first thing this morning, which strikes me as odd. If anyone would turn this into a witch hunt, it would be her."

"She did want to talk to you," Franklin reminded.

"Yes, and I want you to call her office and tell her I'm on my way."

"What do you want me to do in the meantime?"

"Keep the status quo. We don't need the rest of the team getting anxious over this. I want them focused. We're in the home stretch on this project. This is no time to fuck it up."

"I'll do my best," Franklin said, and left the office.

John walked to the floor-to-ceiling windows and stared at the rain pouring down on the foot traffic below. Reflecting on yesterday and this morning's events, he should have been feeling a bit more anxious about the security of his position in the company. What he felt was apathy. Randall had at least one thing right: he was no longer the best person for the case, because, bottom line, he really didn't give a shit anymore. With two of the three senior members of the team riding his ass, he wasn't even sure he wanted to work for the company. And now that Ferguson was back in the picture, the F&A family would solidify and drilling would begin, no matter what had caused him to leave. What John had seen on TV wasn't a triumph reunion of a has-been band; it was Ferguson declaring a promise to his long-lost love.

Still, something in the two lovers' saga didn't quite add up. Why had Ramona married Bob Strong instead of Ferguson? John told himself to just let it go, but it wasn't in his nature. What he needed right now was a kick in the ass to get his head back in the game.

A remembered thought struck him, and he reached in his pocket for the Williston phone number and his cell. Perhaps Ms. Shannon could shed a new perspective on the subject and boost his interest.

He dialed the number.

The scratchy sound of a female voice answered, "Blarney Stone."

It doesn't sound like Shannon, John thought, but there was considerable static on the line, or maybe she had a cold. He said in an affable voice, "Ms. McDonald, John Finch here, returning your call. How can I be of assistance?"

Static filled the line for several seconds; John thought he'd lost the call before Shannon said, "It's what I can do for you. Have you heard about the Indian girl found out at the Altman property?"

He hadn't.

"And why would that be of assistance to me?" John said it without pretense but was already at his office door, waving at Franklin to get his ass in there.

"Not so fast, lawyer. I need something from you as well."

Of course, the hitch. "And that would be?"

Shannon explained what she wanted; then, after John promised his end of the deal, she told him about the Indian girl. It was quite a story, and frankly, a little hard to believe. Getting an accurate read between the lines was difficult when the phone connection was so poor.

When she'd hung up, John told Franklin, "Get your tablet. I need you to get me on the first available flight to Williston."

"Now what?"

"I'll explain while you search."

CHAPTER 20

NATE

Mobbed by crazed fans and media, it was dawn before anyone could leave the club. By the time Nate arrived at the place where Kat and Mindy were staying, they were long gone. He tried calling each of their cells several times—everything went straight to voicemail. Next, he checked Kat's itinerary on her book website. She had a signing in San Diego the following day. It was all the further he got in his quest. Awake for the past forty-eight hours and hungover besides, he had no choice but to crash a few hours and returned to Trevor's place.

His head had barely hit the pillow when Trevor roused him out of bed for an impromptu press conference. He complied, but his heart wasn't in it. It was only for the sake of the audience he hadn't walked out last night. The tension between him and his bandmate was so pervasive, it was a miracle they'd finished the set. Taking up their roles, Brandon tried to keep everyone calm, Tim got stoned, and Rocky kept talking about *obligations*. Trevor, who'd used to side with Nate, joined in Rocky's crusade. Nate told them all to go fuck themselves. It amused the drummer immensely.

The night should have been a triumphant comeback in his music career. It felt more like a noose around his neck. From the moment they'd all met at the studio to when they'd stepped onto the stage, he should have known it had been more than a friendly jam session. The whole business felt like a setup, empty and fake. No longer comfortable with the people he'd once shared the spotlight with, Nate yearned for the days jamming with the cover band back home. At least he'd felt more himself.

There was also the small matter of his whereabouts. Now that the reunion was viral, it wouldn't take long before Massey came for him. In a preemptive attempt to ward off a confrontation, Nate tried calling, then hung up. Christ, what would he say? *Gee, sorry for beating you up after you slept with my girlfriend thirty years ago, can I come home now?* Maybe his brother was ignoring him, still pissed about the broken nose. Perhaps Massey wasn't coming at all. Nate couldn't blame him if he held a grudge, though deep down he knew it wasn't in his brother's nature.

Makeup artists were on hand when they arrived at the club. Nate didn't think anything could make him look presentable after the hellacious night he'd had, until he got a look at Tim's transformation. Hair brushed and styled, beard trimmed and clothes cleaned, Tim looked like a new man. Nate caught the scent of weed on those fine new threads and wished he'd taken up the habit himself. Magazine, television, and newspaper reporters from all over the country were gathered. Marginally aware of his surroundings, Nate's mind kept drifting to what would have made Kat and Mindy leave without saying goodbye.

"Hey, Fergmeister, that was quite a performance last night," a reporter said jovially.

Rocky responded, "Which one, during or after the concert?"

Everyone laughed.

Maybe the girls received a call. Is something wrong back home?

A second reporter asked, "Does this mean you guys have set aside your differences and are officially back together?"

Again, Rocky answered. "Look at your video feeds, you tell me."

"That's not an answer," someone shouted.

Maybe the old man had had a heart attack. Maybe Mony's cancer is back. Was there a drilling accident? The possibilities were endless; the speculation was driving him insane.

"Our concert last night was preternatural fate," Trevor said, taking over the interview. "The lead singer for the headline group had an unexpected illness and the guys were just helping out an old friend."

"Yeah, I heard it was food poisoning," a reporter near the front clarified. "Convenient."

Trevor didn't skip a beat. "If we had been planning a comeback, there would have been considerably more preparation and promotion," he said, schmoozing the audience. "As it stands, think of last night as a celebration for our loyal fans. If anything more comes out of it, you'll have them to thank."

"What do you have to say about the reports MHC was seen coming from your former recording studio, Shooting Star Records?"

Rocky held up a hand. "Just a friendly jam session, not a big deal. That's not to say anyone in the band is opposed to getting back together, but there are a few things that need to be worked out before that happens."

Tim held a closed fist in the air. "Rock on," he shouted, sending the crowd into a fit of laughter.

"I'd like to hear the Fergmeister's thoughts on that," a third reporter shouted over the noise.

The room went abruptly silent as all eyes focused on Nate. Startled by the sound of his name, he withdrew from his introspection and told them what they wanted to hear. "I would be willing to look at a proposal when or if the time comes."

He managed the next hour, cruising through the interview mostly by rote. When the press conference ended, Nate went straight to the guest room and tried to call Massey. No answer. When Mony didn't answer either, he knew something was seriously wrong. Mony always answered calls from him, *always*.

For the first time in months, he needed to talk to his family. He wanted to go home.

Returning to Trevor's, Nate, too agitated to attempt sleep, began throwing things into his duffle bag. He had no idea what he was doing or where he was going; he just knew he had to get out of there. His temporary sanctuary was turning into a jail cell. As he passed through the kitchen, he was contemplating leaving a note when the glowing ember of a cigarette caught his attention.

Dressed in her kimono bathrobe, Gem sat at the kitchen table, waiting in ambush. He wasn't in the mood. Trevor St. James wasn't his warden, nor did he owe him an explanation. He owed Gem even less.

"Where you off to at this hour?" she asked in a tone like a mother who'd just caught her child sneaking out of the house.

He didn't even bother to lie. "I'm going home,"

Her eyes fell on the duffle in his hand. "You can't do that."

Nate was too tired to argue. "You can go to hell."

Gem ignored the barb. "Trevor has a photoshoot set up for later today and—"

"I don't care," he said, conscious of sounding like a five-year-old, and walked to the fishbowl where he'd tossed his keys.

She stood. "Look, Nate, this is bigger than you. Think about the rest of the band and what this would mean for them."

"What did you tell my nieces?" he demanded.

"I didn't tell them anything," she snapped.

Nate dug his hand into the bowl and pulled out his keys, then turned to face her. "Until I get things straight with my family, there is nothing else for me to think about." He reached for the door handle.

"Does that include your mom?"

Nate stopped at a local convenience store, both seething and enlightened by the pointless encounter with Gem.

At least he'd finally come to understand her role in the entire "open relationship" thing. She'd shoved a piece of paper in his pocket, informing him it was a lead on his mom. He'd ended the conversation by closing the door in her face, thinking, *Let her believe she's conned me.* Just because he had a name and an address didn't make it true or mean he was going to follow up on it.

He walked into the store when the cashier shouted, "Hey, Fergmeister, caught your show from the street level the other night. Huge fan. I hope we'll be seeing more of you and MHC here in Vegas. Would you mind taking a selfie with me?"

It was the interview all over again.

He found an abandoned parking lot where he scarfed down the tasteless food. Facing the sunrise reminded him of the morning he'd stayed at the campground in Idaho Falls during his flight to Vegas. Unlike that cold winter morning, today was bright and hot. Somehow the warmth didn't change the agonizing chill he felt inside. Nate took the piece of paper out of his pocket.

It read: *Glory West Sunrise Ranch, Parker, Arizona.*

I must be batshit crazy, Nate mused, but he punched the name and city into his navigation system anyway.

Well, fuck me.

The place was legitimate, at least, but how could he be sure it had anything to do with his mom? It was probably a well-crafted stall tactic dissuading him from returning to North Dakota. Nate made a closer examination of the map. If he took US Highway 95, it was practically a straight shot south from his present position, about 150 miles. Back home, that was two trips into Williston on the same day. Very doable. Things messed up as they were, he considered what little difference a small detour made in the grand scheme of things, and he pointed his wheels south.

With the weather at a moderate 99 degrees, the ride between the eastern edge of the Mojave National Preserve and the Grand Canyon Prashant National Monument was a pleasant drive if your vehicle had AC. Alone in the wide-open space, Nate had plenty of time to reflect. His thoughts turned to Gem. Maybe he'd her judged too harshly. It wasn't her fault he was a coward for not telling Mindy and Kat the truth.

Turning on the satellite radio, he stared out at the arid landscape in front of him. He vowed to keep his promise to make things right with his family, and on the remote chance Gem wasn't a liar, it made sense that journey should begin with his mother. He had no idea what he would say to her if the lead panned out. Maybe the words would come to him like a lyric in a beautiful song. A glimmer of hope filled his heart. "My Forever Childhood Friend" came on the radio, and Nate hummed along.

He stopped in Lake Havasu City for gas, then continued further south on US 95. He'd never been to this part of the state and felt a little conspicuous in his big black truck with North Dakota license plates, then realized it wasn't out of place at all. There were dozens of out-of-state plates driving around from the Midwest. It seemed he'd found where the snowbirds congregated.

Near Parker Dam, he came upon what looked like an irrigated section of land and discovered it was the confluence of another river with the Colorado. He turned off the main highway at the Bill Williams River National Wildlife Refuge and drove along a narrow road that wound through fields of green, sticking to the riparian corridor until he came to an offshoot with a raw iron archway. A sign read: *Glory West Sunrise, private property. Keep out.*

Wildflowers filled the ditches along the lane, kept vibrant by an irrigation canal siphoned from the nearby river. It led to what Nate could only describe as a small hacienda nestled against the base of a low mountain. The shingles were made of brown clay tile, along with stucco siding resembling the color of the surrounding rock. It made the modest estate blend into the side of the hill, appearing like a natural part of the landscape. A six-foot wall surrounded the front of the home, blocking the view of the rest of the house from the road. Off to the north stood a small horse corral and a stable. There were a couple of outbuildings and a small, cabin-like structure set a few hundred feet back from the main home, butted against the mountain. *A guesthouse, or a bunkhouse for a ranch hand,* he thought. It reminded him of the shabin back home.

Parking near the courtyard gate, he beeped his horn. When no one responded, he got out and entered the unlocked gate, which led to an inner courtyard. A fountain made of clay stone dominated the center. Water shot straight up in the air, then fell back into a collecting pond, where a pump recirculated the fountain's supply. Butterflies filled the sanctuary and buzzed with the sound of bees. He strolled across a terracotta tile walkway to the main door and knocked, but no one answered. Lingering a moment, he considered walking around back, then decided to check out the stable. As he exited the courtyard, he caught sight of a horse in the corral.

She watched him—a beautiful creature painted with lush, tawny brown, white patches and a chocolate-brown star on her nose. It made Nate think of Mony, and his heart filled with melancholic joy. She had a horse back on her farm in Minnesota too—also a Mustang, if he remembered correctly, though he wasn't sure. Reaching into his shirt pocket, he said to the mare, "Looks like it's your lucky day, pretty girl."

The horse's ears perked up with interest and she trotted toward him. She was eating the sweet treat from his hand when Nate heard a male voice say, "You have a way with her."

A tall, broad-shouldered man with dark, leathery skin strolled up behind him. His long, black-and-gray hair hung down to his shoulders, and he carried what looked like the beginnings of a woven basket. He was Indian or Mexican or perhaps both. The weathered old man stopped a few feet in front of Nate and squinted. "You look like her," he said, "especially around the eyes."

Nate frowned, confused at the remark. "I look like the horse?"

The old man laughed and startled the mare. "She's a skittish one," he said, pointing to the horse. "Knows who to trust and who not to. You passed the test."

"What was the test?"

Ignoring the question, the old man said, "My name is Jerome Coyote, but everyone calls me Slow Joe, because I'm old and slow. And this"—Joe stepped around Nate and took the horse's snout in his big hands—"This here beauty is Wind Dancer, but Buddy nicknamed her Windy." He patted the horse's nose and held open a flat hand filled with raisins. "She and he got along good. They both liked their sweets."

Nate's brows shot up. "As in Buddy Altman?" It was the first true glimmer of promise he'd felt during this entire misadventure. He extended his hand. "Hi, I'm Nate Ferguson. I know Buddy very well. You might say we're business partners. Do you own this place? Does a woman named Gloria Ferguson live here?"

Joe didn't answer and kept feeding the horse. When the treat was gone, the mare lost interest and trotted off to the other side of the corral. Nate waited anxiously for a response, but nothing was forthcoming. *Could it be that this man knows Buddy and Mom?*

The mare paced in a small arc, waiting for more treats. Joe crinkled his forehead and finally spoke. "I look after Windy. Better check at the house."

"I just came from there," Nate said, flustered. "I should tell you, Buddy—"

"You will find your answers up there," Joe interrupted, pointing two fingers toward the house. "I take care of Windy."

Was he being dismissed? Nate looked from Joe to the house, then back to Joe. He thanked him for his time and dug an old business card out of his wallet. "I'd appreciate a call when the homeowner gets back," he said, writing down his tracker number and holding the card out to Joe. "I have information about Buddy and some questions about my mom."

Joe took the card and stuffed it in his shirt pocket. "Yes, I believe you do."

Nate walked away with a sullen laugh, feeling profoundly disappointed. He should have known Gem had lied to him. The despair which had threatened to overpower him for months stung in the corner of his eyes. He glanced at the house, then at the road that had brought him to where he stood, when he spotted a familiar sight.

Off to the left and nestled among a stand of cottonwood trees sat twelve beehives—to the right, a small garden filled with young sunflowers. He'd been so intent on finding his mom, he'd completely missed the beehives. *Was this where Buddy brought the bees?* The thought of it overwhelmed him and brought tears to his eyes. It was all too much. Standing in a daze, he tried contemplating his next move when his phone vibrated.

Checking the screen, he considered letting it go to voicemail, then decided it was time to face his destiny. He answered with a tentative, "Hello?"

"Nate? Jesus H. Christ. Where the hell are you?"

He heard both restrained anger and relief in his brother's voice.

"I'm near Parker, Arizona. Where are you?"

"In Vegas, looking to kick your sorry ass," Massey barked. "What the hell are you doing in Parker?"

Nate took a strange delight in hearing ferocity in his brother's voice. It was like being admonished for doing something stupid when they were kids. It was better than apathy. He told Massey, "I was following a lead on where I might find Mom."

There was a long pause.

"I swear to God, Nate, if this is some bullshit story—did you find her?"

Nate failed to hide the disappointment in his response. "No, but I think found where Buddy was keeping the bees over the winter. A place called Glory West Sunrise."

Another long pause, then, "How long did it take you to get there from Vegas?"

"Oh, I don't know, about two hours, I think. Why?"

"Do you think you can find a place where you can lay low for a few hours and stay out of trouble?"

Nate considered the ominous request. He'd planned to use the two-day drive back to Williston to prepare himself for a confrontation with his brother. Now that the moment might only be a couple of hours away, his resolve was beginning to waver. He turned toward the corral to see the mare and Joe watching him intently. Nate shouted, "Hey, Joe, do you know a place close by where I can hide?"

Massey said into the phone, "Don't hide too well. I need to be able to find you."

CHAPTER 21

MASSEY

Massey arrived at VGT Airport a little past noon. It felt wrong leaving town with Mony's whereabouts unknown, but there was nothing he could do about it. He had a different mission, and he was eager to get underway. As he stepped out onto the tarmac, the Nevada sun beat down with the intensity of a blast furnace, and he squinted in the bright light. Reaching into his pocket for his sunglasses, he contemplated where to begin the search when he saw a familiar figure standing at the gate's entrance.

"Nate?"

The tall, lean man approached, then removed his aviator glasses and shook Massey's hand. "Hey, Uncle Massey."

Surprised, Massey returned the handshake. "Dane, good to see you. How did you know I was here?"

Dane released his grip. "Kip gave me your flight itinerary. Come on, I've got a jeep waiting."

The two men started toward the exit. "Don't get me

wrong," Massey said warily, "I'm glad for your help, but why are you here?"

They'd reached the jeep; Dane popped the locks with the remote. Climbing behind the wheel, the young man said with equal caution, "Don't be too quick with the gratitude. I have conditions." He held up a finger. "One, you're going to tell me what the hell is going on in Williston. I haven't been able to reach Mom for almost two days, and I just read some bullshit on the internet that F&A found a new business in human trafficking."

Dane was far too perceptive to sidestep that truth, so Massey took one uncomfortable topic off the table and filled him in on the events out at the farm. He hated that he couldn't address Mony's current whereabouts, but that was out of his control, "I suspect she's gone out to the Rez to try and protect the child."

Dane started the engine, then shook his head and sighed. "Man, I wish she'd stick to animals. She thinks she can save the whole world from neglect and abuse."

Massey couldn't disagree. "What's the second condition?"

Dane looked Massey in the eyes. "When we do catch up with dear ol' Uncle Nate, I'm going to seriously kick his ass." His nephew laughed as if it were a joke, but what Massey heard was stone-cold conviction.

He replied, "Not if I get to him first."

They stopped at the Mile High Club first, then the recording studio. It was late afternoon when they reached Trevor's house. People, cars, and media vans lined the streets. Wading through the crowd, there was a feeling of gloom and foreboding. It wasn't what Massey had expected. They passed a group of women camped out on a lawn who eyed Dane with curiosity. One boldly came up to him and asked, "OMG, are you the Fergmeister?"

The hype Massey had seen on the news this morning depicted an upbeat celebratory feel. The energy from this crowd felt more like a funeral. Massey and Dane approached a police officer on-site. After they'd explained who they were and what they were doing there, the officer checked their credentials, then escorted the two of them to the door.

Massey knocked several times before someone finally answered. The door opened a crack and the crowd broke into a frenzy, shouting, "Fergmeister," and "MHC, MHC!" The two men were quickly ushered inside. When the perfunctory greetings were out of the way, Trevor launched into an instant rant.

"Nate really bailed at a critical point in our comeback," he said, not bothering to hide his frustration. "He has an obligation. We need to find him."

Massey wasn't there to discuss contractual issues, if any in fact existed; he was there to find his brother. "What do you mean, Nate bailed?"

A woman dressed in a kimono-style bathrobe joined in and introduced herself as Gem Richards, Trevor's chief security consultant, among other titles. Dane bristled; his response did not go unnoticed. Gem eyed him warily, then turned to Trevor and said, "I thought you said the Fergmeister has only one brother?"

She didn't wait for a response and joined the discussion,

spewing some fabricated story about how Nate's nieces had sabotaged the concert. Dane took the opportunity to introduce himself and relayed his sisters' account of the events. Gem jerked back her head and looked to Trevor. "Are you going to just stand there and let him call me a liar?"

Trevor wasn't concerned.

"He just can't up and leave like that," he began again. "You have no idea the time and money that has been invested into the band's reunion. This is bigger than Nate. He needs to fulfill his obligation."

It wasn't uncharacteristic for his brother to cut and run when he was feeling overwhelmed, Massey thought, but kept it to himself. He glanced between Gem and Trevor. "Why should I believe anything you say? You've been lying to me for months about Nate's whereabouts."

It was Trevor's turn to be indignant, and for a moment, Massey worried they'd exhausted their options. He offered, "Tell me how to get in touch with Nate, and I promise I'll do what I can to talk him into coming back to Vegas to finish the demo." The proposal piqued Trevor's interest and he immediately gave Massey Nate's tracker number.

Opening the door, Massey and Dane were immediately greeted by an uproar of cheers. Over the noise Trevor shouted, "I'm holding you to that promise, Ferguson."

With a clearer direction on where to go next, Dane suggested grabbing a bite to eat before calling Nate. They stopped at a popular eatery famous for its street tacos when Massey received an incoming text from Kip.

Mony's okay, she just showed at the sheriff's office.

That was a relief, except now he had to relay his less-than-positive news to his Dad. He was doing that when two women in their forties came up to them and boldly asked Dane, "Excuse me, but are you the Fergmeister?"

Massey called his brother and was both confounded by the information regarding the bees and relieved to hear he was all right. They set a course for Lake Havasu City. Dane, who was a quiet man by nature, had become unbearably so after the incident at the taco stand. They were nearing the end of city limits when Massey broke the silence and said, "Before we get too far down the road, I need to know what you're hoping to accomplish by coming with me. It's not too late to turn around, hop a flight back to San Diego, and spare yourself the family drama."

Dane clenched and unclenched his jaw, then let out a deep breath. "Uncle Massey, if I asked you something, would you tell me the truth?"

That was a loaded question, Massey thought. "If it's information I can share, then yes."

Dane gave a frustrated huff. "Well, get ready for a Stronghold."

"A what?"

"A Stronghold. It's what Mom used to do to Dad whenever he was holding back information. Instead of nagging him to death, she'd act all nice and suggest they do something fun, like go for a drive in the country or something. When Dad was at the furthest point from home, she would hammer him with questions. He was a captive audience, and she'd wear him down before they got home. He called it a Stronghold."

Massey laughed. "Sounds like Mony. And your dad fell for that?"

"Every single time."

He considered the two-and-a-half-hour drive and said to Dane, "Fire away."

His nephew began with a story.

The hunting trips to Montana had been a tradition for the Altman and Ferguson families for nearly three decades. The participants changed in and out over the years; sometimes non–family members joined them, like the Sanquist twins or Shawn and Shannon McDonald, but the core remained consistent—Buddy, the entire Ferguson family excluding Diana, and the entire Strong family excluding Mony. Not because Mony wasn't a good shot—on the contrary, she was an excellent marksman with a handgun. She'd just liked hanging out with Poppy for the weekend.

"At no point was it ever mentioned or made apparent that there was anything between Mom and Uncle Nate," Dane went on. "There was no animosity between him and my dad. In fact, they got along. They even had shit in common, like their viewpoint against frac mining and other environmental issues."

"Why would you think there would be friction between your dad and Nate?"

Dane snorted. "You and Mom have been dancing around this shittin' topic for a half a year, and I'm sick of it. I know Mom and Nate were lovers at some point, so don't deny it. Plus, it must have been something really bad for the three of you to not be talking to one another. You need to fix it. The family oil business will never survive divided like this." Massey opened his mouth and Dane held up his hand. "Kat and Mindy said this 'Gem' told them Nate beat you up, pretty bad, then ran out on Mom without a word."

Massey considered his words carefully. "Nate was told a lie about me and your mom having an affair. He got pissed, punched me, and left. Is that what you want to know?"

Dane became irritated. "Look, Massey, there has to be more to the story to make Nate believe you'd do such a thing. What it feels like is that someone is either trying to hurt Mom or trying to hurt this family. My money's on both. This is no time to be secretive. We have to stick together."

Dane made a good argument. Massey had also been thinking along those same lines for months. Still, it was hard to know what to share without betraying Mony's trust. "Is that all of your conspiracy theories?"

Dane wouldn't answer.

"Do you really believe your mom would have, *could* have, betrayed your dad?" Again his question was met with silence—he realized he was in a Stronghold. Massey sighed. "Okay, you're right about Nate and your mom being in a relationship. But it was before she met your dad. I won't say long before, but before. She never betrayed your father, I swear it."

Dane said, "Tell me something I don't know."

He wasn't sure if his nephew was being sarcastic or fishing for more information. In any case, Massey said, "Mony had some trouble back in college before she met Bob, and he'd helped her through it. A relationship blossomed between them, and your dad won her heart away from Nate."

"Why hadn't Nate been there for her?"

"Logistics. Nate was still in high school back in Williston."

"My dad stole Mom from Nate?"

"In a manner of speaking."

Dane glanced at him. "You know what the trouble was?"

"I do, yes."

"But you're not going to tell me?"

"That's Mony's story to tell."

"Someone hurt her, didn't they?"

Massey couldn't avoid the direct question. "Yes."

"Was it Nate?"

When Massey didn't answer, Dane reached into his pocket, pulled out a small piece of paper, and handed it to him. "I found this in my mailbox the afternoon you and Mom must have found that girl out at Grandpa Buddy's farm. No writing on the outside, no name. Just this little piece of paper inside an envelope. Read it."

He glanced at the paper. It read, *Who's your daddy?* "Where did this come from?"

"Was it Nate who hurt her?"

"Goddamn it, no," Massey barked. "My brother was heartbroken when Mony didn't come home for Christmas and married your dad. He quit high school and ran away, just like now—joined a rock band, became a star. You don't know what they are to one another."

"Someone needs to tell the truth," Dane said, his tone resolute, and stuck the paper back in this pocket. "What am I supposed to think when I get something like this? I'll tell you what I think. Someone else out there knows the truth, or thinks they know the truth, or they're trying to manipulate a fragment of the truth to hurt my family. Tell me you're not thinking the same thing. Do you know who told Nate the lie about you and Mom and why?"

Dane was shocked to learn a family friend told the rumor, but she hadn't instigated the lie. That would be Cindy Van Dyke, Mony's former college roommate and friend, a name connected to the present under the alias "Hitch." Cindy had married the family's biggest nemesis. It was beginning to make sense.

"I'd rather hear the truth from you or Mom than from some random asshole. Can you please just help me understand what the hell is going on?"

Dane was right—there'd been too many secrets kept under the guise of sparing heartache, and it was completely backfiring. "I guess there's something to this Stronghold," he said solemnly. "I'll tell you everything, but first we find Nate. I'm only telling this story once."

CHAPTER 22

JOHN

John went straight to Ferguson's office, located in the airport annex, and found the place closed. Disappointed but not dissuaded, he then hurried to the courthouse to see if there was any further development on the whereabouts of the missing title and deed. Closing for lunch, the clerk was not pleased to see him. She neither confirmed nor denied whether the courthouse had the actual papers but did say ledgers indicated Altman's purchase of the property back in the early 1980s, mineral rights intact, as the last recorded transaction. John asked for a copy of the public record, which the clerk reluctantly provided, and headed for the hotel.

He was pleased the accommodations had improved remarkably since his last visit and sprawled himself out over the ample surfaces of the business suite. Examining the ledger notes and information Franklin had uncovered on Altman's property holdings, it was easy to conclude the probate hearing was just a formality. John considered the ramifications of losing his first case in over three years, then blew it off. For whatever reason, the prospect of seeking new employment carried little weight on his pros and cons list. Perhaps he was overdue for a change. It was a welcome thought.

He contacted Shannon McDonald shortly before four o'clock; she seemed genuinely surprised by the call, then invited him to dinner. It struck him as odd, but he accepted the offer, curious about her motive.

Arriving at the given address, he found Shannon's residence was a loft above the bar. She had a private entrance; still, anyone watching from inside would know he was there. He climbed the long flight of stairs to a deck facing the back parking lot. She was working a large gas grill and said over her shoulder, "I didn't peg you for a beer drinker, so I have a single-malt Irish whiskey sitting on the table next to the ice bucket. You pour while I finish up here." John picked up a heavy crystal decanter and set them up each a healthy glass.

He handed her a glass and stood beside her, admiring her skill at the grill. Was she planning to seduce him with food and alcohol? It wasn't entirely an unpleasant prospect. She wore no makeup or fragrance, essential weaponry when enticing men into making bad decisions, but she had other assets. The tight-fitting Blarney Stone T-shirt and faded jeans hugged her lovely curves. Her wild red hair, hanging loose from her ponytail, made an alluring package.

After the meal, Shannon offered a slice of rhubarb pie. He asked, "Where do you find the time to bake?"

She laughed. "I don't. Poppy made it fresh for me this morning."

"The senator's wife?"

"Yup. Kip would have a major shit fit if he found out who I was serving it to." The irony added a delightful flavor to the pie.

"I was wondering when we were going to get around to the topic of the Altmans and Fergusons," he said.

Shannon broke off a piece of crust and savored it in her mouth, then said, "John, I'm going to go out on a limb here and say I consider you a fairly decent guy. More intelligent than your counterpart Monroe, at least. So I'll tell you: Monroe Oil has nothing to gain challenging Mony Altman over ownership of her dad's property in this probate hearing."

John took a drink of his scotch. Anyone with an objective eye and half a brain could draw the same conclusion. What he wanted to know was, what was motivating Shannon's sudden willingness to talk? He said, "You need to tell me something I don't already know."

"Do you know Massey left for Vegas this morning? He'll likely have his brother in tow and back to North Dakota by this evening." John gave a casual shrug. Shannon scowled. "Make no mistake, despite their precarious relationship, the family will pull together and Kip will have his way about drilling a new oil well. This scam, or whatever Monroe has going out at the Altman farm, isn't going to stop it from happening, so you may want to sever your ties quickly."

She's fishing, he mused, disappointed. "How do you know Altman and the Ferguson's aren't pulling their own scam?"

Shannon ignored the question. "People are damn sick of outside conglomerates ruining our community," she said angrily. "We especially won't tolerate human trafficking, and that includes Indian kids."

He straightened. "Wait. Tell me more about this human trafficking business. What does that have to do with Ramona?"

"Human trafficking is just the tip of the iceberg," she spat. "Someone on the outside is conspiring with someone locally to fill the vacuum of illicit profiteering left when the oil boom officially goes bust."

"And you know this how?"

She told him the whole story about the Indian girl and the speculation that a friend named Cindy Van Dyke-Mitchell was using her position in the county to feed the trafficking business. He considered this new information along with what he knew about Dwight Mitchell. The guy hated the Altmans and the Fergusons, ranking him high on a short list of people who would love nothing better than to dethrone the mighty F&A Oil Empire. Add Jason Monroe to the mix, and it wasn't difficult to postulate Mitchell and Monroe teaming up and using Altman's abandoned farm as a base of operation to discredit the family.

"It seems to me someone needs to talk with this Indian girl. Has anyone done that, or does anyone know where she is?"

"Well, Mony went out to the Rez this morning and the word is she—"

"Wait, Ramona's still here?"

Shannon looked exasperated. "Isn't that why you're here so early?" John didn't answer immediately, and she didn't bother hiding her contempt. "Look, I know there's something between you two. I was there when you dragged her out of my bar last winter. Naturally, I assumed you and her—anyway, she was pretty pissed the sheriff didn't offer protective custody to the kid. Then Nate shows up on national TV, Massey's off to Vegas, and it all went to shit."

John rubbed his hands over his face. "Is she staying at the farm?"

"Over Kip's dead body," Shannon retorted. "I'm pretty sure she's staying with him and Poppy."

He made an audible sigh of relief and brought the conversation back on topic. "How do you know so much about this? And do you have any proof to support this conspiracy theory?"

Shannon's lips curved into a sly smile. "I know everything. And not so fast, bub. You have to do something for me first."

John recognized the setup but was too curious to back out now. "All right, Shannon," he said, "what you want?"

She hesitated, then said quietly, "Cindy's missing, and I need your help to find her."

John reared his head. "Are you shitting me? You don't need me for that. Just call the police."

Shannon reached over and tapped his head. "Don't you think I'd have done that? You really aren't as smart as I thought."

The tap didn't hurt as much as it pissed him off. He'd

have walked out, but he needed the rest of the story. Shannon obliged without solicitation. "Hitch hasn't been missing long enough to be"—she made air quotations with her fingers—"officially missing."

"Wait—who's Hitch?"

"Will you keep up? It's Cindy Van Dyke. Anyway, she's gotten herself into a real mess this time. She came to the bar yesterday, wanted to talk in private; said she was done with Dwight and his harebrained criminal activities."

"What sort of activities?"

"Embezzlement, racketeering, bribery, fraud, prostitution, drug trade, you name it. You asked for proof? She has it, documents, phone records, receipts, photos. She started making a bunch of calls from the pay phone. I don't know who she was talking to. After that, she left. I haven't seen nor heard from her since."

"How long ago was that?"

"Yesterday afternoon."

A little over twenty-four hours, he thought. "Do you think she may have skipped town or gone into hiding? If what you suspect regarding her involvement in the human trafficking bit is true, it would make her an accessory."

"Maybe," Shannon confessed. "But you didn't see her eyes. I'm scared for her, John. Dwight's a crazy son of a bitch. It's hard telling what he might do if she decides to blow the whistle on him."

"Has she threatened him?"

"She didn't say," Shannon murmured.

What a soap opera, he grumbled inwardly. *Rejection, jealousy, revenge.* "Why are you telling me this?"

"I told you. I want you to find her Finch," Shannon demanded. "I can't ask the Fergusons because—well, Hitch told some pretty bad lies about Mony and Massey. Plus, she's married to Mitchell."

"Can you blame them?" He didn't especially like defending the Fergusons, but Shannon was really beginning to sound like a nutjob. "Are the lies what instigated the fight between the brothers?"

"You know about that?" she said with an incredulous tone.

John gave her a cynical look.

She nodded.

"And who, pray tell, was the asshole who told Nathan Ferguson about the lie in the first place? It couldn't have been Van Dyke; he would have never believed her." When Shannon's eyes skidded away, he had his answer. *Jesus, was Shannon conspiring with Van Dyke?* Then another thought occurred to him. "You wanted to believe the lie because you're in love with the rock star."

"I didn't say that," Shannon defended. "I think Mony would say or do anything to protect Massey."

He heard the implications in her tone. "But Ramona isn't lying, is she?"

Shannon refused to meet his gaze. "No."

Of course not. "So you let your feelings for the rock star cloud your judgement, and now you're in a panic because you've backed the wrong person. Is that it?" She had the decency to show remorse, and he almost felt sorry for her. "Well, Shannon, how exactly am I supposed to help you?"

"It's how I can help you. But first, we need to find Cindy."

"How does finding a woman who's involved in child sex trafficking possibly help me?"

Shannon winced. "You asked me for proof earlier. Well, Cindy Van Dyke is the key. She's only involved in this human trafficking thing under duress. Mitchell's threatening her family, blackmail or something. Anyway, she's gone along with him to protect her family. She also knows about Mitchell and Monroe's plan to burn down the Altman farmstead."

John eyed her skeptically. "Van Dyke has lied before. How do you know she hasn't fabricated the whole story to save her own sorry ass?"

"She's not lying," Shannon insisted. "She says there's incriminating evidence somewhere on Buddy's property they would have destroyed if the runaway hadn't been found hiding out by the shabin. Time's a-wasting. As soon as the heat dies down with this Indian girl, they'll make their move."

John's head was spinning. He wasn't sure if it was from the alcohol or Shannon's crazy story. "Shannon, be realistic. If you can't find her and you're her friend, what makes you think I'm going to—" A thought suddenly occurred to him. "Did you call my office yesterday afternoon?"

Shannon furrowed her eyebrows. "No, why would I do that?"

"And Cindy was calling from a pay phone at Blarney's, right?"

"Right—"

"A woman called me yesterday afternoon from a crowded Blarney Stone, claiming to be you."

"Impossible, I was tending bar and—wait—do you think it was Cindy?"

"The timeline fits."

Shannon stood and began pacing. "If Cindy called you, she must think you can help her in some way." Her face brightened. "If she called you once, maybe she'll try again. You won't have to look for her; she'll come to you. Then you'll get your proof, and maybe Mony in the process. That would be a win for both of us."

He should have left when the scotch was gone, but he didn't. Except for the adulterated sex, the rest of the night was a blur. He felt disoriented and a little more than used when he gathered up his scattered clothes and slipped away early that morning.

At the hotel, John checked in with Franklin for an update. The sound of his voice was glum.

"No one knows where he is," Franklin whined. "The paparazzi are on-site at the Mile High Club and the private home of Trevor St. James day and night. No one has seen him coming or going, and Trevor refuses to talk. Honestly, I'm very worried."

It seemed overdramatic. Still, Nathan Ferguson's presence or lack thereof was pivotal in more than a few projects beyond the oil business. John said, "He'll surface sooner or later."

Franklin wasn't appeased. "What if something

happened to him, like he's been kidnapped or something? The guy's worth an awful lot of money."

Shit. That was all he needed right now, a media frenzy based on fabrication. "Franklin, not another word unless you have something factual. I don't have time for conspiracy theories. I've got enough of those already."

Franklin moved on from the subject and asked about the meeting with Shannon McDonald. John filled him in, leaving out the part about having sex. Preferring men, Franklin never found John's conquests very appealing, though he may have liked this one, since John had been the one subjugated.

Franklin said, "Do you think she's setting you up?"

"It's not entirely impossible, but I don't think so." It was mostly true; still, there was something about the timing of the missing rock star and the information Shannon had spewed that left him vexed. He couldn't help feeling something very bad was about to happen.

CHAPTER 23

MONY

Her mind racing all night with thoughts of Nate and Sissy, Mony finally got up and dressed for the day. She moved quietly through the house so as not to wake Kip and Poppy. It was too damn early for a confrontation. They were still pissed at her for going out to the Rez, even though she'd left word exactly where she was going. She defended, "What's the matter with you people? Doesn't everyone leave their messages on the fridge door?"

She figured they'd have less to gripe about this morning, since she was going out to service the Piper. She had to do something. This sitting around waiting for shit to happen was driving her crazy. Despite the security on the hangar, it was unnerving having the Piper sitting unattended out at the farm. This entire violation of private property gave her a renewed feeling of vulnerability.

Her stealth had been for naught, she realized as the smell of fresh-brewed coffee wafted from the kitchen. Kip sat at the table, absorbed with his electronic tablet. Mony walked to the cupboard, grabbed a mug and said over her shoulder, "Good morning. Whatcha reading?"

Kip grunted a greeting and took off his reading glasses. Setting them brusquely on the table, he said with irritation, "Trying to find out where my younger son has run off to. This social media thing is bullshit. Now they're claiming Nathan's on a beach somewhere in Costa Rica. It's ridiculous. Have you heard any news from Massey?"

She filled her mug, capped off his cup and sat down at the table across from him. Mony had heard from Massey; unfortunately, she couldn't share it. He'd given specific instruction to keep the side trip to Arizona under wraps for now. He hadn't met up with Nate yet, and there was no sense building up false hope for his parents. She felt guilty about the deception but understood the precaution. "You know Massey will call when he has him." Kip's uncritical acceptance of the ruse was alarming, not to mention remarkably uncharacteristic. She asked, "Are you worried?"

Kip set down the electronic device with more finesse and rubbed his eyes. He looked tired despite the caffeinated lead; she wondered if he'd gotten any sleep at all. "I don't know how anyone can tolerate looking at a screen all day. No wonder people have so many eye problems." He looked up at her for the first time and said, "Where are you off to?"

Mony braced for the pending argument.

"Karl and I are going to check on the Piper this morning." Karl Lindgren was a former Air Force mechanic during Kip and Buddy's time in Minot. He also worked part-time for F&A when Nate wasn't available and was a skilled pilot in his own right as well as captain of the aerial firefighting brigade.

Kip grumbled his approval and moved onto the next subject.

"Are you ready for the probate hearing?"

Mony nodded, then shared her thoughts from yesterday. "The excavation of the limestone silt from the quarry is scheduled for next week. I'm not sure it will be enough for drilling, but it'll be a good start. Who should I get in touch with at F&A to make the transportation arrangements?"

Kip's lips thinned in a ghost of a smile. She was pleased she could still surprise him. "I'll have Gary get in touch with you." In an afterthought he said, "If you're planning to meet Karl, you'd better get going."

She checked the clock on the stove and nodded. Then, because she felt like it, she walked up to him, hugged his shoulders, and kissed him on the side of his head. "Keep an eye on Shep for me. I'll see you later."

The maintenance and safety check lasted only a couple of hours. Mony flew Karl back to the main airport, dropped him off, fueled the Piper, and thought, *Now what the hell am I going to do with myself?* Without something to keep her mind busy, it ran wild with worry and speculation on what might have happened to Sissy. Maybe the teenager had gone back to the farm. That was the first hopeful thought she'd had all morning.

Eager to escape from the watchful eye of those who meant well, she retreated to her own personal sanctuary and set a course for the Lake Zahl wildlife management area and home.

From the air, she could see farmers busy plowing and planting. It looked barren now, but in a few months the fields would be lush with spring wheat, sunflowers, dry edible beans, and soybeans. As she flew over the abandoned Swenson farmstead, Mony considered the plight of many area landowners. Unlike Sissy's people, whose land was confiscated, many of the large ranchers and farming operations invested all they had in a drilling project gone bust, then sold off their mineral rights to pay off their debt. Some of the lucky ones received a stipend from the oil conglomerates, but they were basically squatters on their own property. Her family had been one of the lucky ones. Passing over the dilapidated barn, she remembered how she'd buzzed the roofing crew that day she'd taken Nate flying without permission. The story was legendary. It seemed forever ago. It was. She wondered how she and Nate had moved so far away from the bond they'd created that day. He'd placed absolute faith in her, knowing she'd return him to the earth safely. Now, he couldn't even trust her or his brother enough not to know there'd never been more between them than a sibling's bond. That was her fault. Had she come clean with the truth right away, perhaps their relationship wouldn't be the mess that it was. Somehow, she had to find a way to fix it.

She crossed from Ferguson to home airspace, over the plot of land with the missing deed. It was easy to see why Nate and her dad had selected the location to harbor the beehives. Safe in the refuge, they had a chance to thrive unhindered by herbicides and pesticides. Thinking about the bees, it struck her odd that as conscientious as Massey had been with all her dad's legal affairs, he hadn't had this particular piece of paperwork in hand. Maybe it had something to do with the Hernández deed. Hopefully Massey would know more after he found Nate.

She was approaching from the south end of the lake when her eyes caught sight of something floating atop the dam. Bobbing in the water's natural current was an object unnatural in both color and size. There was no way it could be misconstrued for branch debris, since there were no trees in the region. Her stomach clenched in a hard knot. *The carcass of a foolish young deer,* she thought, caught in the mire of soft earth during the wet season; it had died when it was unable to escape. It must have floated with the lake's current toward the outlet, but it didn't feel right. She could neither confirm nor refute her speculation from her current altitude and considered flying in for a closer inspection, then thought better of it. The low fly would only disrupt the waterfowl roosting in the grass—then she'd really have a mess. Instead, she set a course for her home landing strip and radioed the Williston airport to report her findings. She was mid-landing cycle when Kip's voice boomed over the radio.

"Don't I have enough on my hands with my two rouge sons? Now I have to deal with you too?" he shouted without preamble. "I told you not to go out there by yourself. Couldn't you just for once follow orders?"

Kip hadn't exactly ordered her not to go by herself, but she'd understood the implied directive. He'd only let her leave in the first place because Karl had been with her. "That's why I radioed in," she said, ignoring the militant tone. "I won't go checking it out on my own without backup—"

"Don't get cheeky with me, young lady. Do not, I repeat, do not land that plane, Mony Altman—that's an order, or I swear I'll—"

The rest of the remark cut out, probably by the air-traffic controller reminding Kip that use of inappropriate language was unsanctioned by the FFA. His voice came back less volatile. "The sheriff and I are boarding a chopper right now, ETA in twenty. For God's sake, Mony, do you think you can stay out of trouble for that long? Over."

She acknowledged and aborted her landing approach. Contemplating what to do for the next twenty minutes, she thought about flying back over the lake when she spotted an unfamiliar vehicle sitting in her driveway. There were no signs of human activity, but whoever was down there, would have surely seen her. Then, the *someone* stepped out from under the cover of the porch. As she flew overhead, the person looked up, shielding their eyes from the morning sun. Again her altitude proved a disadvantage, yet there was something strikingly familiar about the intruder.

John Finch walked out to the landing strip, smiling as he approached. Mony wondered if he was that good an actor, or that clueless. Either way, she'd retrieved the handgun from the locked box before deplaning and stuffed it in the inside pocket of her flight jacket. She approached with caution. He sensed her lack of enthusiasm and responded in kind.

"What's the matter, Ramona?" he asked, casting his gaze around the open field.

It was a beautiful spring day with the temperature in the midseventies, yet a shiver ran down her spine. He quickened his pace and took hold, banding his arm around her waist, escorting her quickly toward the cover of the hangar. If he'd felt the gun, he said nothing.

She tried not to bristle at his aggressive behavior and said, "Nothing's the matter." It sounded weak. She kept up with his pace; she didn't like the manhandling, but nor did she like being an easy target on an open airfield. *Is he luring me away from or toward danger?* she wondered. Mony considered the countless times she'd trusted him in the past. Giving him the benefit of the doubt, she asked, "What are you doing here, John?"

He said he'd flown out to Williston to get a jump on the pending court case and ventured a trip to her place in hopes he'd find her home. There was a scripted tone to his voice, and her trust waned a little. She had no doubt part of what John had said was true, but there were pieces missing.

"John, this isn't a good time for you to be here," she said, struggling to keep her voice neutral. "You know, with the upcoming court case and all. What are you hoping to gain by ambushing me out here?"

He seemed affronted by the remark. "Ambush? I just wanted to see you, Ramona, that's all. I don't give a damn anymore about the court case. You've already won. I want us to start seeing each other. You know, like dating."

She snorted in amusement. "Dating? There's a word. I told you in Chicago there wasn't much hope of building a relationship between us. I'm in love with—"

"You're throwing your life away to a man who runs off at the first sign of trouble," John finished angrily. He released his hold and stood rigged in front of her, as if blocking her from escape. "My God, Ramona, can't you see that? While I'm standing right here, ready to accept you for who you are."

She stepped back. "And who exactly do you think I am?"

John pursed his lips.

"You don't know me," Mony snapped. "You only know what I want you to see. And you're changing the subject. I'm going to ask again. What are you doing here?"

He tried to reach for her, and she took another step back. She'd hoped he'd respect her boundaries, but he bowled right through them, the way he had outside the Blarney Stone and when he'd picked her up out of the snow. She resisted at first, then slowly melded into his arms.

She told herself she was buying time. It was a lie. There was something about his assertiveness that lent comfort and eased her troubled mind. If he'd meant to harm her, this was his chance. Instead, he pressed his body closer and took her mouth, kissing her fervently, savoring the tension building between them, mistaking it for passion. His embrace was intoxicating, powerful, a perfect combination of want and need. It was a delicious challenge, his hands roaming along her torso, caressing, worshiping. She'd forgot about everything, the object floating by the dam, bees, oil, Nate, danger. He slid his hands up under her jacket, finding flesh, and brushed against the outline of the gun.

"What the—?"

Mony shoved him away and instinctively drew her weapon. The shock and dismay on his face were heartbreaking. She pointed the gun at him. "Goddamn it, John, put your hands where I can see them."

He did so slowly, without argument or question. His hurt expression morphed into something unreadable, detestable. "I'm going to ask you one last fucking time. What the hell are you doing here?"

The whirl of a helicopter and wailing sirens came from somewhere off in the distance. He neither acknowledged it nor seemed concerned. *The cavalry,* she thought despairingly, but maybe it was for the better. She'd lost all objectivity; her head filled with lust and need. She had to get a grip and ascertain whether he had any involvement with whatever was out by the dam.

Sadness returned to his face and he said coolly, "It seems you've already formulated an opinion about that."

She had wanted to share with him what she saw on the lake. Now she wanted to slap him. What she needed was for him to tell her he had nothing to do with the awful possibilities floating around in her head. Instead she said, "Are you Hitch?"

The implacable mask returned, and he assumed a power stance. It was a closing-argument persona, one she imagined he'd used to sway a jury. In that moment, she both despised and feared him. Whatever his true purpose had been for coming to see her, it no longer existed. He raised a hand, shielding his eyes, looked in the direction of the helicopter, and said dispassionately, "It was clever having your pal Shannon throw me off guard with her little seduction scheme. I must say, bravo." She had no idea what he was talking about, and she wanted to punch him.

Weapons drawn, Kip and Sheriff Wagner deplaned the helicopter simultaneously, her dog Shep alongside them. The sheriff took hold of John and frisked him before handcuffing his wrists behind his back. The attorney made no move to resist and let himself be escorted to the waiting squad car idling in the driveway.

Mony holstered her gun and walked to the porch, where she plopped down on the top step, propped her elbows on her knees, and watched the disaster unfold. Shep followed her and sat by her feet. The farmyard began to fill with search-and-rescue vehicles, fire trucks, and first responders. Among the crew were the Sanquist twins and Shawn McDonald. A truck pulling an airboat roared through the driveway, swung past the hangar, and continued toward the shabin, where they would access and launch. From there it was a short distance to the dam and whatever she'd seen caught in the current.

Kip nudged the dog aside and sat on the step next to her. Relieved of his duty, Shep wandered off, sniffing the parameter. They sat in silence. Mony looked over at the squad car where the sheriff had taken John for questioning. He hadn't asked her a single question. She said to Kip, "Don't you think this is all a little overkill?"

Kip placed a big burly arm over her shoulder. He was a few years older than her dad, with the build of a linebacker and the strength of a man in his prime. He and her dad were as opposite as two men could be both in personality and physique. Mony drew comfort from him nonetheless. He said, "I'd want to take you and shake—" Instead of finishing, he said, "I'm relieved you're all right."

She barked out a nervous laugh and leaned her head against his powerful chest, feeling safe, protected, and guilty. *How could she accuse him of overkill when she'd overreacted?*

"You did the right thing, protecting yourself," Kip said, reading her inner angst. "Now let the sheriff protect the lawyer by taking his statement. If he doesn't have any involvement with what you found, he'll be cleared."

"It's the handcuffs," Mony said despondently. "They weren't necessary."

"Maybe," Kip said.

Mony felt the sting of tears pooling in her eyes, angered by the whole misunderstanding. "I know what it's like being restrained against your will."

Kip gave her shoulder a bear-hug squeeze. "I know, Mony, I know."

She stood to walk to the patrol car when Shep began barking wildly from somewhere in the yard.

"What the hell is wrong with your dog?" Kip asked with alarm.

Mony closed her eyes. She simply didn't want to know.

Shep rounded the corner of the house, dragging something in his mouth.

CHAPTER 24

NATE

Slow Joe's idea of "laying low and staying out of trouble" was a place called the Desert Bar. Out in the middle of nowhere, it was a perfect hideaway. Built circa 1975, the bar stood on an old copper mining campsite and was something of an oasis in the desert community. The bartender brought Nate a beer and they struck up a conversation. Familiarizing him with the surroundings, she pulled out a detailed map and described some of the key landmarks and popular jeeping trails in the area.

He pointed to a mountain range and said, "On the other side, over here by the Bill Williams River, is where my bees are wintering."

The bartender eyed him skeptically, "There's only one piece of private land within the refuge that has honeybees," she said, "and it's owned by Buddy Altman. You're not him."

"Nope." He extended his hand. "I'm Nate Ferguson, Buddy's partner."

The bartender gave it a hearty shake. "Sorry, but I

thought Buddy's partner was Hernández."

Hernández—finally he had a name to reference. "I'm Buddy's partner from North Dakota, but I'm looking for Hernández. Can you tell me anything about him?"

The bartender looked at him, puzzled. "Him?"

The server, a woman in her midforties with a halter-style blouse and camouflage shorts, interrupted the conversation and brought him his food. She took a long look at him. "Say, aren't you that guy from the band that was on TV yesterday?" He smiled, and her eyes widened. "Yeah, you're the piano player from Mile High City. I love your music." She hollered to the bartender. "Hey, Billie, did you ever get the old piano tuned? We have a celebrity in our humble establishment."

The bar closed at sundown; Nate joined the patrons heading for the parking lot. He was disappointed he'd never gotten the chance to chat more with the bartender about Hernández, nor had his brother caught up with him, which was odd. He checked his phone messages and—*Shit.* Four missed calls. Nate hurried to his truck and got in the line of traffic.

The prospect of trailing behind dozens of cars churning up enough dust to choke a horse didn't thrill him. *Thank God for AC.* While he waited, he checked his bars again. Still no signal. He'd have to wait until he got closer to civilization to call.

In the quiet truck cab, Nate contemplated what he would say when he finally met his brother face to face. For his part, he would be satisfied if Massey punched him in the nose and had him beg for his forgiveness. It would be a just dessert. He accepted that. He'd grossly misjudged his brother and Mony. It would take a long time to earn their trust again, and now he needed his brother's help. Nate was contemplating the right words to use when there was a sharp rap on the door. Startled, he rolled down the window.

"Hey," the familiar bar server said in a friendly voice. "Just to let you know, a compact took the wash way too fast and got hung up on the embankment. It's a clusterfuck. Not sure if the axle is broken or what. Anyway, there's a group of guys trying to lift the car off the rocks. It will take a bit, so sit tight. We'll get you out of here in a jiffy."

He thanked her for the info and asked, "Is there anything I can do to help?"

She shouted over her shoulder, "Nope, unless you've got some major-ass equipment in that tool chest in the bed of your truck."

He didn't.

Slightly relieved he didn't have to do anything, Nate killed the engine and took in the tranquil evening. As the sunlight faded, the night stars shone like diamonds in heaven. It was a sharp contrast to the glowing artificial lights over the Vegas skies. Looking out over the landscape, he surmised it would be easy to get lost, venturing too far from a light source. His mind began to formulate lyrics to a song, but they sounded too depressing.

He spotted three young men hurrying toward the truck. They weren't big guys, just tall and lanky, and he could make out their leathery skin even in the dim evening light. They each sported the bleach-blond hair of people who spent a lot of time in the sun. The too-tight T-shirts, long cargo shorts, and sandals suggested beachwear more than the nighttime desert.

The spokesmen said, "Hey, can you help us? One of our guys is missing. We think he might have go gone off the trail."

Nate was about to decline when the guy behind the leader, a dull-eyed character with a snaggletoothed grin, said, "Our friend took the trail heading toward the Gray Eagle Mine marker. You know, on the back trail. We should hurry, he might be lost or something." Then, as if a lightbulb had winked on, he added, "Hey, aren't you that guy from the bar everyone was talking about? Ya, ya, you play in that rock 'n' roll band or something, right?"

"Not today," Nate told him. "Just a regular guy having a burger and beer, enjoying the desert like anyone else."

"No, you're that guy from Vegas," the third one said. "You're all over the internet. Wanna see?" The man held up his phone in various positions, trying to get a signal. Nate was about to tell him to forget it when the spokesperson snatched the device and stuffed it in the guy's shirt pocket. Nate brought the conversation back on topic.

"Who else knows about this? Is anyone else looking for him?" As a certified first responder for the William County search-and-rescue, Nate knew the first rule to any successful rescue was to never go it alone.

"Could you at least come with us and check it out?" the spokesperson persisted. "He might be hurt."

Nate got out of the truck. *I don't have time for this bullshit,* he grumbled inwardly. This guy was probably somewhere close by, passed out drunk. Still, having been in similar predicaments himself on more than a few occasions, Nate remembered the random strangers who had helped him along the way and figured he should pay it forward. "One of you should find a saloon employee and tell them what's going on," he suggested. "If your friend really is missing, we're going to need a lot more help."

The two men deferred to the spokesperson. "You heard the man," he snapped to the guy with the cell phone. "Get going, and then join us on the trail."

Nate reached back into his truck, opened the glove compartment, and retrieved his first aid kit along with his military-grade flashlight. Grabbing his F&A flight jacket, he tucked the supplies in the inside pockets, gestured, and said, "Lead the way."

The snaggletoothed guy chattered nervously while the spokesperson walked along quietly. Few things were as useless as a rubbernecker tagging along to a rescue. Still, an extra set of eyes was better than nothing. They reached the ATVs; Nate took a seat behind the spokesman and they sped off into the darkness.

It took longer than he expected to reach the trail's ridge. Maybe it was because his driver was poorly skilled with the ATV. He considered walking the rest of the way, but they finally did reach the summit. From their vantage point, he could see the saloon glowing across the valley like an island in the middle of a black sea. The taillights from the departing cars marked the main road, making Nate wish he'd been among them. Massey might think

Nate was avoiding him by not returning his call. He sent up a petition prayer that the guy they'd sent for help had found someone and the cavalry was already on its way.

The three men spread out and started calling out for the missing friend. Nate ventured off following the beam of his flashlight, while the two compadres stayed close to the headlights of the vehicles. He had no idea where he was going or where to look and tried to identify landmarks that might be helpful. In the dark, it all looked the same—dirt, more dirt, rocks, and an occasional tuft of plant life as far as light could reach. Walking along the rocky ridge, he carefully canvassed the area as best he could. The last thing he needed was a twisted ankle. It seemed strange the ATV outfitters hadn't had some sort of safety kit in case of such an emergency; then again, judging from the young men's demeanor, they likely waived the extra insurance to save a few bucks in the name of adventure. He used the sound of the two men's voices as a means of keeping his bearings and ventured further from the trail.

He'd gone about a hundred yards when he detected the pungent odor of gasoline and hollered, "Is anyone out there?" There was no sound except the two men's voices and the occasional call of a nocturnal predator. "If you can hear me, make some noise." He listened again; this time he thought he heard something and moved toward the sound.

When he came to the edge of an embankment, he was glad he hadn't an audience as he ungracefully slid down the loose gravel on the seat of his pants. The smell of gasoline grew with his descent. "Sure hope no one lights a match," he muttered to the desert night, and moved in the direction of the sound.

An overturned ATV was a couple of yards beyond the edge of the embankment; past that, a young man lay only a couple of feet beyond the wreck. Covered in dirt, his eyes stuck out like two pieces of coal in a snowbank. He'd managed to prop his back against a large rock, with his contorted legs stretched out in front of him. Even in poor lighting, Nate could see they were broken. "Holy shit." Nate quickly introduced himself, then asked the young man how he was doing. When no answer came, he felt the victim's skin. It was already cold and clammy.

Without protective headgear, the young man had sustained a large gash above his right eye. Nate waved the flashlight in front of his face. His pupils didn't respond, remaining fixed and dilated. Nate checked for a pulse, which was weak and thready, the other man's breathing shallow and fast. He was clearly in shock. To compound matters, the man reeked of alcohol. Nate would have helped him lie flat and elevate his legs to treat the shock had it not been for the compounded fracture in both limbs. The prognosis was grim. If he didn't get the victim advanced medical attention soon, he was a goner.

The young man stirred. "I'm okay, I guess," he finally said with a slurred voice, "but my head hurts like a son of a bitch."

Nate made him hold the flashlight as he cleaned and dressed the laceration over his eye. It was the least of the young man's problems, but it gave them both something to do. He kept talking, hoping to keep the victim oriented, and asked easy questions. The responses were slow, but mostly appropriate, until Nate made a reference to Evel Knievel. He was closing his kit when the young man asked, "Got any good drugs in there?"

Nate suppressed a laugh. "You'll have to wait until you're in the ER for that. On the upside, be glad it hurts; at least you know you're alive." He kept the tone of his voice light as he finished his assessment; then came the moment of panic. "I'm going to have to leave you now and get some help. Your friends are just above on the ridge and—"

The young man clasped his arm and dug in his fingers "They're not my friends."

The hairs stood on the back of Nate's neck. He took the young man's hand and felt more than just an urgent need to get him medical help. He was feeling a sense of dread.

"Listen to me. These guys offered to pay for me and my girlfriend's rentals—if we let them join us. They seemed cool at first and even paid for our beers. But when my girlfriend didn't come back from the bathroom, and these guys tried to tell me she'd left with someone else, I knew something wasn't right. I got worried and started driving the trail looking for her. That's when they ambushed me and pushed me over the cliff. They left me here in the dark as bait for you."

Nate killed the switch on the flashlight, plunging them into complete and utter darkness. *Christ, I've been duped.* Not only that, but he and the victim were both sitting ducks. The gravity of their situation must have solidified in the young man's mind; he began to sob, "Please, you have to find Kara."

The sound of crushed rock underfoot some thirty feet behind them had Nate placing a finger to the victim's lips and slithering behind the rock. He had no idea how he was going to get the young man or himself out of this mess, but he had to come up with something.

The voice of the spokesmen shouted out from the darkness. "You're not dead yet?" He yelled to his partner, "What did you do with the bitch anyway?"

The nervous talker shouted back, "I didn't do anything. Tony took care of her, took care of her good." He made a series of vulgar sounds, which made Nate conclude things hadn't gone well for Kara.

A light from a low-watt flashlight flickered to life and swept the perimeter around the victim. Nate held his breath. The spokesman said, "Where's Ferguson?" The light was too dim to capture his shadow behind the rock, and Nate shrank further into the darkness. The young man bought him a few seconds, refusing to respond, earning himself a decisive blow from his tormentor. Between his cries, the spokesman asked again, "Where's Ferguson?"

Nate clenched his fingers around the only weapon he held in his hand. In an audacious challenge, he snapped on the flashlight, blinding the man standing over the victim. Using brute force, he bashed the flashlight over the man's head and sent him crashing down on the victim's already crumpled body. With both men unconscious, he switched off the light and fled into the darkness.

At a full out run, Nate stumbled over the uneven terrain, amazed he hadn't tripped over the loose rock. For a split second he thought maybe luck and the dark were on his side, until he heard the report of a gun.

He felt the sting between his shoulder blades, dropping him to his knees. The sting quickly swelled into an enormous weight and he gasped for air under its pressure. His face met the dusty earth, clogging his mouth and nose with dirt, but he hadn't the breath to spit it out. The menacing voice of his soon-to-be killer drew closer, and he tried to imagine who he'd pissed off so badly that they'd wanted him dead.

A bright light shone above him unexpectedly, illuminating the entire desert floor. His last thought was one of wonderment. Was it the light at the end of the tunnel, people of near-death experiences claimed to see, or was he already dead?

CHAPTER 25

MONY

They stood along the shoreline, waiting for the airboat to dock. Mony clutched Sissy's tattered denim jacket, the one Shep had found, and braced herself for the worst. From her peripheral vision, she noticed John approaching with the sheriff. His hands were uncuffed, an appreciated relief, being that there was nowhere for him to run anyway. John stood several feet away and joined the vigil, his expression indecipherable. Everyone else seemed to ignore him, except for her. He neither spoke nor looked in her direction. She didn't blame him. After all, she'd just pointed a loaded firearm at him and basically accused him of murder.

What else could I have done? She tried to justify her actions by telling herself he hadn't really clarified what he was doing come out to her farm, but it landed weak in her head, especially since the last time he'd come to her, it had been out of fear for her safety and to warn her. *Is that what he's doing now?*

Mony shook the thought from her head and walked

over to Kip and the sheriff. They abruptly stopped talking as she approached. The three of them stood in an agonizing silence. Without looking at her, Kip finally said, "This could be you we're fishing out of the lake." The suppressed fear and anger in his voice were undeniable. They felt like a punch to the gut.

The rescuers brought the body ashore a little past noon. There'd been a reason Shannon McDonald hadn't responded to the emergency call. It was difficult to say what Mony felt as they laid the woman's pallid, naked body out on the ground. They weren't close friends. Some would even say they'd been rivals, but that didn't mean Mony would have ever wished her any harm, most certainly not this. She wasn't a forensic expert, but she could tell Shannon hadn't been in the water long. Shawn must have drawn the same conclusion and began CPR. The rest of the team joined in the effort, though everyone knew it was futile. After forty excruciating minutes, the rescue team's lead finally called it. Shawn went berserk. It was painful to witness.

The multiple pools of blood were a sign she'd been beaten before she died. A preliminary assessment revealed a blow with a blunt object to the back of the head, and her crushed windpipe was consistent with strangulation, another causal factor. The official cause of death would have to be determined by the coroner. Shawn postulated his own cause and lunged at John, slamming him to the ground, and smashed his fist into his jaw. It took four guys to pull him off and a set of handcuffs to restrain him.

As the day unfolded, Mony learned the gest of why Shawn went after John. It seemed John had been with Shannon the night before. No one knew the reason. Shawn had his own speculation about that too, and he wasn't afraid to share his theories. It seemed Shannon had valuable information she hadn't shared with her brother. There was no way of determining whether she'd told it to John or whether the death had occurred during or after his visit. Not without an autopsy. It didn't matter to Shawn. He and John traded places on the way back to town, Shawn in the back of squad car, John in the rear of the ambulance.

Mony tried to make sense of the chaos. She knew John in the most intimate possible way. He was no killer, nor was he capable of such a heinous act. She should have told them that before they hauled him off to the ER. She should have trusted him, defended him. Now it was too late. Her contemptible behavior would forever stand between them, an irrefutable final act of betrayal.

It took several hours to secure the grisly scene before the search for Sissy began. Mony walked alongside the lakeshore with her dog, hoping he'd pick up her scent. It was late afternoon when the sheriff finally called her off the search and asked her to ride along with him out to the Rez. She wasn't entirely sure why he did that—she'd made only a tenuous connection with Sissy's family at best. But the sheriff's sudden motivation for finding Sissy Moonbeam was encouraging. It was about damned time. She hid her suspicion when he became all cryptic in his response to her simple questions, like, "Did John tell you why he was on my property?" It left her with the distinct impression he knew more than he was letting on, and it pissed her off.

Grandmother Moonbeam sat stoic in her wheelchair and listened while the sheriff made a futile attempt to gather and convey information. Mony took Lil Sis outside. They sat on the front step along with Shep and her mutt Rainstorm and made small talk. Mony learned Rainstorm was a rescue dog too, found abandoned in an open field during a spring downpour. Sissy had saved the pup a summer back, and the two girls had nursed the fledgling canine back to health. Mony shared Shep's story and told Lil Sis that she was a veterinarian. It was common ground. Safe. It would have been nice to develop a deeper, more trusting relationship with the girl, but time was of the essence.

She was surprised when Lil Sis shared her information willingly. The adolescent gave remarkable detail describing the man with whom Sissy had been associating. Mony didn't know the Indian word she used for him, but she heard the utter contempt in the child's voice. "I followed Sissy after she told me not to, to the white man's camper parked near the casino one day," Lil Sis began. "He caught me spying, but he was nice about it and invited me in. Sissy was already in the camper along with another white woman. They both looked very sleepy."

Mony took a moment to describe Shannon McDonald's features. She'd felt guilty about that, but she had to know one way or another whether the fiery redhead was involved. The relief she felt when Lil Sis said she didn't recognize the depiction astonished her.

"The white man promised some fun and gave me a strong fruit punch that made me feel strange and sick to my stomach. Afterward, he took off the woman's clothes and made me and Sissy kiss her private parts. When it was over, he gave me a ten-dollar bill. I threw the money at him and ran home. I never followed Sissy after that."

"Do these bad people have a name?"

Lil Sis became quite a long while, then said, "They told me they'd hurt Sissy if I told anyone."

"When, when did they tell you this?" Mony demanded.

Lil Sis averted her eyes. "They came to our house after you left."

Shit. Mony's heart began to race. "Lil Sis, if you tell me a name, I swear I'll keep your secret."

Lil Sis's eyes began to well with tears. She said, "I remember the man calling the white woman *Hitch*."

When it was time to leave, Mony begged the sheriff to provide some sort of protection for the family, but the sheriff kept giving her the runaround, saying, "Not much I can do. It's the Rez, not my jurisdiction."

She wanted to punch him. Instead, she took matters into her own hands and fabricated a lie. She told Lil Sis she needed to do some traveling and needed someone to watch over Shep for a while. She told her it would be good for Rainstorm to have a companion and that Shep could show the mutt how to be a good watchdog. It was a partial truth. When Lil Sis told Grandmother Moonbeam, she saw through the ruse but accepted the offer.

Lil Sis said earnestly, "I promise to take good care of

Shep until you come back for him." It took every ounce of willpower for Mony not to cry. Then Lil Sis decimated all her resistance when she asked, *"Yaku' kta he?"* Are you coming back?

It was probably a gross violation of American Indian custom, but she didn't care. Mony took the child in her arms and hugged her tight. She was so overwhelmed with the senseless waste of life, the loss of youthful innocence, she had to cling to something that offered tangible hope. The entire situation infuriated her, resurrecting memories of her own sexual trauma. She had to get a grip on her rage if she was going to be of any help to Lil Sis or Sissy. Mony had been much older when her sexual assault occurred, and she worried how such an event would affect a young child. It was too early to tell Lil Sis not all men were scum. She sent up a little prayer that, one day, the child would learn that for herself, the way she had when she met Bob.

Mony and Sheriff Wagner headed back west and rode in silence. It was fine by her. His behavior was absolutely confounding. She couldn't understand how he seemed eager to find Sissy, then denied the obvious need to protect her family. She began questioning the good sheriff's abilities as well as his loyalty.

Despite Kip's explicit instructions she go straight to Williston, Mony insisted on a ride back to her farm to retrieve the Piper. She didn't know why, but something in her gut told her to have a quick mode of transportation at the ready. Massey hadn't called yet saying he'd caught up with Nate. It was worrisome. After considerable argument, plus a call to Kip, the sheriff complied with her demand, but not without reservation. He waited the near–half hour she took to prepare for flight. She wasn't in any hurry. What she really wanted to do was look around her own property unimpeded. Daylight was fading, and any clues that hadn't been trampled underfoot by the rescue teams might be gone by morning.

It wasn't until her wheels left the grass runway that the sheriff pulled out of her driveway. She considered landing again and resuming the search, but Kip would ream her ass if she didn't beat the sheriff to town. Hopefully, she'd have a better vantage from the air.

After ten minutes of circling, she was beginning to think she'd lost her mind. She wanted desperately to find something out of place, but everything looked as it should for early spring. Even the garden was freshly tilled, though whoever had done it did a piss-poor job. It must have been a foregone conclusion in Kip's mind that she would come home eventually, so he'd made it ready. It was a thoughtful gesture. She made a mental note to thank him when she got back to town, then hire someone else to finish the job. Still, it niggled at her; something wasn't quite right. Then again, nothing made sense about today. She banked left and set a course for Williston.

It was after sunset when she got back to Kip and Poppy's home. A wave of fresh-cooked rhubarb, baked bread, and cinnamon rolls greeted her at the door. *Poppy's stress cooking.* They sat down to a poor man's supper consisting of pot roast, potatoes, and carrots. Despite the delicious aroma, no one could eat.

Mony and Poppy were cleaning up the kitchen when the house phone rang. Kip answered. The two women huddled together, each holding her breath. Mony's thoughts immediately went to Sissy when Kip shouted, "Speak up, Massey, I can't hear you over that noise." From across the room Mony recognized the unmistakable sound of a turbo engine engaging. Suddenly, the color drained from Kip's face and Poppy hiccupped a sob. To Mony, he said, "Get the plane ready. They've found Nathan."

CHAPTER 26

MASSEY

His parents aged twenty years when they entered the room where his brother lay unconscious. Nate had tubes coming from everywhere. One IV line kept him hydrated, the other carried blood. A catheter hose dangled from the side of the bed, connected to chest tubes to keep his lung inflated. Massey's dad clasped a hand over his chest, and at first, the attorney thought he was having a heart attack.

They stayed for about thirty seconds before a security guard escorted Poppy and Kip to the ICU lounge. Massey followed, giving Mony a moment alone with Nate. Dane Strong stood by the lounge window, looking down on the crowd of reporters gathering in front of the hospital entrance. It had been that way the moment the medical helicopter arrived, their presence a nagging source of irritation. Dane muttered, "Vultures."

They exchanged a quick round of greetings. Poppy went immediately to the young man and touched the gauze wrap around the site where he'd donated blood, her expression one of sadness and gratitude. "Thank you," was all she managed to say before her voice clogged with tears. Dane stood expressionless, as if at a loss for words. Intuitively he wrapped his arms around her, enveloping her in a hug. Poppy began to sob uncontrollably. Dane gave a beseeching glance to Kip, who rescued him, taking Poppy from his embrace—but not before clasping him by the shoulder and saying, "I'm proud to call you my grandson."

A Latino woman wearing surgical scrubs entered the room with a purposeful stride. She brought them up to speed on Nate's condition. Because of the proximity of the bullet to his spine, Nate's surgeon kept him in an induced coma, intubated, and on a respirator. He was in the final preparations before wheeling him to surgery to remove the bullet. Before that happened, the woman whisked Poppy and Kip off for one last visit.

Mony entered the lounge; already she looked bone-weary. It was only just beginning. An awkward silence fell between mother and son as she approached him by the window. Mony did what Poppy had and touched Dane's bandaged arm. "I'm so glad you're here, Dane. At least now Nate has a fighting chance."

Dane didn't hug his mother right away like he did Poppy. If Mony felt injured by the lack of sympathy, she didn't show it. Instead, she wrapped one arm around her son's waist and stood quietly beside him looking out the window. Then, she leaned her head against his shoulder and began to cry. Dane rested his chin on the crown of her head and said to her quietly, "Save your energy for Nate, Mom. This conversation can wait."

Over the next several hours, there wasn't much any of them could do except pray, drink bad coffee, and wait. Huddled together in the corner of the lounge, Massey explained as much as he knew about the events surrounding Nate's shooting.

"Dane and I were there when the search-and-rescue team found him in the desert. Investigators are out there piecing together the crime scene. So far, we know there's two dead, Nate and one other man are critically injured, and a woman is missing."

"What in the hell was Nathan doing out in the desert at night?" Kip asked.

"I'm not sure. We were supposed to meet at the bar, but I'd been delayed when a car got hung up on some rocks blocking the road and I had to go around it. I got a little off course when I started off-roading. Anyway, by the time Dane and I got to the bar, a server told us Nate had ridden off with a couple of guys on an ATV. We heard gunfire in the direction he was last seen traveling and immediately called 911. From what I could tell at the scene, there'd been some sort of accident. A wrecked ATV lay overturned at the bottom of a cliff nearby, along with one of the two dead victims."

"And the other person?" Kip inquired.

"Killed when he opened fire on the rescue helicopter."

"Jesus. Do you know why?"

"No. But it's possible he was the one who shot at Nate."

"Do you think Nate was trying to help the other victims?" Mony asked.

"Probably. His first aid kit and Maglite were at the scene."

Kip said, "What about the other injured person?"

Dane picked up the story. "Here's where things get weirder. The guy was hit over the head hard enough to put him out. He's the one in the room down the hall, still unconscious. There were traces of blood found on Nate's flashlight. The lead medic told us the investigators are analyzing it right now, but the police aren't telling us anything. They still need to question Nate and the other survivor."

"Wait—are you suggesting they consider Nathan responsible?" Kip snapped. He stood probably ready to storm off to the police station, but Poppy clenched his hand. Massey also intervened.

"No, Dad, that's not what Dane is saying. The police found Nate's truck at the bar, which shows he'd arrived separately from the ATV riders, and the server I mentioned earlier corroborated that story. He'd been waiting in line to leave like the rest of the patrons. My theory is, Nate was either asked or forced to help. So far, there's nothing to suggest force. I think coercion would be more accurate. He had the wherewithal to grab both his flashlight and the first aid kit out of his truck."

"What about his gun?" Kip asked.

"Still locked in the toolbox, in the bed of his truck," Dane said.

When they'd rehashed the topic ad nauseam, Kip shifted gears and brought Dane and Massey up to speed regarding the devastating news about Shannon McDonald. Massey felt a sense of profound shock. He had always liked Shannon. She and her brother Shawn were close family friends and had accompanied them many times on the annual family hunting trips to Montana. To compound the tragedy, Mony relayed the status of the missing Indian girl and her concern for the little sister and the grandmother's safety. She was furious with the sheriff and spoke plainly on her thoughts regarding his dodgy behavior. She looked at Dane and said despondently, "I left Shep with the girl's family to protect them. It was the only thing I could think to do."

When Mony finished, Poppy, who was still hanging onto Kip's hand, asked, "Do you think the attempt on Nate's life and Shannon's death are connected?" The question gave them each pause. It sounded paranoid to be sure, but in Massey's mind, the events seemed too premeditated to be coincidental.

Kip gave voice to his thoughts. "Without a doubt."

The post-surgery hours were brutal. They took turns sitting with Nate while he lay unconscious, except for Mony, who refused to leave his side. The nurses finally gave up offering a cot and let her sleep in the chair. Kip secured a place in town for the rest of them to crash as they waited out the vigil. Massey had never seen someone fight their way back from the brink of death before. Fading in and out of consciousness, Nate mumbled, thrashed, kicked and punched while being weaned from the breathing device. He went into respiratory arrest a couple of times during the process—once, Massey even had to leave the room. Witnessing his family's reaction, however, was decidedly a million times worse.

Dane dutifully stayed until Nate had been successfully extubated and was breathing on his own. "A family sticks together, no matter what," he said, quoting Bob Strong; the sentiment made Massey feel both grateful and sad. Despite his stand-in status, Bob Strong had never behaved like a surrogate father. He felt genuine, real. It was a comfort.

Toward evening, Massey and Dane were walking down the hall toward the pop machine when a flash of light caught the attorney off guard. Dane, however, reacted lightning quick and was on the perpetrator in an instant. He rushed after a man pushing a linen bucket and dressed in a pair of loose-fitting scrubs, tackling him to the floor; then he confiscated the digital camera bulging from his pocket. Massey began digging through the basket and found two more cameras. He began stomping them with the heel of his boot.

The incognito paparazzo began yelling, "Hey, that's my property." Dane lifted the phony laundry attendant off the floor by the scruff of his shirt and shoved him at the security guard racing toward the commotion. He threw the digital camera he'd seized at the wall, snapping off the zoom lens. "You're gonna pay for that," the paparazzo shouted, even as the security guard cuffed him.

Dane boldly stepped into the man's face and said, "If I see even a blurry picture of my family on social media or anywhere else unsanctioned, you're going to be out more than just a couple of cheap cameras."

Massey had to lead Dane away by the arm, as the security guard grappled with the reporter over another camera.

Nate woke briefly hours later. He managed to whisper, "Mony, could you help me with a drink of water?"

Of course he'd call to her first.

During the next forty-five minutes, a medical team bustled around Nate, poking and prodding before the rest of the family could get near him. When they'd finished, Poppy was the first to plant a big kiss on Nate's cheek. She tried to smile, tried to be brave. She cried instead and told him through a teary voice, "Don't you ever leave us like that again. Do you hear me?"

Massey came next and placed his hand on brother's shoulder. "Glad to have you back, man. But don't think for one minute this in any way negates the ass-kicking I owe you. When you're feeling stronger, we'll talk." He quickly stepped aside and made room for his dad.

Kip dispensed with the pleasantries. "What Poppy said." To everyone's astonishment, he leaned over Nate and gave him a hug, which made them all cry. Mony waited and sat on his bed. Nate tried to speak, but no sound came from his mouth. She pressed an ice cube against his lips, and he grimaced as he swallowed the melted water.

"Sorry, hon," she said gently, "but you have to start slow with the liquids."

Nate managed to whisper, "I'm okay." It sounded more like a question. He continued to cough and choke as he sucked on the ice cube, trying to be a good patient. When he'd had enough, Mony pulled it away from his lips.

He said in a raspy voice, "I love you, Mony."

The words weren't surprising as much as disconcerting. By now, everyone in the room knew what Mony meant to Nate, including Dane. It was much too early to know how the young man felt about the matter. They were all still functioning in crisis mode. Time would be the teller of that tale. What troubled Massey was the fear and desperation he heard in his brother's voice, the unfocused gaze as Nate searched his lover's face expectantly. He wondered if Nate would feel the same way after learning the truth about Dane.

Mony wrapped her arms tenderly around Nate's neck and kissed him gently on his dry lips. If Nate had been afraid, her actions put his mind at ease. "I—I will always love you, Nate Ferguson."

It was at that point Dane decided to make his presence known and said, "Can you two wait until everyone has said hello before sucking face?" Nate gave a look of surprise then delight as his unbeknownst son came closer to the bed. Dane took hold of his biological father's hand and said, "You really should focus on getting well. You gave us all quite a scare."

Nate flexed his fingers around Dane's hand. An alarm started beeping, and Dane loosened his hold, stepping away from the bed. A short-statured woman with a bombshell figure no boxy pair of scrubs could hide took Mony's place at the bedside. More prodding and probing ensued. When the nurse had finished, she elevated the head of the bed, affording Nate a better look at his surroundings. His gaze fell on Massey and he muttered, "Thanks for coming for me. Thanks for saving my life."

Massey couldn't tell if Nate meant this as finding him in the desert or more generally. He was about to clarify when the nurse said, "I wouldn't give your brother all the credit," injecting something into an IV line. "A lot of that goes to your surgeon, and the rest to your son." The nurse nodded toward Dane. "With your blood anomaly, finding a donor would have been next to impossible. If it hadn't been for him, I doubt we'd have been able to perform the surgery at all."

The room fell deathly quiet, except for the beeping and hissing of pumps and monitors. The nurse looked up from her task at the shocked expressions on everyone's face. Confused by their response, she held up the empty syringe and said, "Don't worry. It's just a little something to help manage the pain."

Mony came over to the bed and sat facing Nate trying to gauge his reaction. Already his eyelids were growing heavy. Still, with a hoarse laugh he managed to say to her, "Did you hear that, Mony? The nurse thinks Dane's my son." With that, he drifted into unconsciousness.

The surgeon held a press conference early the next morning reporting on Nate's status. Only Massey and Kip attended from the family. Dane took advantage of the diversion and had Mony take him to the airport. There was too much to say between mother and son in the short span of time. When she returned, Massey could tell she was still anxious about the words left unsaid between them. He reminded her that she and Bob had raised a good man and that Dane would come to forgive her deception with time. It was a hell of a bomb learning Nate was his biological father while in the same breath being asked to save his life. Yet for some reason, it didn't seem as shocking to Dane as one might have expected. Massey couldn't answer his nephew's question as to why Mony had kept the identity of his biological father a secret all these years, but it wasn't because she didn't love him. Massey had assured Dane before he left that he would keep the promise he'd made to him on the drive to Lake Havasu City when the moment was right. Dane told Massey he would hold him to that promise.

Mony became teary when she told him Dane had offered her a hug and kiss goodbye at the airport. Massey threw his arm around his pseudo sister's shoulders and said, "I told you he was a good man."

They'd started walking back to Nate's room when Mony said passively, "At least I have one piece of good news in all this."

He paused and turned to face her. "I could really, really use some good news right about now."

She used the sleeve of her shirt to wipe her eyes and nose, smiled at him, and said, "I just found out Nate and I are going to be grandparents."

CHAPTER 27

JOHN

John sat in the small interrogation room with a warm ice pack on his jaw, two ibuprofen, a glass of water, and his thoughts. He was tired, hungry, and in pain. He cursed his injuries for not being severe enough to hold him in the hospital overnight for observation. Being handcuffed in a hospital bed would have been more comfortable than his present accommodations. Then again, out there he was vulnerable; at least inside there were cameras and the law. He slouched back in his chair, accepting he was better off where he sat.

Two detectives from the state crime bureau out of Bismarck had rousted him out of his holding cell early that morning, taking on the role of bad cops. John was familiar with the approach, though he'd only seen it on TV—his area of expertise was in real estate and divorce law, not criminal defense.

The detectives had badgered him with the same set of questions asked in different ways. He'd tolerated the redundancy. It gave him time to sort things out, and maybe force the investigators to focus their attention elsewhere. What he focused his thoughts on was who he could trust. He didn't dare call his law firm or Monroe Oil, which would surely send up a red flag toward guilt. After all, why would he need a lawyer if he didn't have something to hide? No, patience was his best ally. Only when he ran out of options would he call Lyn and have her initiate the instructions he'd given. John returned from his introspection when the sheriff entered the room for the next round of questioning.

"Good morning, Mr. Finch. I trust you were able to get a couple hours' sleep?"

John studied the sheriff, who didn't fit the stereotypical, donut-eating rural cop image. He was a tall, lanky man closer to the retirement side of sixty. He looked as tired as John felt; it bought him comfort. The bloodshot eyes with dark circles underneath and more than a five o'clock shadow denuded the sheriff's authoritative persona and made him more human. John pushed aside thoughts of how bad he looked and sat up straight in his chair.

"I was afraid to shut my eyes for fear I have a concussion," he replied calmly. "That so-called assessment I received at your medical facility was far from adequate. After this entire farce is over, you can be assured I will be filing a grievance."

The sheriff took note of his statement. "Perhaps we should wait a bit and continue the interview when you're thinking more clearly?"

John picked up the ibuprofen and popped them in his mouth. He hadn't slept a wink. The blow to the face had triggered a raging migraine, something he hadn't experienced since his college days. Nothing had ever touched them, except maybe some weed, a dark room, and three days' sleep. He washed the analgesic down with the tepid water. "Is that what this is, an interview? I have nothing more to say than what I've already told you."

"Perhaps you can humor me and go over it one more time."

He breathed an exasperated sigh—it wasn't a request—and recounted the sequence of events. "I had dinner with Ms. McDonald by her invitation, and I spent the night with her, again invited. I left around four o'clock in the morning."

"You say Shannon had invited you to come to her place. Why?"

The same question plagued John's mind as well. Shannon hadn't initiated the meeting—he had, when he'd mistakenly assumed her the caller from the bar. The whole thing was a setup initiated by Shannon's friend Cindy Van Dyke. The very woman Shannon had asked John to help her find. She claimed she didn't trust anyone local to help find her friend. He didn't doubt that. Finding Cindy Van Dyke would expose some ugly secrets about their quaint little community—secrets that no doubt were a source of major humiliation and embarrassment. Why this was so important to her, she wouldn't say. Out loud John said to the sheriff, "That would be Ms. McDonald's story to tell. Unfortunately, neither of us fully know that answer."

The sheriff clenched his jaw, poorly masking his

frustration, and blurted, "Did you have sex with her?"

The question was irrelevant, but the answer was bound to show up on Shannon's autopsy. He went with, "Consensual, yes."

The sheriff absorbed his answer, then said, "Did she ask you to leave?"

"We'd come to a mutual endpoint. When I left, Ms. McDonald was very much alive, and we had no further contact after that. The hotel security camera will verify my timeline. I was just as shocked as everyone else when the rescuers fished her out of the lake. It's as straightforward as that."

"Nothing is straightforward, Mr. Finch. You're the last known person to see Shannon Mc—"

"No, goddamn it, I was not the last person to see Ms. McDonald," John countered. "Her killer was, and you're wasting precious time trying to pin it on me because it's the easiest path. I am not her killer. So do your job and—"

"Do not tell me how to do my job, Mr. Finch," the sheriff snapped. "What were you doing out at the Altman farm?"

John took a deep breath and reined in his irritation. He would get nowhere right now if he lost his composure. "I've explained that as well," he said in a more modulated voice. "In an attempt to divert a full-blown legal battle that would cost my client a shitload of money, I'd wanted to discuss the upcoming probate hearing with Ms. Strong. There is little hope of Monroe winning the case, and I wanted to reduce the risk of a countersuit on F&A Oil's behalf."

"Mony would never talk to you about business without Kip or Massey," the sheriff said in a tone of repugnance.

John already knew that, but he wasn't about to share the real reason with the sheriff, not until the guy proved himself trustworthy.

"Plus, when I arrived, you weren't talking anything," the sheriff continued. "Mony pointed a gun at you. Why?"

It vexed him as well. She would have likely seen Shannon's body from the air when she flew in, but why had she suspected John as the killer? "You'll have to ask her that question," John said flatly. "Look, I've been detained for nearly twenty-four hours, and I haven't even been read my Miranda rights. If you're going to press charges, best get to it or cut me loose. Your window of opportunity is closing." He didn't begrudge the sheriff doing his job, and if arresting him on suspicion of murder would get things moving forward, so be it. But time was of the essence. The man clearly supported team F&A. What troubled John was the sheriff's lack of direction without a Ferguson present. He appeared to be in a state of free fall, grasping at straws on what to do next, and it made the attorney nervous. John considered what advantage his current predicament presented and changed his tactic.

"I assume you've gone through my hotel room and rental car?"

The sheriff didn't answer, but of course his personal belongings were being searched, as well as Shannon's apartment, the rental car, the mileage on the odometer and the grounds around the lake—everything. There would be no tread marks from his rental anywhere on the property, other than the ones that had led him to Ramona's doorstep. *Is that why they're drawing out my incarceration?* He focused on his time at Shannon's apartment. *What will they find?*

A sense of foreboding brought a bead of sweat to his brow. It was a variable out of his control. Shannon McDonald's murder had been particularly brutal. The blow to the back of the head hadn't killed her. Her killer had watched the life leave her eyes as he strangled her. *A crime of passion.* "Tell me, Sheriff. What's my motive for killing Ms. McDonald? You must have a working theory by now."

Again, the sheriff said nothing. John prided himself at reading people. He could see the internal strife behind the sheriff's eyes. Unfortunately, before he could elaborate, there was a knock at the door. A young deputy poked his head in and said, "Sir, a word."

The sheriff stepped out and returned a few moments later. His face was glum when he sat down in the chair across from John. He turned off the recording device and looked him in the eye. "I don't believe you personally had a motive in killing Ms. McDonald, Mr. Finch, but what about Mony Strong or Nate Ferguson? It seems to me Monroe Oil would have much to gain with one less Ferguson or Altman to contend with. Perhaps Shannon's death was a diversion from a grander scheme."

John tried not to visibly squirm, for he'd considered that as well. The sheriff noticed his discomfort, and his lips thinned into a smile. *Was Shannon an unfortunate causality?* He was beginning to feel the hinge of trap closing. *Who is setting me up?* He ventured a test of trust with the sheriff. "You may be right about Shannon being a diversion. She'd asked me to help her find a missing friend. She seemed to think the friend had incriminating knowledge against a high-profile member of this community and that friend's life may have been in danger. The killer could be someone who didn't want her to learn this information."

"Why would Shannon ask your help?"

John spliced a couple of half-truths together. "She told me she didn't trust anyone around here to uncover the truth, and she knew Ramona and I were in a causal relationship."

The sheriff suppressed a laugh. "You and Mony?"

"Yes," he said impassively. "It is not in my best interest for anything bad to happen to Ramona or to anyone important to her. I don't know if Shannon McDonald's death has anything to do with what's going on with Nathan Ferguson, but I—"

"What do you know about Nate?"

The terse response put him on edge. "I don't know anything, except I heard he was in the news this morning."

The sheriff gave a disgruntled snort. "All right, Mr. Finch. Let's suppose for a moment I believe your line of BS. How about telling me your theory of what's going on?"

"First, I'd like to speak with Ramona—in private. I—"

"You can't do that."

"And why not?"

After a moment of hesitation; the sheriff filled him in on the family's sudden departure for Arizona to be with

Nate.

John slumped back in his chair. *It's worse than I thought.* For reasons he couldn't understand, he'd felt less vulnerable thinking the Fergusons or Ramona were around. Despite their misgivings toward him, he'd come to trust the attorney. Matthew Ferguson had an integrity not often found among peers. "What happened to the rock star? Is he hurt?"

"Mr. Finch, I'm not answering any questions until you answer a few of mine."

For John, the conversation had reached an impasse—without new information, there was nothing more he could share, leaving him with a choice of either sitting around with a finger up his ass or taking a calculated risk. He straightened in his chair. "I'm done talking, Sheriff. Press charges or cut me loose. I have work to do."

The sheriff leaned back. "I doubt very much you will be conducting any business around Williston today, Mr. Finch."

"Says who?"

The sun was high in the sky when John was officially released from custody. He wished he'd had his sunglasses along but quickly realized that was the least of his worries. He was about to step out the front door when he saw the hostile mob and reporters gathered outside the main entrance.

The sheriff begrudgingly offered him a lift to the impound. He'd have been a fool to turn it down. They slipped out the back, and the sheriff had the civility to allow him to sit in the front seat. The formality was fleeting, however. As they passed around the building, John crouched down in his seat and peeked out the window, taking in the full effect of the crowd. They wanted blood. He was out of jail, at least, but once he left the sanctuary of the squad car, he was jumping from the proverbial frying pan and into the fire. It was a disquieting prospect.

They rode past several implement dealerships, drilling companies, and other small stores. Everything supported the oil business, John noted; even the hotels were located further out of town. Near the edge of the city limits, the sheriff said, "You saw for yourself what sort of cooperation you can expect trying to conduct business around here. If I may suggest, how about having a conversation with someone who will actually listen to what you have to say?"

John turned to face him. "And who might that be?"

The sheriff's mouth tipped into a smirk. "Tell me what your theory is regarding Shannon's death."

He snorted, "So you can hold it against me later?"

The sheriff's face sobered. "Do you know what makes Matthew Ferguson such a successful lawyer?"

"What does the attorney have to do with any of this?"

The sheriff continued, "He's humble and honest. Doesn't wear his pride like a badge of honor the way you do, Mr. Finch. You come to our part of the country thinking you're better than everyone else because you're well educated and live in a big city."

"That's your perception of me, not the other way around."

"Then what on earth possessed you to sleep with Shannon? Or were you just taking advantage?"

This conversation is going nowhere, he thought. "How do I know you won't feed me to the lions anyway?"

"Nate Ferguson was shot last night."

"What?"

"Yeah, shot in the chest. He's made it through the surgery, but I've been too busy with this investigation to hear an update. It's bad enough we've lost Shannon. If we lose Nate—" The sheriff's words caught in his throat, and John watched the man age before his eyes. This was a personal matter, he realized; the sheriff's closeness to the situation clearly placed him at a disadvantage.

The sheriff's attempt at regaining his self-composure was discomforting. He said, "Nate and Shannon were in a relationship, very similar to what you described between you and Mony. But you must know by now, Nate and Mony have always loved each other. I doubt that will ever stop, no matter what information Shannon had hoped you'd helped her uncover."

"She thought Cindy Van Dyke's treachery may have stemmed as far back as college, when she and Ramona were roommates," John confided.

They turned onto a gravel driveway and drove around back of a one-story warehouse building. The sheriff pulled up to the chain-link gate and waited for the security guard, saying to John, "What does any of this matter in the grand scheme of things? It doesn't change the past or the current situation. Did Shannon truly believe unearthing a thirty-year-old secret would change anything?"

"Apparently she did," John said thoughtfully, "and it cost her life. She also mentioned a person named Hitch who might have something to do with all this, as well as the disappearance of the young Indian girl."

The sheriff slammed the palm of his hand unexpectantly against the steering wheel, startling him. "Goddamn it to hell. First Mony, then Shannon, and now you. Why can't you people just let it go? How many people have to die before you stop interfering and let law enforcement do their job?"

John had no idea what the sheriff was talking about, but considering the sheriff's outburst, he had no intention of letting Hitch go.

CHAPTER 28

MONY

The dietary aide collected Nate's tray, and he began dozing. Mony sat in a chair next to his bed, trying to focus on her Cork O'Connor novel, when a verbal confrontation exploded in the hallway.

"Tread carefully, Detective. I didn't spend nearly five hours in surgery pulling Mr. Ferguson from the brink of death for you to wipe him out in his first few hours of consciousness."

Mony smiled at the doctor's vehemence.

The smile quickly morphed into one of surprise when a young woman entered the room. In her late twenties or early thirties, she was of middle height, lean and fit, with jet-black hair pulled back in a severe ponytail thick as a horse's mane and braided down the middle of her back. Her dark brown eyes and warm smile were friendly; her big hoop earrings and street clothes did little to conceal her authority or detract from the sidearm under her lightweight jacket. She entered the room, making eye contact followed by a hearty handshake.

"Hello, my name is Gabriella Gomez. I'm with the Arizona Criminal Investigation Division, or CID." She handed Mony a business card. "I'd like to ask Mr. Ferguson a few questions about the events that happened near the Desert Bar and what he remembers."

Mony joined Poppy and Kip in the ICU lounge while Massey stayed with Nate during the interview. Poppy lay down on the sofa and fell into an immediate sleep. Without looking, Kip said to Mony, "I've chartered a plane back to Williston tonight. I need you to stay and look after Nate."

He wasn't asking, but Mony took no offense at the command and heard the relief in his voice when she readily agreed to the task. With nothing better to do, they watched TV in silence, but after a few minutes, Mony became bored with the mindless activity. Making conversation, she said, "By the way, thanks for tilling the garden for me. Not sure if I'll get a chance to do any planting, but you and Poppy can use it if you like."

Kip looked at her puzzled. "What are you talking about?"

A young volunteer entered the lounge to notify them the interview was over. Mony shrugged off Kip's confusion, got up, and then looked back at Kip when he didn't follow. "You go on," Kip said. "I'm going to let Poppy rest awhile."

An unsettling queasiness churned in her stomach, and she made her way toward the restroom. Finding the place empty, she locked herself in the end stall. The burger and fries she'd eaten earlier sat like lead in her gut and for a moment she felt as if she might vomit. As she took a few deep breaths, the sensation subsided. *Probably nerves,* she thought. Taking a few extra minutes to finish her business, she considered how the stress, worry, and fear was getting to all of them. For the first time in days, she thought of home.

Trundling out of the stall, she was surprised to see Detective Gomez standing in front of a sink and applying a liberal amount of lip gloss. Clearly, she was standing there in wait. Mony walked to the other sink, trying to hide her shaky hands. She could sense the weight of the detective's gaze on her profile and kept her eyes focused on the mirror, grimacing at her reflection. She tried for a little small talk: "Was Nate able to answer your question?"

Detective Gomez's voice was soft, almost friendly. "Not all of them. Mr. Ferguson's brother is very protective."

"And smart," Mony added, then kicked herself, hoping the remark didn't sound like a challenge. The detective seemed to take no offense.

"Did you know the man Mr. Ferguson clocked over the head is a small-time heroin dealer? Imagine this *pistolero* crossing the border just to shoot your musician." The detective shook her head. "Another stupid gringo playing a dangerous game."

Mony wasn't sure if "stupid," was referring Nate or the *pistolero*. Either way, it made her bristle.

"Why do you suppose anyone would want to shoot Mr. Ferguson?" the detective asked conversationally.

Mony kept her eyes trained on the mirror. She didn't care for the woman's informal approach. "I believe that's why you're the detective," she said failing to hide the irritation in her voice.

"You are correct, Mony. May I call you Mony?"

Now she really didn't like her. The flippant request to use the familiar term of endearment chaffed on raw nerves. "It seems you just did, Detective. If you'll excuse me." Mony stepped around the woman and swiped off a piece of paper towel too small to dry her hands. She tossed at the wide-mouth basket and missed—irritated, she had to walk past the detective to pick it up. She froze when Gomez's fingers brushed her forearm.

"I'm not your enemy," the detective said quietly.

Mony looked down to where the woman had touched her, then back at her face. "Honestly, I don't know who you are. What I do know is trying to chum up to me in the bathroom like we're girlfriends won't get you answers to the questions you should be asking someone else." As the detective stepped back allowing her to pass, Mony placed a shaky hand on the doorknob.

"There's strong probability the murder of Mr. Ferguson's former lover, Shannon McDonald, and the attempt on his life are connected," the detective said.

She didn't respond. Gomez was on a fishing expedition, and she was throwing her lure in the wrong lake. Mony wasn't interested in possibilities. What she wanted was proof and a conviction.

Mony's uneasiness hadn't abated when she walked to Nate's room. She immediately noticed the foggy stare and glazed-over look in Nate's eyes and turned to Massey for an explanation.

"Detective Gomez told him about Shannon."

Shit.

Mony sat on the edge of the bed, cradling his head to her chest while he cried tearless sobs. "I'm sorry you had to find out that way," she said quietly. Both she and Massey let him have some time to grieve. The family had agreed earlier to wait until Nate was a little further out of the woods before telling him about Shannon. It seemed the detective was of a different opinion.

When he was worn down from sorrow, Nate asked, "How is Shawn holding up?"

Massey said, "I spoke with Virgil just before the interview. He and his brother have been managing the bar, so Shawn and his family could make funeral arrangements. They said he's holding it together—with a couple bottles of Jameson a day. The guys are pretty worried about him, especially after he'd learned about your incident. I told Virgil I'd have you call him as soon as you were up to it. I hope you don't mind. I didn't know what else to tell him."

"You can tell Wagner to send that fuckin' lawyer straight to hell," Nate said angrily. He started coughing, and Mony reached for the ice chips on the nightstand. He took a few, and when his breathing had returned to a normal rhythm, he pushed her hand away.

She set the cup aside and gently cupped his cheek in her hand, trying to reason with him. "I know how you feel about Finch, but we need him right now. He was the last person to see Shannon before her killer, and his cooperation is paramount, narrowing the timeline. For whatever reason, Shannon confided in him before she died. We need to know what he knows." Mony turned to Massey. "Tell him I'm right."

Massey came over and stood beside her. "I've already told him that. We can't bring Shannon back, but we can find her killer and bring him to justice, North Dakota style."

A slight smile crooked in the corner of Nate's mouth; it quickly faded. "Mony, your silly white-picket-fence life with Bob has made you gullible. I've seen the hunger in that man's eyes. He's a predator, out to ruin you and take your money." Nate pulled his cheek from her hand and turned away. "I need to rest a while. This pointless chatter has worn me out." He closed his eyes, ending the conversation.

Mony withdrew from the bed. "I need some air."

Massey said, "I'll come with—"

"No," Mony snapped, then exhaled sharply. "Please, no." She tried to stay calm, tried not to take her hurt out on Massey. She'd be no good to anyone if she couldn't keep her shit together. "I'll be okay, I just needed a little space, that's all." She wanted to leave before she started to cry, but she wasn't that lucky. She could feel moisture building in her eyes.

"I'm sorry," Massey whispered, and took her arm in his, "I—I can't let you do that." She stared at him confounded and angry, but he persisted. Eventually she let him have his way.

They walked together arm in arm along the temporary privacy wall that had recently been erected to block the back of the building from the street. Mony made no move to pull her arm away, nor did Massey let go. Near the end of the wall, her pseudo brother turned to her and said, "I'm hanging by a thread, Mony. If anything were to happen to you too, it would destroy me."

She tried to recall if she'd ever seen Massey cry. She must not have, for it would have been a memorable event. They held each other for a while, both aware they were crying. They'd been white-knuckling it for too long. They needed to loosen their grip, she thought, at least a little. She said to Massey, "Let's grab a beer after we drop off your folks at the airport. We both could use it."

Massey rubbed his arm across his eyes and said, "You're on."

They continued to walk for a while in silence until, curious, Mony asked, "What did you think of the detective?"

"She's young," Massey said contemplatively, "and aggressive. She uses her looks to charm and disarm but becomes too impatient when the interviewee doesn't take the bait. She's smart enough to recognize it but not yet mature enough to keep it in check."

Mony agreed. "Did you know she ambushed me in the bathroom?"

Massey raised his eyebrows. "Ambushed?"

"Yeah, well, it sort of felt like it. I think she might have thought she'd find solidarity with another female. Anyway, did you get an inkling if she suspects Nate of murder?"

A commotion on the other side of the privacy partition drew the attention of two security guards.

"I can't say with certainty," Massey continued, eyeing the scene, "but I don't think so. Nate has several alibis to corroborate his story. He voluntarily told the detective he'd hit the man while defending the victim he'd rendered first aid to. The first aid kit at the scene and the medics lend credence to his story; I don't see where she'd suspect him of lying. I'm concerned about the shooter. His actions could suggest Nate had come upon or been a part of some sort of dealings gone bad."

"Did Nate say anything to her about being lured into a trap?"

"No. His only witness to that remark is dead. Besides, we don't need the investigator wasting time on something we can investigate ourselves. I think we should drive out to the bar tonight and see who we can talk to."

She nodded. "The detective asked me if I thought Shannon's murder and the attempt on Nate's life were connected. She said nothing about Sissy Moonbeam."

"Interesting."

"Did she ask about me?"

Massey was about to answer when a belligerent couple arguing with the two security guards interrupted their discussion. Two more guards joined in the ruckus, drawing the attention of the hospital staff outside on break. The male half of the two looked up and made eye contact with Massey. He yelled, "Hey, Ferguson, can you help a guy out? We're here to see the Fergmeister."

Mony saw the perturbed expression on Massey's face. "You know that guy?"

Massey took a deep breath and rolled his shoulders

back. "That," he said with disdain, "is Trevor St. James. Next to him is his head of his security, Gem Richards."

Mony squinted her eyes at the couple. "Shit, more vultures."

CHAPTER 29

MASSEY

Massey and Mony dropped his parents off at the airport and said their goodbyes. He could tell they were wavering on their decision to leave. Mony gave Kip and extra-long hug and encouraged, "It's best for Poppy. Don't worry about Nate, I've got this." It was easy for her to say—she didn't harbor worries for their safety the way Kip and Massey did.

With his parents onboard the plane, he punched in the GPS coordinates for the Desert Bar. Mony was quiet as they navigated their way back toward city limits, still stewing about the conversation with Trevor and Gem. It hadn't gone well. Trying to get her to focus on something else, Massey said, "We need to talk."

She bristled, "If you're going to give me hell for losing my shit today, don't. No way was I going to just roll over while that Gem talked trash about my girls."

"She did know how to push your buttons," Massey said observantly.

"I'm so pissed right now, I could spit. I don't need—"

"Stop, Mony. Just stop," Massey said, kind but firm. "Forget about her. Trevor knows what's at stake if he tries a stunt like that again. We have more important things to discuss. What are your plans after Nate's discharge?"

Mony took a moment to rein in her anger and said with more deliberation, "He doesn't want to go back to North Dakota, that much he made clear. He told Shawn to go ahead with Shannon's funeral, which I think is a good thing. Nate's condition is far too precarious even for travel by private plane. When I suggested we stay at the condo Kip rented out, he seemed indifferent to the idea. My thinking is that he can at least finish out his therapy here in Lake Havasu City. We can decide the next step later."

Massey nodded. Keeping both Nate and Mony away from North Dakota would be prudent. It would allow the McDonald family some much needed time for closure and private grief. It would also afford Sheriff Wagner unmitigated resources to focus on Shannon's murder without having to worry about the community's two biggest celebrities.

"Has the detective said anything more to you about the investigation?" Mony asked.

"No, but I sense she's still indecisive about whether or not there's evidence to suggest Nate had been involved in foul play. Wagner will clarify that subject when the two of them talk tomorrow morning; then they can start putting the pieces of the puzzle together. Did I tell you Cindy Van Dyke is missing too?"

Mony's eyes widened. "Really?"

Massey relayed what the sheriff told Kip over the

phone. Her coworkers thought nothing of it when Cindy called in on a Friday, since she was habitually absent before and after the weekend. But when she didn't show up by midweek, her supervisor became concerned and called her contact numbers. There was no answer. No one had seen or heard from Dwight Mitchell either. "It fits with Finch's claim that Shannon was worried for Cindy's safety and wanted his help in finding her."

"It feels like someone is tying up loose ends," Mony said introspectively. She didn't comment on Finch's involvement. It was just as well; Massey would rather she not think of him at all. His gut reaction supported Mony's conjecture: the situation was far from over.

They crossed over a channel onto London Bridge Road. It was a beautiful evening, and Massey puttered along taking in the sunset like a farmer checking out cornfields in July. He glanced in the rearview mirror, aware the leisurely pace might be holding up traffic, and noticed a car tailing a little too closely. His grip tightened on the wheel. Mony took notice and said, "What's the matter?"

Massey kept glancing in the rearview mirror. "I don't know. But I think we're being followed."

She stiffened. "Don't be paranoid. No one knows who we are."

"Mony, we're driving a truck with a North Dakota license plate," Massey offered bluntly. "It wouldn't be difficult to figure it out." He slowed his speed.

"What the hell are you doing?"

"Testing a hunch." When the car wouldn't pass, he pulled over to the side and waved at the driver to pass.

The car simply stopped when he did. The standoff went on for several seconds before he resumed driving, the car keeping pace with the truck.

"We can't lead them to where we're going," Mony said fervently.

Massey shared the thought. "Pull up the police station address on the GPS. I'll head there." He continued along the boulevard, the car still tailing close behind.

Am I being paranoid? After all, they were driving the only outlet from the airport. Maybe, but the hairs standing up on the nape of his neck told him otherwise. "See if you can make out the license plate number and write it down. We can give it to the officer on duty when we get to the station."

The low sun on the horizon caused a glare in the rearview mirror, obscuring the car from Massey's view. Unable to see his pursuer made him nervous, and for the first time, he thought about Nate's gun in the locked toolbox.

"Damnit, no front license plate," Mony complained.

He glanced in the mirror. "What about make and model?"

She huffed. "Jesus, Massey, I don't know cars." But after a moment, Mony described the car in detail, including the customization on the rear spoiler. That made him smile.

They were about to cross the highway on a green light when, from out of nowhere, a black SUV came barreling into the southbound lane and cut in front of them. Massey swerved a hard right, marginally avoiding a collision and forcing them to take the highway. They were heading southeast, with the car and the black SUV falling in behind.

"Holy shit," Mony shouted, still clinging to the dash, "I take it back about the paranoia. Either these guys are major assholes, or we're definitely being followed." She looked out the back window and then back to Massey. "I don't suppose we can outrun them?"

"I doubt it. We have a V-8. They have a Hemi. That car's meant for speed."

Unable to hide the panic in her voice, Mony asked, "Should I call 911?"

It seemed desperate, but things also felt that way. Massey had no idea who they were dealing with or if they were in any real danger. If he'd been alone, he would have pulled over, grabbed Nate's gun out of the back, and asked. Aggressors generally backed down when confronted. But with everything that had happened, he wasn't taking the risk—not with Mony along.

"This sort of aggression doesn't speak of an adoring fan," she said flatly. "I'm calling it."

As Mony began dialing, the sound of bullets ricocheting off metal pierced the air.

"911, what is your emergency?"

Mony began talking frantically while Massey punched the pedal to the floor and tore down the highway. He was driving excessively fast and wondered why the chase hadn't drawn the attention of a local cop or highway patrol car. The Charger easily kept pace. Massey couldn't be sure which vehicle had fired off the shots and avoided weaving in and out of traffic, not wanting a stray bullet to hit an innocent. At his first opportunity, he took a good long look to see how many vehicles were following him. Only two, the Charger and the mysterious black SUV, still several car lengths behind.

The traffic began to thin near the end of city limits. The car swerved into the outside lane, attempting to cut them off. The black SUV came up quickly from behind, closing the gap. The dispatcher kept repeating to stay calm and firmly instructed them not to engage the pursuers. Mony wasn't having it.

"Are you kidding? They've already shot at us, and now they're trying to box us in." She muted the receiver and said to Massey, "We need to get off this highway, somewhere we can kick up some dust and rocks to back them off."

The Charger effectively passed him before the highway dropped down to two lanes; now it was setting the pace. They were still driving nearly 100 miles per hour. The sun had dropped below the horizon, making the surrounding environment more difficult to see. Massey tried to back off the Charger once, but the SUV riding his tail prohibited it. They'd traveled three or four miles like that when Mony said, "They're taking us somewhere. We can't let that happen."

Massey concurred—they needed to make a stand in a place of their own choosing. He considered their options. The choice would have been easy back home; out here, he had no idea. He assumed there were dirt, rocks, and more desert. The problem was he couldn't get to them. The unpredictable spacing of the guardrails lining the road flip-flopped from one side of the lane to the other depending on where the washes and small gulches were more prevalent. Plus, their speed prohibited any abrupt deviation from the straight path without the potential for a rollover. He'd resolved on taking their chances on the highway when Mony said, "I've got an idea."

Off-roading was a popular recreational pastime in the desert community, and several trailhead markers were dotted along the highway. They'd passed one such site already. "Watch for the next mile marker," Mony said. "We'll see a kiosk on the left-hand side marking the upcoming trailhead. If we can make the turn, we should be able to ditch the Charger easy enough and just have the SUV to deal with. I'm pulling up a trail map on the GPS now."

Lacking a better option, when they reached the mile marker, Massey drifted easily across the oncoming-traffic lane and onto the gravel road. The approach wasn't nearly wide enough—fortunately, he didn't need it. The parallel surface to the road was hard-packed dirt and made for a relatively smooth transition. As predicted, the Charger kept speeding along the highway. But that wasn't all. Hell-bent on his mission, the driver of the SUV hadn't anticipated the deviation in course—it sped along behind chasing the Charger. Shocked that her plan had worked, Mony let out a shaky whoop of triumph, but they weren't out of danger yet. Massey slowed his speed while she relayed their location to dispatch and they decided what to do next.

Dispatch instructed them to head toward the staging

area, then take the trail northeast, passing along the edge
of the gravel pit. According to the trail map, the wash held
a northeast course and narrowed between two mountains
in a little over two miles. "You should have enough
clearance driving a truck," the dispatcher cautioned, "but
I wouldn't rule out the possibility of bogging down in the
sandy washes. There are a couple of old mines about four
miles out. We're sending a helicopter to that location.
You're to hole up at the mine and wait."

Mony muted the phone again and turned to face
Massey, her taut expression illuminated by the dashboard
light. "Should we trust it?"

It was a good question.

There seemed no clear reason not to, and yet Detective
Gomez's silence on whether she suspected Nate of any
wrongdoing in his attack niggled at the back of Massey's
brain. These people didn't know them, and given their
current situation, they could easily be misconstrued as
being involved in some sort of illegal activity. Sure, there
were probably some witnesses who could attest to them
being chased and shot at, but that didn't absolve them
from being suspect in a drug run or worse.

When they reached the staging area, Massey took the
trail, following along toward the gravel pit. The soft sand
forced him to slow his speed considerably. He checked his
rearview mirror and said, "It won't take long for them to
figure out where we've gone."

Mony examined her GPS. "Dispatch wants us to
rendezvous here"—she pointed to the screen—"but what
if the police channel is being monitored? We'd be like

sitting ducks for the police and whoever is chasing us. I think we should find a place to hunker down and wait. If the SUV does take the trail in, we can loop back out once they pass on one of these other trails. In the dark, there's no way for them to know we didn't follow the original trail, and being far enough in the lead, the lack of dust won't give us away."

It was a tense moment—put their fate in the law's hands or choose one of their own.

Massey said, "I like your idea, but I have one more thing to add. We grab Nate's gun from the toolbox the first chance we get."

Mony left the perpetual chatter of the dispatcher's growing irritation muted and said, "I like it, but a gun won't do us much good unless we're in close range. You can't see a damn thing out here except what's in the headlights. Are you sure we want to make it that personal?"

The trail began to climb steadily, and Massey shifted into a lower gear. The surface was solid, at least—the drawback was that the considerable amount of loose gravel made the climb treacherous. He didn't want to blow a tire or bust the axle. The higher elevation allowed for a better view of the highway, but it also made them easier to spot. He glanced again in the rearview mirror. This time he saw two sets of headlights turning onto the road leading to the trailhead. He didn't worry about the Charger continuing, but the SUV—

"The Charger will probably wait by the staging area and let the SUV flush us out," Mony said, giving voice to his thoughts. "And they probably can see our taillights by now. Hopefully, the trail drops a little over this ridge and we can confuse them, maybe set up an ambush."

Massey found such a spot behind a rock formation near the peak of the trail, then killed the lights and engine. It was impossibly dark. To his disappointment, they had to rely on the flashlight from Mony's cell phone in order to see into the toolbox; he hoped it wasn't bright enough to give their location away. The contents of the box, however, were anything but disappointing.

"Thank you, Nate!"

Massey begrudgingly continued driving along the trail, minus his passenger, trying to recall a time when Mony had ever relinquished the role of bait. He was uncomfortable with the arrangement. It wasn't that he didn't trust her aim with a firearm—to the contrary, she was an excellent shot. It was just that, for the first time, he felt extremely vulnerable and out of control of the situation. *Is that how Mony felt?* He couldn't imagine it. She always seemed so cool posing as the bait and took her role to an extreme measure without thinking twice about it. He would have to ask her secret the next time he had the chance.

The trail rimming the gravel pit became even more rugged and forced him to a crawl, but he wasn't in any hurry. He didn't want to be too far from the action when Mony unleashed hell, and he rolled down his window to listen. The desert was ominously quiet and black as obsidian. The only sound was the crunch of gravel beneath his wheels; he rolled the truck to a stop, ending the noise. He heard the whine of the SUV's engine off in the distance as it trudged through the wash at too high a speed. A few minutes later, he made out the slip-sliding of wheels on gravel as their pursuer made its ascent toward Mony's location. His breath became quick and shallow, and he had to consciously breathe deeper to calm his heart rate. It sucked being the prey.

The headlights, obscured below the ridge, reflected off the rock formation at the peak; Massey knew they were close. He tapped the brakes a couple of times, hoping the SUV driver would see the flashing of his taillights. "Come on, you bastard, come on. Just follow me. Don't worry about that little sniper waiting for you behind those rocks."

The SUV stopped suddenly, along with Massey's heart. He thought, *Shit, was the trap that obvious?* Then, an eruption of gunfire pierced the quiet night.

Massey scrambled out of the truck and crouched on all fours next to the wheel well. Using his phone flashlight, he duck-walked his way back up the hill. His lack of stealth made an easy target, but he didn't care. Fortunately for him, no one had been looking his way. A moment later, more shots rang out, followed by a man's pained scream. Massey got to his feet in a full-out run.

As he got closer to the trail's summit, the SUV headlight illuminated enough of an area for him to move between boulders while keeping out of sight. He wanted desperately to call out for Mony, to know if she was hurt. He didn't have to. She must have heard him coming and whispered in the dark, "Massey?"

He found her right where he'd left her, perched atop

a rock large enough to conceal her. She lay in a prone position, her arms outstretched in front, a gun gripped between her hands. Using the surface to maintain a steady aim on her target, Massey followed the line of sight and saw three bullet holes clustered in the driver-side windshield; the driver was slumped forward over the steering wheel, motionless.

"Jesus, Mony," he muttered. "Is that the only one?"

Mony didn't move, didn't take her eyes off her target. She said softly, "The other one ran off, right over the cliff."

CHAPTER 30

NATE

Nate took his evening pills and tried to sleep, but he mostly tossed and turned. His relentless brain wouldn't shut down, lamenting the last words he'd spoken to Mony, sparked by anger and jealousy. The same thing had happened between him and Shannon, a regrettable action he could never take back. He understood what Mony was trying to explain about the advantage of using the attorney against his own client. But why couldn't she see his point, that Finch was nothing more than an egocentric moron?

In a moment of drug-induced unconsciousness, his mind drifted to familiar, happy thoughts of him, Mony, and Massey. The reprieve was fleeting, however, as memory morphed into nightmarish images of Shannon's drowned, battered body and unthinkable harm befalling his family. He felt cursed and vowed to make it right between him and Mony at the first opportunity.

Around midnight, he had given up on sleep altogether and began flipping through channels when he heard the unmistakable sound of turbo engines engaging. His heart rate quickened. Mony wasn't back yet. It made him anxious.

Typically, the night staff would bullshit with him during rounds. Tonight, no one stayed longer than required. It felt punitive and isolating. When he casually asked about the helicopter, the orderly gave the preempted spiel regarding patient confidentiality. Nate didn't give a rat's ass about other people's business—he just wanted to know his family was okay.

A little after one o'clock, a gurney whizzed past his room, followed by a code blue. Nate broke into a cold sweat, and his breathing became erratic, setting off the monitor alarms. A nurse came to check on him, keeping her eyes trained on the monitors. Feeling ignored, Nate lost his temper and shouted, "Jesus Christ, just tell me if my family is all right."

The nurse answered by giving him a sedative.

He woke up groggy the next morning, when his favorite lab tech, a diehard MHC fan, came in to draw his blood. Always good for gossip, she greeted him with a cheery smile and began filling him in on the night's events. "The state patrol caught up with the car chasing your truck near the trail staging area. One guy was killed at the scene, the other one's down the hall." She prattled on about an SUV driver being shot and the gory details of some guy falling off a cliff. Nate didn't give a flying fuck about those people.

"What about Mony and Massey?"

The lab tech held up a finger indicating *Hold that thought* as she jabbed the needle in his arm. Nate pinched his face in a grimace, annoyed by the stick and his growing impatience. It wasn't as if Mony or Massey were obligated to be there around the clock. It was just that, emotionally, he'd come to rely on their presence. He drew comfort knowing where they were and that they were safe. *Maybe Mony's still pissed at me*, he mused, or maybe she was just tired and needed some sleep. He tried to convince himself of the latter, but it didn't feel right. Reining in his scattered thoughts, he muttered, "How the hell did I get to this place?"

The lab tech looked up from her work with a puzzled expression. "Don't you remember? You were airlifted from the Desert Bar—"

It wasn't what he meant.

His life had become one big clusterfuck after Buddy died—or maybe it had been a mess all along, and his old friend had anchored him somehow in the stormy sea of sanity. For reasons Nate couldn't comprehend, the idea of Mony and Massey off again, leaving him behind, ate at his brain like acid. Just like when they were in college, it felt as if they couldn't wait to be rid of him.

"I shouldn't be telling you this," the lab tech said, bringing him back to the present. "But . . ." She continued her story with the conversation overheard on the police scanner. "They never showed up at the rendezvous, I'm guessing because of the ambush." She applied pressure to the puncture wound in this arm. "Word is, the gun used to shoot the SUV driver is registered in your name. Good thing to have an airtight alibi, right?"

His favorite phlebotomist was starting to piss him off.

"What do you mean, they didn't show? Are they all right? Who fired the gun?"

"No one's saying, but your girlfriend had gunfire residue on her hands when she was seen in the ER for minor abrasions."

He exhaled in a rush, "Abrasions from what?"

"That's all I know," she said, packing his tubes of blood in her tote. "Anyway, I need to finish my rounds."

Nate caught her hand. "And Massey?"

She looked down at him and smiled. "As far as I know, he's okay. He hasn't come through the ER, anyway. Gotta go, Fergmeister. Catch you later."

Detective Gomez showed after breakfast, carrying a satchel. Her clothes were filthy, and she looked exhausted. "Where are Mony and Massey?" Nate asked without preamble.

The detective plopped herself down in the chair next to his bed and took a long drink from her water bottle. Her jacket fell open, and he noticed she wasn't carrying her weapon. She said, "They're at the police station giving their statements."

Nate clenched his jaw. "Are they under arrest?"

Gomez gave a derisive laugh. "Ms. Strong has too good an aim for that."

The comment made him smile. "You know, that's always people's problem when trying to size up Mony: they tend to underestimate her."

"I'll be sure not to make the same mistake," the detective said, her tone more serious. "Especially on a shooting range."

He wasn't sure why he said it, but Nate confided, "Do you know she's never shot a living thing in her life?"

Gomez lifted an eyebrow. "Interesting."

Curious about her involvement in the shootings, Nate said, "I see you're not carrying your gun. Why?"

The detective liberally shared her participation at the staging area, admitting she'd discharged her weapon. She gave no details about Mony and Massey's ambush, except to say it happened simultaneously. When she finished her account of the events, she walked to his bedside table, set the satchel down, and pulled out some photos. "I'm trying to fill in some missing puzzle pieces. Can you look at some pictures?"

He wanted to talk more about Massey and Mony but obliged the detective. He immediately recognized the SUV driver as "Cell Phone Guy" from out at the Desert Bar. The detective informed Nate that he was the younger brother of the one whom Nate referred to as "Snaggletooth." He didn't see the resemblance. His favorite lab tech told him Snaggletooth awoke from his coma sometime yesterday to discover himself handcuffed to a hospital bed. The detective said that after having his Miranda rights read, authorities informed him of his brother's involvement in the car chase and shooting. He became very cooperative after that, promising all sorts of information in exchange for immunity.

"They're part of a white nationalist group currently monitored by the interstate crime bureaus," the detective said, handing him more pictures. "Murder wasn't part of the duty roster, unless you count the attempt on your life, Mr. Ferguson. There're also strong imputations connecting them with the murder of three Jewish people killed in Kansas but no hard evidence. That case is ongoing. Your sheriff believes they're all connected to a neo-Nazi group trying to establish a foothold up in your neck of the woods."

"You've talked with Wagner?" Nate asked with surprise.

"Early this morning. He says these guys may be associated with the same white supremacist leader who's been trying to take over a small town in southwestern North Dakota."

Nate remembered the story. Before Buddy died, some wacko on the run from Canada for hate crimes had been buying up abandoned buildings and properties in a small town south of Bismarck, planning to create some sort of white enclave. "I thought the leader was sitting in jail after being arrested for carrying a shotgun and terrorizing his neighbors."

The detective shook her head. "A plea agreement was reached late last month. He's on a four-year probation with his movements tracked via a GPS device and prohibited from carrying a firearm. Even if he were still in jail, that doesn't stop his cronies from carrying out their missions and finding the perfect white supremacist community. Wagner thinks one may have moved in on a small town in your county."

Nate found that news unsettling, and it only increased his anxiety for his family's safety. Then a thought occurred to him: "Could these guys be the same people responsible for Shannon's murder?"

The detective hesitated, then said, "It's possible. According to your sheriff, a man known only as 'Gunsel' had been instigating more than a few barroom brawls with talk about organizing against the non-Caucasian workers at the drilling company he'd been working at, claiming they were taking away the white men's jobs. He was also allegedly spouting obscenities at a first responder about a month back for rendering aid to a young Indian girl found unconscious behind a rural bar. The sheriff didn't give a lot of details except to say some of the patrons suspected this 'Gunsel' may have been responsible for the girl's beating. Unfortunately, he'd fled the scene. Your local law enforcement has been looking for him since."

Nate digested the information, trying to put it all together. "Was the first responder male or female?"

The detective eyed him, curious. "Female, why?"

Nate closed his eyes, feeling a headache brewing, "You'll want to follow up on that story. Can you tell me what happened to the guy I patched up in the desert and his girlfriend? I never saw the woman, but the guy I tried to help wasn't white."

Gomez shook her head. "Collateral damage."

A wave of nausea began roiling in his gut. "Did you cut a deal with the two brothers?"

"Not yet. Why?"

Nate recounted the conversation between Snaggletooth and the leader for the group, more crystallized in his mind now that he'd seen the photos. "The guy Mony shot probably killed the girlfriend. I hope she was examined thoroughly during autopsy." Nate leveled a cold look at

Gomez; she understood the subtext of his remark.

The detective revealed the body count for the supremacy group so far, and Nate didn't even bother hiding his relief. The leader, gunned down during his rescue, was a coldhearted son of a bitch, and part of Nate wished Mony would have finished off the brother as well. The detective seemed to read his thoughts.

"Don't worry, Mr. Ferguson," she said, collecting the photos. "These guys are going to jail for a long while." Nate didn't share her confidence.

Massey and Mony entered the room. Passing the detective, they each came up to Nate and gave him a hug before taking up sentry stations next to his bed like he needed the protection. They looked exhausted, scruffy, and in desperate need of a shower. Mony had both hands wrapped in gauze. It was a relief to see them.

The detective gazed at them intently, seemingly struggling with an internal debate. She sighed and said, "I'm really under a lot of pressure to close up this case and get the three of you out of Arizona. Mohave County doesn't even see this much action during spring break. So what's it going to take for you to go home?"

Massey's jaw tightened. "You need to ask better questions than that, Detective, or I'm going to insist you leave."

The lack of finesse from his brother was unexpected. Massey never lost his composure, ever. It was difficult to decipher whether he was overtired or he simply didn't trust the detective. Nate, however, did. He'd had a lot to think about lying around in a hospital bed, and one thing was glaringly obvious. They needed an outside perspective, badly. He was about to point that out when Mony said, "We are no great mystery, Detective. If you need the Cliff's Notes, we're just an ordinary family who own a privately managed oil business."

"Ordinary is not a term I would use to describe your family," the detective said wryly. She turned to Massey. "If this is an acceptable question for you, Mr. Ferguson, why are a bunch of neo-Nazi wannabes trying to kill three very white people like you?"

Massey didn't answer. Nate responded for him, "They're hired thugs."

The detective asked, "Hired by whom?"

Mony and Massey exchanged glances and didn't answer. Nate wondered what they were hiding. Again he took the lead and answered, "Monroe Oil."

Mony's temper flashed. "You don't know that."

Nate's anger flared in kind. "My God, Mony, why are you ignoring the obvious? Or are you still defending that asshole Finch? He could have killed Shannon as easily as anyone."

"I will defend him," Mony retorted. "We should be searching for the real killer instead of wasting time on him. Everyone's so stuck on pinning this on Finch that no one's looking for Sissy or Cindy. We need to—"

The detective asked, "Who are Sissy and Cindy?"

Mony went ballistic.

"Are you fucking kidding me? Is the CID or whatever you call yourself too busy to bother with a victim of human trafficking just because she's an Indian?"

Nate saw the expression on the detective's face harden, the allegation hitting her like a bucket of ice. Massey took hold of Mony to calm her down.

"John knew nothing about Sissy," Mony went on, trembling as she spoke, "but he knew about Cindy. So did Shannon, and she's dead for it. She had a theory—"

Massey interrupted Mony. "Can we follow up on this later, Detective, after we've washed up and had a few hours of sleep? It's been a rough night."

The detective took her cue. "You have my card, Mr. Ferguson. Call me when you're ready to talk." She began walking toward the door, then turned to face the three of them. "Sheriff Wagner never told me about the Indian girl or this Cindy. I'm not sure why, but I plan to find out. And Ms. Strong, I take the exploitation of children very seriously, regardless of ethnicity. Nathan, you've given me a good start—thank you. I'd like to go over some more photos later when you're up to it. I want to see if I can find this Gunsel in our database. Actually, I'd like all of you to have a look if you're available."

Nate answered for all of them. "My therapy ends at two o'clock. Let's plan for after."

An awkward silence fell between the three of them after the detective left. Massey had let go of Mony, and they plopped in opposing chairs, each slipping deep in their own thoughts. Their exhaustion was evident, but Nate couldn't tolerate the tension between them any longer. Taking it upon himself to break the ice, he asked, "What's going on between the two of you?"

Massey and Mony each returned from their personal

reverie enough to register a blank expression. He knew they'd heard him. Massey said, "Nothing is going on between us, except for maybe you."

"Bullshit," Nate said flatly. "I'm talking about back in college. What happened that would make Shannon believe Cindy that the two of you slept together?"

Mony visibly rallied. "Cindy was never my friend. She only hung out with me to be close to Massey. She must have made up the lie when they broke up."

Nate felt the fury building inside him. "Why?" he persisted.

Mony gave him an incredulous look. "How should I know? I suppose she thought if she could make people believe there was something between us, it would hurt him somehow. Where are you going with this?"

He watched their subtle body language, a silent exchange passing between them. He tried to stay calm, tried to take the high road. It was useless. He was up to his eyeballs in lies and withheld truths, and he demanded, "Why?"

Mony suddenly began to tremble again, tears filling her eyes. It was distressing for Nate to watch, especially after everything she'd been through—some caused by his own bad behavior—but he refused to back down. "Goddamn it, Mony, stop protecting me and just tell me the truth."

She began weeping uncontrollably, and once again Massey approached her taking her in his arms. He looked to Nate and said somberly, "What makes you think you're the one she's protecting?"

His brother was right: Nate didn't know—that was the

problem. Maybe it wasn't about his protection. But Mony's quandary still had to do with him, and he deserved to know the truth. Nate pleaded with his brother, "Massey, for the love of God, please, just tell me what happened."

Massey's face turned hard as stone. "She was gang-raped the night I took her back to my apartment and had her stay with me until the next morning."

All the breath left Nate's lungs as his self-righteousness fizzled; he deflated into the bed. It wasn't at all what he'd expected or wanted to hear.

As the truth of his brother's words seeped into his brain, a rage began to coil in his gut at the mere idea of anyone violating Mony. He wanted to break something. His body grew hot and rivulets of sweat began rolling down his forehead. His heart began pounding in his chest and his breathing became erratic. A nurse walked quickly into the room, her expression critical when she asked him, "Mr. Ferguson, are you all right?"

Mony lifted her face from Massey's chest, took one look at him, and came to his bed. She wrapped her arms around him his neck and sobbed. "I'm so sorry, Nate. I wish—I wish—"

Tears welled in his eyes as he held the woman he'd loved all his life tight against his chest. As she cried, it occurred to him that, since his mother left, he'd always turned his head away from witnessing a woman's tears. Cursed to follow his father's footsteps, Nate too had left the woman he loved exposed and vulnerable in order to hide his own failings. It couldn't be like that anymore between them. Nate stroked her hair gently and whispered, "My God,

Mony, I should be apologizing to you."

Massey came to the bed too, sidestepping around the nurse, and sat down next to Mony. Wrapping his arms around them both. "I failed you both," he murmured, his voice choked with sorrow. To Mony, he whispered, "I should have protected you better, should have taken you to the ER right away despite your protests. It's a decision I will regret for the rest of my life."

They sat several minutes holding one another like that. All the emotions of a lifetime—fear, loss, regret, and failure—coalesced and purged in their solidarity. It was the way things were supposed to be between them, the trio of trouble. There was incredible power in their unity such that Nate felt something shift in his universe. Aided by the two people he loved most in this world, he understood his brother for what he truly was—Matthew Ferguson, secret keeper, protector, whose compassion held no limits. It was both burden and gift, a duty which Massey accepted with the greatest humility.

The nurse finally interrupted their hug fest to check Nate's monitor and vital signs. When she was satisfied he wasn't having a cardiac arrest, she left the room without asking questions.

Mony grabbed a wad of tissue from the nightstand and blew her nose long and hard while Massey pulled himself together privately in the patient bathroom. When he returned, the two stood next to each other beside his bed. This time, Nate didn't feel the jealousy that had plagued him most his life whenever Mony and Massey were together. He accepted their relationship. Massey did love Mony, just not in the way Nate had always feared. His brother had been there in her greatest hour of need. Nate would always feel an underlying twinge of envy and love for his brother for that. He reached for both their hands and said, "You two should get some sleep. We can talk more after our meeting with the detective."

Mony leaned her head against Massey's shoulder and squeezed Nate's hand back. "All right," she said, the low tone of her voice filled with resolution. "When I come back, you and I also have a lot to talk about."

CHAPTER 31

JOHN

John felt the *snap* in his spine as he drove the old rust-bucket van along the pock-riddled township road. A sharp pain began shooting down his leg, and he knew immediately that his lower lumbar was out of alignment. "Shit," he muttered, clutching at his thigh. He thought about his masseuse René and chiropractor Karen's skillful hands back in Chicago, a thousand miles away. It would be weeks before he would have access to decent health care. He was on a fool's errand, solidifying the acrimony he'd felt the moment he'd stepped off the train toward the desolate landscape of Dakota.

His journey began when Sheriff Wagner dropped him off to pick up his rental a couple days back, he'd received an anonymous tip informing him the location of the missing murder weapon. The alleged tool of death turned out to be the leaded crystal decanter Shannon used to pour—correction, *John* used to pour the whiskey from. It was enough evidence that if the sheriff had decided to, he could have arrested John on suspicion of

312

murder, in the first degree.

He didn't.

Instead, Wagner created a new living hell by letting everyone think John was guilty, then coercing him into the sting he was presently in. The sheriff believed he could pass off John as some sort of anti-Semitic fanatic from Illinois vying for control of the sex-trafficking business. The sheriff claimed he needed a non-local he could trust to infiltrate a white supremacist group trying to establish residence in his county. The plan was sheer folly—one, neither man fully trusted the other, and two, John was sure the sheriff watched too many procedural cop shows if he believed he could pull off said caper. John's maternal grandfather was a Holocaust survivor, for crying out loud. Anyone with a computer and half a brain could look that up. Nevertheless, he'd accepted the assignment eagerly, determined to find out who exactly set him up. If Shannon's murder could be pinned on a bunch of bigoted Jew-haters, so be it. It was better than sitting on the sidelines in a jail cell.

Early that morning, the sheriff had informed John a Detective Gomez from the CID in Arizona had called to update him about the attempt on Ramona and attorney Ferguson's life. The detective then used her connections to provide John with a cover and backstory. John called Lyn and let her know what was going on; the conversation was a train wreck. She told him he was insane for agreeing to such a reckless plan, and then she started to cry. He felt her pain. He knew nothing about undercover work, drugs, or human trafficking, nor could he argue with the inherent danger of his mission. His only experience with illicit drugs was smoking a little weed on occasion. But he'd be goddamned if he was going to be patsy to Monroe or that vindictive weasel Ethan Rice. John's earbud crackled to life, retrieving him from his introspect.

The whirling sound of a helicopter blade in the background nearly drowned out the sheriff's voice when he said, "Mr. Finch, have you reached the turnoff for Dead Dog Slough yet?"

John's teeth rattled as he spoke into the mike wire. "I have no idea. Are you sure you this guy isn't making this shit up as he goes along, sending me on a wild goose chase?"

"Just stay on course toward Lostwood National Refuge, and take the next right," the sheriff reassured him.

"Stay the course," John muttered sarcastically and mused, *I could be in Canada for all I know.* Up until six months ago, he'd never even seen a tractor that wasn't in a picture. Now dozens of tractor cabs dotted the landscape, pulling gigantic disc plows, planters, and sprayers. He met one such monstrosity driving toward him on the narrow road, so big he nearly drove into the ditch to avoid a collision. It sparked a thought. "Detective Gomez is right about dealing with the lower rung of the group," he said, watching for the turnoff. "Who else would live back in these marshes? What we need is someone higher up the food chain."

"Good idea, but not likely," Sheriff Wagner replied in his ear bug. "Massey thinks there's another go-between buffering Monroe's involvement."

Ah, the great Matthew Ferguson, John thought sullenly. He'd been wondering when his name would pop into the conversation. He said, "That doesn't mean we shouldn't try. I know Jason: he has an impetuous nature compounded by a Napoleon complex. He's going to get directly involved, mark my wor—"

The sheriff interrupted. "Just a minute."

John heard Wagner say something to the pilot, then to him, "I can believe it, but some might say the same about you, minus the short-man syndrome. Look how easily you fell into the trap making everyone believe you're the killer. Though Shawn's animosity toward you certainly didn't hurt."

John subconsciously rubbed the side of his face where Shannon's brother had jacked his jaw a week ago and asked, "By the way, how did you convince him I'm not his sister's murderer?"

"No, toward Tioga," the sheriff said to the pilot. To John, "I didn't. Mony did. Said she stopped thinking you were a murderer the moment I slapped those handcuffs on you. She knew it was a setup when—"

"Did she say that? Did she say, 'I stopped thinking John was a murderer after the sheriff put the handcuffs on me'?" John snapped. "Because that's not the way I remember it." The memory of steel biting into his wrists was nearly as bad as Ramona's implacable expression when she pointed a loaded gun at him, making him pissy.

"I believe her words were—"

"Why should I believe you?" John said, his mood

turning bitter. "People around here will say anything to cover her ass."

The sheriff released a deep breath before saying calmly, "No, Mr. Finch, they won't. But we will do what we can to protect her. Just think how easily she could have been the killer's target, especially in light of the recent attempt made on her life."

John had thought of that. In fact, the idea never left his head, especially after hearing about the ordeal in Arizona. He took a deep breath and said with greater deliberation, "Can we talk about something else?" He didn't want to think about Ramona right then. She was his Achilles' heel, and he needed all his mental faculties to focus on his current situation.

"In less than a mile, you'll make a right," the sheriff prompted. "It comes up quick, so keep your eyes peeled, Mr. Finch."

John wound up making a hard turn off the lousy gravel road onto an even lousier one. The whole van shimmied as he muttered, "I feel like my brains are being scrambled in my skull."

The sheriff ignored the comment. "You should be able to see the trailer by now, Mr. Finch. Stay focused, and remember, you must convince Gunsel you can deliver on the goods or he's liable to shoot you on the spot. Can you do that?"

John didn't need the reminder. "I'm a lawyer," he said with phony arrogance. "I can convince a pregnant mother the baby she's carrying doesn't belong to her. Will there be anyone else?"

He felt worse than an angsty teenager, worried about being recognized. Once the sheriff had traced ownership of the heirloom canoe found in Ramona's lake back to Dwight Mitchell, it wasn't difficult connecting him to the missing Indian girl. The problem was, no one had seen or heard from Mitchell for the past week. That wasn't the only connection. Mitchell's wife, a.k.a. the infamous Hitch, was facing criminal charges for using the county social service system to feed the human trafficking industry. Since the time of her employment, at least ten girls ranging from ages twelve to seventeen had gone missing under her watch; eight out of the ten were Indian children. The couple was clearly the inside connection, if either of their sorry asses could be found. The question John wanted answered was, who were they collaborating with? Gomez and Wagner had narrowed it to some bigot named Gunsel who was believed to be hiding out somewhere in the county. What they needed now was proof.

"At this point, I'm not sure of anything," the sheriff cautioned, "so for God's sake, be careful."

Four mangy dogs barked viciously as John pulled the van in next to a ramshackle trailer. Sticking out like a sore thumb in the middle of nowhere, it sat along the shore of a lake smaller than Ramona's. The beasts started jumping up on the door, scratching at the fiberglass, and John's heart leaped into his throat. He hated big dogs and scanned the yard for an owner. There wasn't a soul in sight, not even a car. The hairs on the nape of his neck prickled; he felt increasingly certain he was being set up.

He shifted the van into drive and was about to pull away when a man wearing a sleeveless T-shirt, dirty jeans, and greasy smile with a swastika buzzed into his hairline opened the front door. A *consigliere* he was not.

John rolled down the window a crack and hollered, "You Gunsel?"

The smile on the man's face wavered. "Don't call me that. Name's Harland Richards," he said, waving at John to come in.

John shook his head and shouted, "I'll talk from here."

Richards started to laugh, reigniting the dogs into a frenzy. John felt like a clay pigeon trapped in the launch position. He imagined it was the desired effect. This went on for several seconds until a rifle report silenced the lot of them, sending a shiver down his spine and scattering the dogs.

A hulking figure whose head sat between his shoulders like a melon in the sand stepped out from around the side of the trailer. John recognized him immediately, and his heart sank.

Dwight Mitchell held the gun with both hands in front of his body, the barrel up, a finger on the outside of the trigger guard. He looked menacing, wearing desert camouflage and black smudges under his eyes. Mitchell approached the driver's side window and said, "I was wondering when you'd be coming around to making a deal." He turned and yelled to the man by the door. "Richards, get your ass over here."

The plan was simple. John would disclose credible, damaging information regarding Monroe Oil Company and their presence on the Bakken in exchange for Sissy Moonbeam. Simple, had it not been for Mitchell's presence. It wasn't clear where his allegiance lay. *Too late to worry about that now.* John turned on his Chicago charm and got the dog-and-pony show started.

"I believe you backed the wrong horse," he said to cordially to Richards. "Ethan Rice may tell you he's got the Altman probate hearing wrapped in a pretty bow, but he's lying. I have a credible source that says Monroe's case is already lost. F&A have everything they need to win, so Ferguson and Altman are going nowhere."

Richard's snorted a laugh. "Yeah, what source?"

John glared into Richard's stony eyes. "Me. With their land grab out of the picture, you won't be getting that perfect community he promised, and Monroe will be scrambling to find another oil company to usurp in order to keep his foothold in North Dakota. The last quarterly business report showed a 40 percent drop in production. His wells are drying up. He either must risk sinking more money drilling deeper at his current location or find somewhere else. I have the documents here in an envelope outlining who, what, and where he plans to target next, for a price. Are you interested?"

Richard's shifty eyes drifted from John to Mitchell; then he took a step back. Mitchell stepped forward and said, "Now, who should be asking for my favorite little cocksucker?"

John held his poker face. "I am. I need proof of life for my associates—proof that you're not some fly-by-night business operation."

Mitchell scratched his chin as if deliberating; then he gave a sharp whistle. John braced himself for another dog attack. Instead, a sullen girl stepped out of the house. She wore a baseball cap pulled down over her face, a halter top, and way-too-short shorts. She marched with her arms crossed in front of her budding chest, walked around the front of the van to the passenger side, opened the door, and climbed in. John handed over the envelope.

It was too easy.

Before anyone could change their mind, John started the engine and said, "Thanks. I'll be in touch." Then he got the hell out of there. The drive back down the lane felt twice as long then when he'd arrived. He kept checking the rearview mirror, but so far, no one followed. Releasing a deep exhale, he finally looked over at the young girl. She sat quiet with her arms crossed and her head down. He said, "You're going to be all right, Sissy. No one's going to hurt you anymore."

The girl didn't respond.

They were near the end of the driveway, and his breathing was becoming less shallow when the young girl broke into a maniacal laughter that sounded like an evil clown. John began to wonder if the child was crazy. She finally looked up at him, her dark, almond-shaped eyes unfathomable. She said, "Mr. Mitchell wants me to tell you Sissy's worth a lot more than a lousy piece of paper."

Abruptly, she jumped out of the moving vehicle. John slammed on the brakes and jumped out of the van after her. He stumbled when he hit the ground as a spasm shot down his leg, limping around the front of the van to check on the girl. She'd already taken off in a full-out run back to the trailer.

He was about to give chase when a bullet shattered the back window. He cleared the bumper and hit the dirt with a thud. Crawling backward on his belly behind the shelter of the van, he peeked around the corner but couldn't see the shooter. The sheriff began shouting into his earpiece, "Mr. Finch, are you all right?"

Pinned down next to the side of the van, John watched helplessly as the young girl fled back to her tormentor. He thumped his head against the door and said to Wagner, "Yeah, I'm still here."

The sheriff yelled, "Well, get the hell out of there. Mitchell missed you on purpose."

John slinked back inside the van and tore off down the rest of the driveway. Turning onto the pock-riddled township road, he slammed the heel of his hand on the steering wheel. "Shit." Never in a thousand years would he understand Stockholm syndrome. "I had her. I had Sissy Moonbeam. She was in my grasp, and I let her away," John complained into his mike. "Now what are we going to do?"

The sheriff was radio silent for a long while; John worried he might have lost the connection when Wagner finally said, "Another opportunity will present itself."

John didn't share his optimism. He looked over at the vacant seat where Sissy once sat, then noticed the piece of paper she'd left behind. It read:

Altman for Moonbeam, or no deal.

CHAPTER 32

NATE

"Come on, let's go for a walk."

Mony helped Nate with his slippers before he had a chance to argue. He'd just come from therapy and was already worn out, but he complied. With discharge a day away, he wanted to be ready.

It troubled him that he still became winded with the least amount of exertion, and his pain was only marginally controlled. But he'd already begun to rely on the hospital as a sanctuary and knew he couldn't hide there forever. The staff seemed eager for him to move on as well, disguising their frustration in well-meaning encouragement. He played along, being the good patient and hiding the anxiety bubbling just under the surface of his cool, easygoing exterior. It was unsettling worrying about the press hounding him. It was terrifying knowing he might still be a target.

His hospital exit had been coordinated with the utmost secrecy. Leaving under the cover of night, Nate and Mony would stay at the condominium his dad had rented. Situated in a gated retirement community, it came equipped with the necessary accessories to support his convalescence and would be relatively quiet. Massey and Mony noticed his pent-up anxiety, and Massey often tried to lighten the mood, harassing Nate by calling him *cougar bait*. It was nervous energy. His brother harbored worries of his own.

Scheduled to leave the day after next, Massey would be the sole representative for the Ferguson-Altman family at Shannon McDonald's funeral. It killed Nate not to be there to support Shawn and pay his last respects to a woman he'd considered more than a friend. He wasn't the only family member out of commission. After they'd returned home, Kip took Poppy straight to the hospital, where they admitted her with exhaustion and dehydration. Nate felt some culpability for that. It was another blot in a litany of transgressions he'd have to atone for.

He also held an edge of disappointment that he hadn't had more time to settle the rift between him and his brother. After Nate, Mony, and Massey got things out in the open, the reveal of Mony's rape all but shut her down emotionally, and he could have used his brother's advice on how to be a better support for her. Denial through secrecy was her protective shield; it was going to take a tremendous amount of patience to get her to speak her truths. At least she'd agreed to stay during his convalescence. He wasn't sure if she'd done so freely or if it was out of some sort of obligation. It didn't matter. He was grateful for her presence. Maybe they could find healing together.

When they returned to his room, Mony perched herself on the windowsill, staring out at the desert city while he did his spirometry treatment. She was a million miles away, and he wanted to ask what was on her mind, but he was afraid. It seemed she no longer confided in him; perhaps she never had. Maybe the love between them had all been in his head, a wishful dream of a sad and lonely little boy.

Nate finished his therapy and Mony set the spirometer aside. Sitting on the bed next to him, she took hold of his hand. His pulse raced with apprehension when she said, "We need to talk."

Nate squeezed her hand and went for it. "Is this where you finally tell me Dane is our son?"

She looked directly into his eyes. "I'm so sorry, Nate. I should have told you a long time ago."

Somewhere deep inside him, he could feel the anger bubbling—not just at this secret kept for so long, but at everything. At himself for leaving in the first place; at his mother for leaving *him* long before that; at Mony for keeping him from knowing, *really* knowing, his son for all these years. Yesterday, he probably would have let his emotions overcome him.

But as Mony spoke of the mistakes she'd made, he watched the shame bloom in the shadows of her eyes. When she confessed the dehumanization of one's soul that came from being a victim, he remembered the rage and pain that had flooded through him at the revelation of what had been done to her.

Anger won't help anything. He kept his mouth shut,

willing the fire within him to die down.

Mony's jaw tightened with her own anger as she conveyed her refusal to abort the pregnancy, even though everyone had thought it was best. She cried, justifying her marriage to Bob, and mourned his death as if it had occurred only yesterday. She told Nate with utter conviction, "Bob was a good man and a wonderful father to our son."

Nate lost the words partway through her confession as tears stung the corners of his eyes, the last of his anger seeping away. He should have been there for her instead of Massey or Bob Strong. Part of him insisted he should still be furious at being deceived or feel grief for the years lost with his son. Instead, he reflected on the time he'd spent with Dane, and how every one of those moments brought his heart joy—Mony not once denying access. He thought about the day Mony put the homemade Christmas decorations away, how she'd held the clay cast of Dane's handprints as if it were a living thing. He wanted that kind of connection, an extension of himself. He'd thought he'd found it in music, in his brief marriage, in farming, in the bees. He was wrong.

After his mom had left him, his greatest dread was that he would never find love again. Mony and Massey eased that fear. It was a terrible struggle when they each left home; he'd grown to rely on their presence. When they'd moved on to have families of their own, he tried to be satisfied with the relationships he shared with his nieces and nephews, but deep down, he'd always wanted more.

For the past half year, rage and remorse had ruled the

spaces in his mind and in his heart. It was exhausting and brought no value to his life. His near-death experience reinforced the triviality of playing the wounded victim, changing him for the better, he hoped. There was nothing he could do to change the past; he'd have to accept that. But he could damn sure take control of his future. The fact his own son had saved his life was a good start.

Nate took hold of the mother of his only child, a woman he'd loved all his life. Clearing the tears that clogged his throat, he said, "I can't pretend to understand or agree with your justification deceiving me all these years, but I don't want to dwell on that right now. What I do care about is you. I won't waste the second chance I've been given to show you how much."

"Second chance?" Mony asked and gave a bitter laugh. "How can you be so sure you've got one?"

His heart swooped downward. "Mony, what are you talking about?"

"You're not in love with *me*, Nate. You're in love with a version of me. A version from before . . ." She broke away from him and swept her arm in a wide gesture, encompassing all that had built up in their lives in the last few decades—*Hell*, Nate thought, *in the last few days*. "All this. I'm not the same person I was. I can't ever be again."

Nate took a step closer. "Mony, I—I am so sorry for what happened to you. Really. I can't imagine what you must have been through. But if you think that means I don't love you—"

"Where is this going, Nate?" she interrupted, her eyes filled with tears. "You ran off for *months* when you thought those rumors about Massey were true. How are we supposed to build something—something that *lasts*—now that you know what actually happened?" Shaking her head, she continued, "We're not kids anymore. Pretending that we are, acting like we are, won't get us anywhere."

Taking another step forward, Nate once again took hold of the woman he loved. "Mony, you're right. We're not the same people we used to be. But that doesn't mean we can't build any kind of life together. I mean, look at Dane! He turned out pretty great, and I wasn't even trying."

Mony snorted a reluctant laugh through her tears.

Gently, Nate brushed his hand along her shoulder. "You're right, you're not the woman I thought I loved. But that doesn't mean I don't love you here, now. And don't think it means I won't come back for you."

He cupped her chin and kissed her fervently on the mouth. And then, after a moment's hesitation, Mony responded in kind, wrapping her arms gently around his neck and kissing him back.

"Don't you two know to put a do-not-disturb sign on the door?" Massey asked with a playful *tsk* as he entered the room.

Mony disentangled from Nate and slithered into the chair next to the bed. She countered, "Don't you know you're supposed to knock?"

Massey sat in the folding chair next to her. "Be glad it was me who caught you necking. I met the detective in the parking lot. She's on her way with those pictures."

"She's a tenacious one, I'll give her that," Mony said,

combing her fingers through her tussled pixie locks. "Especially the way I treated her this morning."

"We treated her," Massey corrected.

"You're both forgiven, if you can give me a lead," the detective interjected from the doorway. "May I come in?"

They spent the next hour passing around more photos while the detective brought them up to speed on the investigation. "Your sheriff doesn't think it was Sissy at all in the van with Mr. Finch," she said, handing an eight-by-ten glossy to Mony. "And Mr. Finch wouldn't have known, since he'd never met the child."

"I'm inclined to agree with the sheriff," Massey said. "It seems unlikely a pimp would hand over his most prized possession, even if he was confident in getting her back."

Mony held up a picture. "Who's this?"

Nate leaned over her shoulder for a closer look. The shot was one of those broody guys with a chiseled chin, a model's good looks, and the body mass of an athlete. The detective asked, "Do you recognize him?"

Mony shook her head. "No, but he has a face a woman would remember."

The detective nodded sagely. "When he's working within the parameters of the law, he is a self-employed private detective, and goes by the name Anton Kuznetsov. When he's out in the field working as a mercenary, he goes by several different aliases. He's not a white supremacist, but we've been monitoring him ever since the unexplained death of a political consultant for a Texas senator about a year ago. There's evidence he may have been involved. What makes him interesting to you three is that the dead consultant was an outspoken opponent of Monroe Oil."

Massey said, "Can I take this picture? I want to show Finch when I get back to Williston and see if he recognizes him."

They continued for a bit when Nate came across a photo with a pair of familiar eyes. He handed the picture to the detective. "Who's this guy?"

"That's Harland Richards," she said with a hint of disdain. "He's a rodeo circuit has-been from Casper, Wyoming. He's one of the early recruits for that white supremacist group in North Dakota. A couple of years ago, he was overseeing a small prostitution ring servicing the oil workers between Wyoming, Montana, and parts of Oklahoma. Then he slid off the radar. Your sheriff thinks he's the guy who may have beaten Sissy Moonbeam. Your hunch was right about the first responder. It was your friend Shannon McDonald who was involved in the verbal altercation with Gunsel, a.k.a. Harland Richards. Mr. Finch just confirmed he's working with a couple by the name of Mitchell."

Nate examined the picture. Through the pale skin and emaciated body of a heroin addict, it was very different to see any family resemblance, yet the eyes were undeniable.

"Do you know this person?" the detective asked.

"No, but I think I know his sister."

They all looked at him, puzzled.

"Detective, I think you need to talk to Trevor St. James's head of security."

Nate wasn't sure how much, or even if, Gem was involved in the white supremacy organization, but it was evident she had something to hide. She'd lied to him about her twin brother's death. There were several possibilities as to why; it was up to the detective to find out which was true. Mony became furious at the implication Gem may have had some culpability in Nate's shooting. Nate and Massey told her to let it go for now, at least until the detective got the whole story.

Within the hour, Detective Gomez made plans to head for Vegas, but before that she promised to prioritize the search for Sissy Moonbeam as well as Cindy Van Dyke once she got to North Dakota. Mony pulled the detective off to the side and made it a point to apologize for her bad behavior the morning after the car chase. The detective was sympathetic and recommended a counselor she'd used after being involved in her first shooting. Gomez also laid out the hard facts regarding the probability that Sissy and Cindy may already be dead. Nate could see Mony struggling to accept that truth, but she seemed to appreciate the honesty. As the detective left, Mony said to Nate and Massey, "I think I'm beginning to like that woman."

Because his truck was impounded, Massey rented a vehicle for the drive out to the beekeeper's ranch. Nate couldn't say why the meeting with the elusive Hernández had him on edge. Maybe it was because Gem had steered him in that direction, building false hope that she'd found his mother; at least he'd found Buddy's business partner. Nate kept the information about his search for his mom to himself for now. Things were tenuous between the three of them right now, and he didn't want to get Mony or Massey all worked up over nothing.

They rode in silence for much of the drive. Massey pointed out the trailhead road he and Mony took to escape their would-be assassins. Nate shared a radical thought: "You know, I've been thinking about that. Maybe I should hold a raffle or something on my truck and give the proceeds to organizations that offer help to exploited children and runaways. That bullet hole in the back might even jack up the value. Don't you think?"

Mony and Massey looked at him skeptically.

Nate felt compelled to defend his idea. "Fame is fleeting. I should do something useful with it while it lasts before I fade into obscurity. The music industry's great for getting behind a good cause. Besides, who wouldn't want to own the Fergmeister's bullet-riddled getaway truck?" Neither Mony nor Massey seemed sold on his idea, but they didn't shoot it down either, and it gave him a strange sort of satisfaction.

Massey turned off on the refuge road leading to Glory West Sunrise. Nestled near the foot of the mountain range, the ranch blended seamlessly into its surrounding; if the road hadn't led straight to it, it would have been easy to miss. Nate pointed out the location of the beehives as they passed it on the driveway, sitting surreptitiously among a stand of old cottonwood trees—another easy miss if you weren't looking for it.

The first thing that caught Mony's eye was the large stable and horse corral several yards from the main house.

Near the corral's edge, an old man with weathered skin stood next to the beautiful Mustang, waiting patiently. Massey parked near the gate and helped Nate out of the truck. He moved stiffly after the drive and took his time walking. Nate approached the old man and shook his hand. "Hey, Joe, remember me?"

Joe gave a toothless grin. "Sure, the beekeeper from the north. I'm glad those bastards didn't kill you in the desert."

Nate laughed at the blunt remark. "Yeah, me too."

Mony and Massey took turns shaking Slow Joe's hands. Joe said, "I see you brought your brother and Buddy's girl with you. That's good. I hear she's a pretty good shot too. It comes in handy when you're being chased by crazies."

Mony looked at Joe, surprised, and said to him, "Have we met?" Joe didn't answer. He just smiled and handed her a couple of apples.

Nate leaned against the corral post, conserving his energy while Mony fed the horse. Massey kept staring at the house and fiddled absently with something in his shirt pocket. The nervous gesture was uncharacteristic. Massey had been so determined to meet the beekeeper; now it seemed he wasn't sure. Maybe Nate was projecting his own uncertainty. He didn't have a problem delaying the visit. From what he could tell, the bees were safe and well cared for, plus there was no one back home to take care of them anyway.

"Did you three come all the way out here to feed a horse?" Joe said, giving voice to Nate's thoughts. "Hernández is at the house. The door is open, just go inside."

Unable to walk the distance without becoming short of breath, Nate allowed Massey to drive him to the house's gate. His face was already flushed from overexertion, and Mony voiced concern that he was pushing himself too hard. "Maybe we should wait until Nate's feeling a little stronger before we meet Hernández," she suggested to Massey. "I'm sure he would understand."

Nate mopped the sweat off his brow with his forearm. "No, no, I'm all right. We're here. Let's get this over with," he said, but his words lacked conviction.

Mony looked to Massey for corroboration, but he seemed equally distracted. When she pressed the issue, his brother said, "I'm with Nate. Let's get this over with."

She let it go, and they walked along the terra cotta cobblestones of the inner courtyard surrounding the fountain. The fragrance of the flowers and native herbs was heavenly, and butterflies and bees were everywhere. When neither Nate nor Massey took the initiative, Mony knocked on the door. It took a beat before the sound of a pair of small feet came pounding across the floor.

The child who'd greeted them had mesmerizing dark eyes and even darker, thick, curly hair. Nate remembered Massey looking much the same at that age, except for the darkness of the eyes. He guessed the boy to be somewhere between eight and ten, about how old his brother had been when they first met Mony. Nate wondered if the little fellow had a playmate, living so far away from town. In a thick, rolling accent, the boy said. "Can I help you?"

"*Buenos días*," Mony greeted him. "Is Mr. Hernández home?"

The boy assessed her with those big, dark eyes, then fixed his gaze on Nate, who was standing back a few feet, guarding the side where he'd taken the bullet. Nate could feel the color draining from his face and was grateful when the little boy said, "Hey, Señor Fergmeister, you need to come in out of the heat."

The coolness of the foyer was heavenly, not artificial air from an air conditioner but something else. Nate sat down on the small bench in front of a half wall which separated the open foyer from the main living space, catching his breath. Gazing into the main part of the house, it was an impressive space with a wide-open floor plan—entry, living room, and kitchen combined. Soft earth tones decorated the living room, with splashes of brilliantly colored throw pillows.

While Mony conversed with the boy in broken Spanish, Nate took notice of the wall behind them covered with framed photos in various shapes and sizes. Some pictures had ornate frames, while others were encased in wood, metal, or cheap plastic. The photos took up the entire wall space and looked like one big collage. Massey noticed it too and helped Nate to his feet to take a closer look.

Distantly, Nate heard the little boy say, "I'll go get Nana," and scuttle off across the living room, then bound through the kitchen and out of sight. Mony joined Nate and Massey at the wall, their eyes drifting from one picture to another. A lifetime of memories hung compacted in that space. One photo held their focus, a large framed picture in the center. Massey took something out of his pocket and held it next to the picture.

"Well, I'll be dammed," his brother said. The picture he held in his hand and the one framed on the wall were a spot-on match.

EPILOGUE

Gloria West-Hernández stood bent over the raised garden beds, prepping the soil for the late harvest plants. Her good friend had built them years before out of old railroad ties, giving her better control over the quality of the soil. It was the best way to raise produce in the desert and much easier on the back. He'd also installed a programmable managed irrigation drip system set on the timer, giving her the freedom to leave for several days at a time. It was one of the luxuries of having a river nearby. Occasionally, she needed to spray with a hose, but that was rare. The six-foot fence kept out the deer, fox, and coyotes but not squirrels, skunks, snakes, scorpions, and tarantulas. The small critters were annoying, but not near as troublesome the scorpions and tarantulas.

Taking a moment to stretch her back, she lifted her face toward the sky and soaked in the desert sun. The warmth felt like a lover's caress on bare skin; she was grateful she could no longer recall the frigid winters of the north, where six months out of the year she could never get warm no matter how much clothing she wore. Sometimes in a bad dream, she remembered the isolation and utter loneliness she'd felt in that desolate place. Thank God for her boys. If it hadn't been for them, she'd have surely gone mad.

Was it any wonder the wingless snowbirds flocked from the north to her little desert community, she thought? Seeking warmth and companionship among like species, the snowbirds found fellowship and respite for their weary bones and joints. It was how she'd reunited with her special friend. Some people in the community found the influx of northerners a nuisance, complaining about how the out-of-state cars clogged the neighborhood streets. It never bothered her. She'd developed many good friendships over the years—one in particular. Her lady friends liked to tease and gossip, calling him a boyfriend with an air of chastisement laced in jealousy. She merely laughed it off, saying she was too old for that sort of business, though deep down it gave her a thrill just the same. Her special friend was long overdue for his visit, with the long winter past; it was time to collect the bees. The spring planting would have already begun, and the wildflowers of the prairie would surely be blooming.

A small boy with dark hair and almond-shaped eyes poked his head out the patio door and shouted, "Nana, there's someone here to see you."

Her heart leapt with excitement. *Finally*, she thought. Slow Joe had told her the beekeeper from the north was coming. She reached over to check the pepper plants and plucked a few jalapeños. She'd make Vietnamese beef pho tonight, she decided, it being one of his favorites.

Straightening, she bundled the harvested peppers

in her loose-fitting blouse and called back to the child, "Be right there, sweetie." She wasn't really the boy's grandma, but she wished she were. He was one of the many abandoned children that had come into her care. Her friends took to calling her a kid magnet with disdain because all the kids nicked named her *mi abuela*. She liked the distinction. Children were very perceptive and could often spot a person willing to offer unconditional love— plus they knew she kept a candy stash.

Before entering the house, she gave her face one more time to the afternoon sun. *Maybe we'll go for a horseback ride this evening if he's not too tired.* The thought made her smile.

Her cheerfulness faded slightly at the sight of three strangers standing in her foyer. Engrossed in the family photos, they hadn't even heard her come in. Not wanting to interrupt, she watched from her vantage as their collective gaze drifted from photo to photo. They murmured quietly between one another, the way people often do when coming upon a memory. They paused from time to time to focus on a photo, bending low or standing on tiptoes to gain a closer look, cataloging the details of the event. They laughed subtly, the kind of joyous sound made by close friends telling an inside joke.

Though strangers, there was something familiar about the three of them; she took pleasure observing them, the way a mother does when her child does something for the first time. One of the men settled on the picture of her boys standing on a raft, taken long after she'd moved away. He reached with his fingers and brushed reverently over the girl who stood between them. The corner of his mouth curved into a wistful smile.

That girl, now a woman, turned to face Gloria Hernández. She didn't wear her hair in a crewcut, and her smile lacked crooked teeth, but there was no doubt the woman who stood before her was the beekeeper's child. The mischief in her hazel eyes gave her away, an exact replica of her father's.

He's not coming, she thought disappointedly, though her friend had sent an incredible gift in his stead.

"Please forgive our intrusion," the beekeeper's daughter said. "Are you Ms. Hernández?"

Both men turned simultaneously. One was as handsome as his father, the other a mirror of her twenty years ago, when her eyes were a brilliant dark blue and her face less wrinkled. The room began to spin, and she suddenly felt lightheaded. *You were out in the sun too long,* she told herself, but she knew that wasn't the reason. When she tried to speak, no words came from her lips and she was terrified. Unconsciously, she let loose the hem of her blouse, and the peppers tumbled to the floor. A salty sting emerged at the corners of her eyes and a sharp pain pierced her heart. It was a bittersweet communication from her dear friend, the beekeeper in the north.

I'm sorry, I can't be with you, my dear friend, but I send you your heart's desire instead.

Lifting her fingers to her lips, she suppressed a gasp and fell on her weakened knees. The two young men lurched toward her, falling to their knees along with her. One scooped her up in his arms while the other hovered in front of her. He cupped his hand to her cheek and kissed her forehead, urging her to rest her head against his brother. They rocked her gently to the rhythm of an unsung lullaby—or had she been humming to herself softly? She felt the melodic sound reverberating in her son's chest; his heartbeat steady and strong. Clutching her tight, he made a mournful sound and began to sob.

"Don't cry, Nathan," she sobbed with him.

He clung to her tighter, so tight she could hardly breathe. She didn't complain. He said, "Then don't leave me ever again, Mom. I promise I'll hold onto you tighter this time."

ACKNOWLEDGMENTS

Thank you to my editor Erik Hane for your patience and guidance in my laborious effort in helping me say more with less to create an engaging story. It's difficult to subject the labor of your creativity to the austerity of the red pen, but necessary for growth and improvement.

To the fabulous Graham Warnken who found a way for me to save my greatest darling—the Lakota dialogue between my female protagonist and a young runaway Indian American girl. After finishing my edit review of chapter 14, I found myself sitting in a puddle of tears. Staying true to the Lakota language brings such poignant intimacy between the two characters, the chapter would simply have fallen flat without it. A thousand times thank you to my wonderful editing team.

And where would I be without Wise Ink Creative Publishing, the best cheering squad an indie author can ever hope for aside from my family. Thank you for connecting me with Steven Meyer-Rassow from across the pond, my cover artist extraordinaire.

Finally, heartfelt gratitude to the lovely Ms. Doris, and handsome Sir Kieran, models for Mony and Nate. The image of your true-life love story illustrated on the cover of this book brings an essence of realism to my fictitious characters, lending credibility to Mony and Nate's unconditional love for one another, and the belief that it truly does exist.

Julien Bradley never aspired to become an indie author, but she does love telling a good story. She used time between jobs to hone her documentation skill and do some freewriting—the exercise resulted in 1,100 pages! Encouraged by her daughter Kimberlee, she pitched the story idea to Wise Ink Creative Publishing; the "draft," after professional editing, became the first installment in the Bakken series.

With over thirty-five years in the health care industry, Julien writes stories that reflect a culmination of real human experiences to create organic women's fiction/chick-lit. Her books give an honest look into the lives of ordinary people, elevates the under-represented voice of women over fifty, and breathe new life into the unexpected depth of the "normal" day-to-day.

Born and raised in Minnesota, Julien lives with her husband atop the bluffs overlooking the beautiful Hiawatha River valley. She is a member of Midwest Fiction Writers and Romance Writers of America. *Between Fracture Lines* is the second in the Bakken series.